THE SECOND GREAT MORTALITY

THE SECOND GREAT MORTALITY

L O N N I E   C O L S O N

The Second Great Mortality

K N Y G H T L Y   A R M E S

PUBLISHING

Denton, Texas

Published by Knyghtly Armes Publishing
111 E. University Drive, Suite 105-150
Denton, Texas 76209

www.knyghtlyarmes.com

Cover: Limbourg Brothers (Herman, Pol, Jean) (fl.1399-1416 CE).
The Horseman of Death. Illuminated miniature from the Tres Riches Heures du Duc de Berry: The Office of the Dead. 1416. Ms. 65, f.90 verso.
Located in the Musée Condé, Chantilly, France.
Photograph by René-Gabriel Ojéda.
© RMN-Grand Palais / Art Resource, NY

Author photograph © Javy Camacho

Library of Congress Control Number: 2016905973

Trade Paperback ISBN: 978-0-9974087-0-6
eBook ISBN: 978-0-9974087-1-3

First Edition: May 2016

Printed in the United States of America

5 4 3 2 1

As odd as it may be to dedicate a tale of zombies, this book is for my darling wife, who has supported *most* of my crazy endeavors, and for our beautiful children whose laughter warms my heart.

And to my parents, I thank them for showing me how to always seek contentment in life and to follow my dreams.

CONTENTS

1436

To my right worshipful Father, the Abbot at Deerhurst, be this letter delivered in haste.

MOST REVERENT AND RIGHT worshipful Father, I recommend me to you, praying that you keep me foremost in your thoughts and prayers. If God grants me sufficient time, I will hereafter record the tragic tale of Sir Richard Colleville, a knight, formerly of Stroud but lately lord of Colleville manor. I have thrice made him swear upon the Holy Scriptures that this is a true and faithful account of what some are already calling the Second Great Mortality.

Never before could any man have imagined the kinds of horrors that we have survived these past several days. This is a story that defies all sanity and reason. I confess that, even now, as I attempt to record it for posterity upon what few scraps of parchment there are to be found, I can scarce believe it to be true, even though I have witnessed much of it myself.

This living nightmare began on the feast of the Holy Innocents, in the year of Grace 1436. Just days earlier, Richard's only son and heir, Thomas, had returned home to celebrate the Christmastide. Although Sir Richard says it seems so trivial to him now, just the chance to spend that unseasonably mild day hunting with his son had felt like the most important thing in the world.

Part One:
Pestilence

28 December

Feast of the Holy Innocents

FATHER," THOMAS CALLED FROM ahead. "It sounds like the hounds have cornered something. A stag perhaps?" His face was flushed with the kind of youthful excitement I envied of him. Life had grown tiresome these last several years since he had gone to Beverstone Castle, leaving only Anne, my wife, as well as our daughters and servants to tediously carry on. He sat tall in the saddle, head held aloft, and carried a steel-prodded crossbow. He had inherited my dark hair and ruddy complexion but his mother's soft green eyes. Hearing the enthusiasm in his voice gave me a momentary surge of energy.

"Listen for the horn," I chided him. "And wait to draw your bow until the huntsmen have it harbored." I was eager to see him make the kill.

"I know, Father," he said, spurring his chestnut horse forward through the oak trees before I could say anything more.

You can't coddle him any longer, I reminded myself. *He is as much a man now as you were when slogging through France with King Harry.* I had not always been the overly cautious man I was that day. Too many years alone in a house full of women had dulled my edge.

"Hah!" I shouted as I kicked Ebon, my black courser, driving him headlong through the copse. Thomas's scarlet doublet resembled a fiery hornet as he kept ahead of me, hurdling fallen logs, darting between tall oaks, and ducking low-hanging branches. My son had left my house a boy and returned a man. He was twice the rider that I was.

The crazed sounds of the hounds grew louder and louder with each stride of my horse. At first I thought the raches had run down a stag; the huntsmen had reported seeing some large tracks earlier in the day. But the closer I rode, the more frantic their calls became.

"Be careful, Thomas!" I called ahead to my son a moment before he disappeared through a dense hedge. "A boar may have gored one of the hounds." The rest of the dogs would be taking turns nipping at its heels. "Let them tire it out and don't get between them."

I should have recognized the unnatural tone in their terrified barks. I have spent many fretful nights since then wondering how things might have turned out if I had only trusted my instincts and called my son back.

"Father!" I heard Thomas shout from just ahead, drawing out the word in a desperate plea. Within a heartbeat I reined my horse to a halt next to his in a small clearing amid a stand of ancient beech trees that veiled the overhead midday sky. Mouth agape, my son appeared to be dumbstruck by an odd figure crouched upon the dark, mossy earth. "Look," he finally stammered.

The man, dressed in the tawny-colored rags of a plowman, was bent over the limp body of a fawn; small tufts of blood-tinged fur roiled in the cool breeze. The four hounds whimpered as they paced warily back and forth several yards behind the stranger.

"You there! Villein!" My muscles tensed with anger. The man had trespassed on my estate and interrupted the first hunt I had been able to enjoy with my son in over two years. "By what right have you taken that deer upon my lands?" He ignored the question and took a savage bite out of the small animal's neck. "Lewys!" I shouted for the master of hounds. He had been in my service since his days as an archer in France. "Lewys, where the devil are you?"

"Coming m'lord," a voice responded from my left. A moment later Lewys Massy emerged with his two assistants in tow; all carried long oaken staves, which they used to beat the brush for game.

"Apprehend that man," I barked, pointing at the stranger who thrashed his head like a mastiff savaging a hare. The sheer barbarism of it all was stunning. I had every right to have the man hanged, but I had never before seen someone so overcome with hunger. I considered letting him keep the wretched deer, but his disobedience could not be tolerated in front of the servants. "Remind him that poaching will not be tolerated and that he must show proper respect to his lord."

Lewys pushed back the hood of his woolen mantle and moved to leash the hounds. He nodded in agreement to the other two huntsmen.

"Oy," Guy Wode, the larger of the two, said as he stepped forward. "Are you deaf, man? Didn't you hear Sir Richard address you?" Tall and brawny, Guy served as my woodward, keeping charge over the foresters who provided the timber for my estate.

"Enough with the pleasantries," grumbled Hugh Eworthe, the younger huntsman, as he slid past Guy and Lewys to give the stranger a strong jab in the ribs with the end of his stave.

It was in that instant I knew a terrible evil had been unleashed upon the world. The grotesque figure raised his head as suddenly as a stag after hearing the blare of a horn. His face was smeared with fresh blood and his eyes were milky white. Without warning, he lunged towards Hugh with lightning speed, tearing at his neck with black, claw like fingers. The lad shrieked in horror as he collapsed under his attacker's weight. His panicked screams sent a chill up my spine.

Guy reacted first. "Get off him, cur!" He delivered several powerful chops about the head and shoulders of the demon-crazed figure, the final one splintering his oak shaft. Hugh's urgent cries for help began to weaken.

"He's going to kill the boy," Lewys shouted as he ran up behind the devil and hooked his stave under its chin. "Help me get him off." With all of his might, he leveraged his opponent backwards while Guy pushed and shoved from the front. The monster, finally separated from its victim, began scratching and clawing wildly at Guy's face and neck.

"Hold the devil still," Guy bellowed as he reached down for Hugh's discarded shaft.

"Forget the bloody stick! He's too much for me! Whip out your pig-sticker and stab the bugger!"

Guy attempted to deflect the madman's savage attacks with one hand while reaching for his knife with the other. Suddenly he roared with pain as he recoiled backwards and collapsed to the ground.

"Stinking saracen bit me!" he exclaimed, clutching a hand to his forearm. The ghoulish figure struggled forward towards Guy with outstretched arms, seemingly indifferent to the fact that Lewys was still dangling from its back. Guy frantically kicked his legs in an attempt to worm his way backwards.

With a loud thud, a quarrel struck the figure so solidly in the chest that only the last few inches of its shaft were visible. The creature flung Lewys to the ground as if he were a maid and then turned towards my son, who was desperately trying to pull back the string of his crossbow.

"Die, you fiend!" I growled as I leveled my spear and spurred Ebon forward. Locking my arm, I drove the tip through the monster's chest and used the momentum of my horse to pin it to the ground. The ghoul continued to thrash around wildly.

"He's still alive," Lewys gasped. "The devil's been seized with an unholy fury."

"Stay back," I said as I slid off my horse and approached the figure, still clawing at the shaft of the lance. Unsheathing my hunting sword, I thrust the blade into its heart not once but thrice with no apparent effect. Finally, I aimed for the milky white of its left eye and shoved until the tip stuck deep into the cold earth below; with a guttural exhale, the creature went limp.

"Lewys, are you all right?" I finally asked the chief huntsman. He rose and brushed clumps of earth from his green doublet and stuck a finger through a rend in his hose.

"Aye, lord. You saved my life." He turned and looked down at the body of Hugh still quivering on the ground; a large hunk of flesh had been ripped from the side of his throat. "Poor lad, he's beyond all hope of saving. No surgeon on earth could help him now."

He's right, I told myself. Hugh's life was quickly ebbing away. It had been many years since I had been forced to watch a man die from his wounds. It had never become easy for me, not like it had for some. *Poor Hugh, he has no wife or family in the village to mourn for him.*

The eerie quiet was broken by the sound of thick fabric being rent. Guy Wode had sliced off the lower portion of his sleeve with a dagger. Thick blood ran down his elbow from a hole in his forearm. He cut the material into several strips, which he then bound atop the wound.

"And what of you, Guy? How badly are you hurt?"

"Nothing that won't mend in a few days, lord. Thanks be to God."

"Father, how is it possible that man should refuse to die so?" Thomas had dismounted and was now standing to one side. He did his best to appear confident in front of the other men, but his grip on the reins was so tight that his knuckles were white.

"I once saw a Welshman keep fighting even after being disemboweled. It was not until he looked down and realized he was stepping on his own guts that he collapsed and died instantly." It was mostly true, but Thomas cocked his head as if unconvinced.

"Do either of you recognize this man?" I asked, turning back to the huntsmen. "Someone from a nearby village, perhaps?" I withdrew my blade from the creature's skull. Strangely, the blood appeared already clotted on the tip as I wiped it on the corpse's sleeve.

"No, lord," Lewys said, once again going about the task of gathering the whimpering hounds. "He doesn't look familiar at all. I can send one of the lads to inquire around, if it pleases you. He looked stark blind to me. Likely as not, he must have wandered here after begging for alms at the priory."

"He killed Hugh and nearly bit Guy's arm off. Those are not the actions of a blind beggar."

"Perhaps he was one of the hermits they say live in the Forest of Dean. There've been stories of fell creatures in those woods since long before my father was a boy." I couldn't help but wonder if Lewys was trying to appease me as I had with Thomas.

"I do not believe in ghosts or evil spirits, but I have to admit there was something very unnatural about his appearance," I replied. The dead man's face, though streaked with fresh blood, was ashen gray and marked by several dark spots. I used the hunting sword to examine the folds of his clothing for any clue as to where he might have come from. "From his manner of dress, I first thought he was a simple plowman."

"Looks more like the canvas shirt and trousers of a mariner if you ask me," Guy commented. "Come to think of it, he looks like a foreigner."

"That makes no sense," I countered. "The nearest port is in Gloucester, and that is nearly twenty miles away. How could he have walked that far in such a wretched state?"

"Saints preserve us!" Lewys gasped after I sliced open the front of the stranger's shirt. He quickly crossed himself to ward off evil. "What sort of disease can do that to a man?" There were a number of large blackened tumors near the pits of his arms, some of which had burst, oozing a mixture of blood and dark bile. My stomach started to churn.

"Thomas, get back on your horse!" My words were shrill.

"What's wrong, Father?" The color fled from his face.

"I fear it is Pestilence, though I confess I have only read of such things in a book once, many, many years ago." The book had not mentioned anything about it causing madness.

"And what of me, Sir Richard?" Guy took a step backwards and clutched a hand to his wounded arm. "Am I to die?"

"I am sure you will be fine," I lied. I had no idea how the Great Plague spread, but I knew it would do no good to create a panic. "Nevertheless, we will take no chances. Let us hasten home to Colleville Manor. Lewys, I want you to accompany a couple of the lads back here with a litter to recover Hugh's body and bring it back to the parish church for proper burial. The other corpse is to be taken to the priory at Stony Heath for the monks to examine. While you are there, I want you to ask Prior Gregory to send a physician to treat Guy's wounds. And Thomas?"

"Yes, Father?"

"Have Master Edmund ensure that everyone is present in the great hall for supper this evening. Depending on what the monks have to say, our Christmastide feasting may be a more somber affair tonight."

On any other afternoon, I would have greatly enjoyed thundering across the grassy moors and up the gentle slope back to Colleville, but on that particular day my thoughts were never far from my wife and children waiting back at home. There was a queasiness in my stomach that refused to go away.

Rather than returning along the curved northern road, we galloped headlong around the dark, shallow waters of the mill pond and bounded over a low hedge to cut across the village's southern grazing field. A hundred yards later, we hurdled a garbage-strewn ditch and flew around the great stone barn to reach the manor green. The trip lasted barely a half-hour, but it felt like an eternity.

Anne and the girls will be fine. There are no other foreign devils wandering the countryside. Still I could not get the image of the madman out of my head. But the manor house was well-fortified; I was confident it would be enough to keep my family safe.

When I first took possession of Colleville Manor—I can scarce believe it has been more than twenty years—I was told that the main house and enclosing walls were already nigh a century old. Over the years I made no small number of modest improvements, many of which were financed with French coins and silver plate gained during my intemperate youth. The most noticeable addition was a small, square gatehouse built in the center of the west wall comprised of golden Cotswold stone quarried from my own lands.

I spurred my courser over the final stretch of land. No man spoke or slowed his pace until after we crossed the short stone bridge spanning the moat and passed through the gatehouse. As we emerged onto the cobblestone courtyard, Edmund Bromeley, my household steward, was already waiting for us. Doubtless he had instructed one of the boys to keep watch and alert him at first sight of our return.

"What're you waiting for, lads? See to your master's horses. Hurry up, now. Don't keep him waiting." Despite an angry scowl directed at the pair of grooms, Edmund's round face and bright red cheeks made him appear jolly. The boys dutifully rushed forward to take our horses and lead them to the stables outside the north wall. "Is everything all right, Sir Richard? I didn't expect you to return until much later in the day."

"Thomas will explain everything," I replied before waving over the porter, Adam Stoney. Impatiently, I glanced up at the large sundial carved onto the side of the gatehouse as the man hurried over. Although great cities such as London have mechanical clocks that chime a standardized hour, we still divided the daylight into twelve equal portions according to the movement of the sun. It was almost the ninth hour.

"Master Adam, bar the gates and ensure that no visitors are allowed to enter without my express authorization." I did not bother to wait for either man to acknowledge my words; instead, I immediately turned and made my way briskly across the courtyard. Once again my thoughts focused on Anne and our three daughters.

I climbed the well-worn steps in front of the hall and pushed open its heavy door. Passing through a line of panel screens, I entered the great hall. The central hearth fire had burned down to embers; only a wisp of smoke spiraled up to the vent in the tier-beamed roof high above. Vaulted stained-glass windows on either side illuminated the room with faint hues of pink and yellow and pale blue.

I paced across the tile floor towards the high table on the far wall, strode up the steps of the dais, and passed through a small door to my private rooms. I knew I would find my wife in the main solar beneath the master chamber.

"Husband, why are you back so soon?" Anne asked as I entered the family room. The air was filled with the aroma of fresh-cut holly and fir. She placed her embroidery down on the window seat beside her before moving to meet me in the middle of the solar. She looked radiant in her blue brocade dress. "There are still a few more hours of daylight. Could you find no sign of game?"

"You would never believe it, but a stranger attacked and killed young Hugh Eworthe in our woods." I was still unsure how much to disclose. There was no reason to alarm her or the girls.

"Is Thomas all right?" a voice called out from the corner of the room. Turning, I saw the concerned face of Elizabeth, my youngest daughter, peering out from behind a needlepoint loom.

"Of course he is, my dear," I said, holding out an arm. "You have nothing to worry about." She ran over gleefully and slid underneath my arm to give me a warm hug.

"Are you that excited to see me or just happy to escape the loom?" She looked up and giggled before burying her head in my chest for another hug. "So where have your sisters gone off to?"

"Ellie's probably under a window somewhere reading a book, and, of course, Bernie is looking in on James."

James Berkeley was the eldest son of Sir John Berkeley of Beverstone. Like Thomas, it was customary for him to receive his education as a squire in another knight's household. I was expected to teach him good horsemanship, jousting, swordplay, and the other requisite martial skills in addition to having him tutored in Latin and French. It was one of the few uses the world had for grizzled old warriors apart from feasting and hunting. At sixteen, James was the same age as Bernice, and she followed him around like a lost puppy.

"Be a dear and go fetch them."

"But," she began to protest. A scowl from my wife promptly quelled her dissent. "Yes, father," she said, a protruding lower lip emphasizing her displeasure. "But I still want to hear about the man who attacked you." She turned and ran through the door and up the stairs.

"How is James?" I asked my wife once the sounds of footsteps had faded. James had felt too ill to join us on the hunt.

"He still has a fever. Mary took him a broth earlier, but I don't think he ate any of it." Mary Barry was the wife of our kitchen steward. She also served as the laundress.

"I asked Lewys to bring back a physician from the monastery. I will have him look in on James when he arrives."

"You don't think his fever is that serious, do you?" she asked, placing a hand to her heart.

"No, good wife, I sent for the monk to tend to Guy. He was injured while trying to save Hugh. It's nothing serious, but I wanted someone from the priory hospital to examine him nonetheless." I had already revealed more than I intended, so I tried to change the subject. "I hope to know more after supper." I turned and exited the room before she could question me further.

"Sir Richard, the lads have returned with a brother Phillip," Edmund spoke quietly in my ear. "He has already been shown to Guy's chamber." I nodded in acknowledgment. The sun had just begun to set; it had taken less time than I anticipated for them to fetch the surgeon. Everyone had just taken their seats in the great hall. As was customary, I sat at the center of the head table with my wife at my side. Thomas sat to my right, next to Bernice, while Ellie and Lizzie were to the left of Anne.

"Please see that he checks in on James as well." I kept my voice low. "Tell the monk that the boy is to be treated as a member of the family."

"Certainly, lord." He hesitated for a moment before providing the rest of his report. "The lads said they retrieved the stranger's corpse from the woods but there was no trace of Hugh to be found." Anne immediately turned towards me, her eyes wide. I held up a hand to subdue her interruption.

"Did it appear that a bear or pack of wild dogs had carried off his body?" There had been far more of them lurking in the woods that winter than I had ever previously recalled.

"They said they didn't find a single track apart from those of you and the men, so they carted the stranger straight to the monastery."

I nodded again. "Have the marshal of the hall show him in when he has completed his work." Edmund bowed his head and then slipped around the table and off of the dais, giving a brief instruction to one of the ushers before taking his seat.

As soon as he moved away, a boy carrying a silver ewer placed a basin in front of me and poured rose-scented water over my hands. Another servant did the same for Anne. We were each offered a linen towel to dry our hands before the basins were moved down the table.

"When were you going to tell me?" she whispered through a forced smile.

"Anne, dear," I replied in a soft but deliberate voice. "I did not want to alarm you or the girls. It was an isolated incident several miles from here."

"And you left Hugh's body alone in the woods?"

"I know," I sighed. "I should have left a man behind to guard him until the lads returned with the cart.

"What could have taken his body without leaving behind a single track?"

"I am not sure, but I will get to the bottom of it."

"You should have told me, Richard." She turned away abruptly. "Sit up straight, Elizabeth. You, too, Elenore."

"Yes, mother," they groaned in unison.

I did my best to smile and appear cheerful as I looked across the room. The smell of boiled fish filled the air. Two long tables had been erected along either side of the hearth, which now blazed high to warm and brighten the hall. At the far end of the room, above the panel-screened hallway, was a minstrel's gallery. Luke, the porter's teen-aged son, was given a halfpence each evening he sat there and played his psaltery.

The guests were seated in order of precedence, extending away from the high table. Edmund had once again taken his seat at the head of the table to my right. Next to him sat William Sorel and his wife, Agnes. Like Lewys, William had crossed the English Sea in my service over twenty years ago, and I had continued to retain him as a feed man ever since. As my marshal of the stables, William was responsible for managing all of the horses and carts used by the manor.

Most of the other men were much younger, many having returned home looking for work after serving as mercenaries in the free companies. I always believed it was good for a lord to surround himself with trustworthy men of a certain temperament.

A pair of lads placed cellars of salt along the tables and filled every cup with sweet red wine imported from Burgundy. A cheeseboard and a dish of softened butter were placed nearby.

The first course consisted of peas cooked in milk with ginger and saffron followed by a pottage of flayed eel cooked in water and wine. Courses of carp, mullet, and sole were brought out one by one, but I barely tasted them. My mind was still preoccupied with the fact that Hugh might never receive a proper Christian burial.

"My lord," a voice suddenly rasped over my shoulder, causing me to jump in my seat. Hal Mydelton, my grizzled old chamberlain, courteously ignored my reaction. "Brother Phillip has completed his treatments and is waiting outside. He says he has urgent news for you."

"See him in, Master Hal." He exited momentarily through the screens passage before returning with a slender man carrying a large satchel and dressed in a plain black habit. The robes signified that he was a member of the Benedictine Order. Hal escorted him to the base of the dais.

"Brother Phillip of the Priory at Stony Heath," he announced before bowing and taking several steps to the side. A hush fell on the room.

"Brother Phillip, what urgent news do you have for me?"

"God keep you, Sir Richard," the monk said in a high-pitched voice. "Regretfully, I must report that your man, Guy the woodcutter, is infected with Plague." There was a collective gasp throughout the hall, followed by a growing din of murmuring. "It is very important that he be isolated from the rest of your household at once."

Impossible! a voice screamed in my head. No disease spreads so quickly. I wrangled with the possibility that the monk was wrong, but then another thought crept into my head. *If you really thought it impossible, why did you send for a surgeon in the first place?*

"Please," I said with authority. "Everyone remain calm. Continue dining." Anne's hand clutched my thigh. "Are you certain? He appeared healthy a couple of hours ago. We only summoned you here to treat the wound to his arm."

"He is feverish and complained of nausea and a headache. I examined him and found lumps around his neck and thighs."

"And you are certain that means he has Plague?" I searched his eyes for some sign of doubt. James, my young squire, had been feverish and complained of aches, and Anne had permitted Bernice to pamper him all day.

"The lumps," brother Phillip said, opening a large wood-bound tome that he produced from his satchel. "The lumps will develop into tumors that will fill with blood and pus and turn black. They will eventually split open and ooze. He will bleed internally, which will create black spots all over his body. Death will very likely come within days. I wish I could say that I was less than certain in my prognosis, but the evidence is dreadfully clear." He turned the book around to show me the illumination. Even from across the table, the gruesome depiction of a plague-ridden corpse was easily recognizable. It looked identical to the stranger in the woods.

What the devil have I done? It was as though the monk had stabbed me in the gut with a dull knife that he twisted over and over with every word. *I've been such a fool. What will become of my family?*

"The Great Mortality has returned to our shores," brother Phillip continued, oblivious to my mental anguish. "It hasn't been seen for many generations, but I'm afraid that this is now the second case I have seen today. The body your men brought to the monastery this afternoon was also infected. That's why Prior Gregory sent me here in such haste."

"He must go!" a woman shouted near the far end of the hall. She was quickly hushed by those next to her, but it was hard to ignore the growing storm of frantic whispering.

"And what of James?" I asked forcefully, attempting to exert some sense of control over the situation.

"Squire James only has an ague. His humors are out of balance, so I've given him almond milk and an infusion of mandrake to help him sleep. He should recover fully within a day or two. If he doesn't, I may have to bleed him, but it shouldn't be anything to worry about."

"That is good news," I replied, turning to give Anne an encouraging nod. I reached down and patted her hand still gripping my thigh; it trembled softly. A heartbeat later, she jerked her hand away and reached for her cup without bothering to take a drink.

"Thank you, brother Phillip," I said in the most reserved tone I could muster. "If you would be so kind as to stay on for a few days to treat Guy and ensure that the disease does not spread within our walls, I would be most appreciative."

"But I was only supposed to—" he began to protest but stopped short. "Very well, with my prior's permission."

"Good. I will send a man at first light to ensure that you have it." The thought of harboring such a deadly disease just across the courtyard from my family was terrifying, but, by locking Guy in his quarters, at least it would keep the Pestilence bottled up. To toss him out now would be like rolling a powder keg into the midst of the village. Pushing my chair back, I stood to address the hall.

"Each and every one of you is assured of my good lordship. I would not put out my wife nor son nor daughters; neither will I send one of yours out. Guy Wode has been kept in his room since his return from the hunt. There is no reason to believe anyone else could be infected. Am I not right, brother Phillip?" I gave him a stern look to ensure his cooperation in calming the crowd.

"Yes, Sir Richard," he said meekly. "I will ensure no one other than myself enters his quarters."

Anne was waiting when I entered the bed chamber. She was seated on the side of the bed gently running an ivory comb through her long, golden hair. I had spent a couple of hours pacing around in the upper hall before coming to bed in the hope that her anger might have subsided. Her tightly pursed lips told me that it had been in vain.

"Why not have your chambermaid do that for you?" I asked.

"If I left it to Sarah, I would have no hair left. I doubt you would like me very well if I were bald." I chose not to respond. Instead, I went about my nightly routine of chasing out the dog, changing into my sleeping shirt, and then warming myself by the fire.

"What do you intend to do about the Plague?" she finally asked, setting down her brush. The features of her alabaster skin softened as tears welled up in the corners of her eyes.

"Dearest Anne." I gently wiped my thumb across her cheek. "You know I can't stand to see you cry. You have to understand that Guy is a member of this household, so I will afford him every opportunity to recover, no matter how dire it may seem."

"Even if it puts your own children at risk?" Her words were a slap across the face.

"Guy was infected because he was following my orders, and he's been kept secure in his quarters since our return. You yourself heard brother Phillip. He's keeping a close watch on Guy. There's no reason for you to be afraid."

"What about Lewys Massy? Didn't you say that he fought with the stranger as well?"

"Yes, but he wasn't bitten like Guy."

"Does one have to be bitten to become infected?"

How the devil should I know? I wanted to shout. "I'll speak with brother Phillip in the morning. If he believes that there's any possibility that Lewys has been infected, I'll direct him to remain in his cottage on the other side of the village."

"What if there are more like the stranger lurking somewhere out in the woods?"

"There was only the one, my dear. We found no others."

"But how can you be so certain? You said that you didn't see any deer, but we both know there are hundreds of them roaming the countryside."

"It's not the same thing. The deer bed down and must be flushed out of hiding with dogs."

"But what if there *are*? What will you do then?"

"Then we will deal with them the same way we did this one, and you and the girls will remain safely inside the manor. A small army couldn't get past its high walls and wide moat, so rest yourself easy. Everything will be all right." Her eyes searched my face for any doubt. "Now, Anne, it's late, and I'm very tired. We should get some sleep."

Without another word, I slid under the soft, hare-lined coverlets and pulled the embroidered bed curtains closed. They provided a small measure of privacy from the two servants who slept in low beds across the room. I was relieved when Anne did the same; her doubts had already begun creeping into my mind. May God forgive me, but in that moment I hoped Guy would die quietly in his sleep so that life at Colleville Manor could return to normal.

29 December

Feast of Saint Thomas of Canterbury

ICHARD?" ANNE'S VOICE GENTLY lulled me from a deep and restful slumber and back into a world still shrouded in cold darkness. "That was the bell at Saint Wystan's. It's daybreak."

"Already?" I groaned. It was the first time in years that I had not been awakened by church bells tolling the hour of Matins. My eyes slowly focused on her shadowy face silhouetted against a white pillow. "How did you sleep, my dear?"

"Not nearly as well as you," she chuckled softly. Her small but pleasant smile gave me hope that her worries had vanished during the night. "You barely moved a muscle all night."

"I was exhausted," I replied, propping myself up on an elbow to look down at her. I felt more refreshed that morning than I ever had before, or perhaps that is just the way I remember it now, after the many sleepless nights that followed.

"Ugh, I think winter has returned," Anne grumbled as she pulled the covers over her head. Even inside the bed canopy the air was cold and crisp, a stark contrast to the previous day's mild climate. A faint smell of smoke drifted through the room.

"Matthew, lad, how is that fire coming?" As my personal varlet, young Matthew Scoffe attended to my wardrobe and served as my personal groom; like Anne's chambermaid, Sarah, he was provided a small bed in the corner.

"Just a moment, Sir Richard." There was a faint crackle as the kindling started to burn in the fireplace across the room, its soft glow slowly illuminating the chamber through the bed curtains.

"Time to get up," I said, tugging at the coverlets still clutched over Anne's head. She brushed an icy-cold foot against my leg.

"For heaven's sake, woman! How can anything be so cold and still alive?" I threw back my covers in mock protest as I parted the curtains and slid from the bed. It felt good to stand and stretch. Slipping on a pair of shoes, I shuffled over to warm myself by the now-blazing fire.

"Good morrow, Sir Richard," Matthew said cheerfully. He was seated on a stool nearby, dutifully brushing out my woolen hose.

"And to you, Matthew." I truly liked the boy; he worked twice as hard as any of the other lads. I sometimes could not help but pity his misfortune. Matthew's mother had died in childbirth, and his father had been killed three years ago when his oxcart overturned in the village. It was then that Edmund first brought the 10-year-old boy into the great hall and recommended him for service. Diligent and resourceful, Matthew Scoffe had all the makings of a good squire except for his pedigree.

"That should be fine, Matthew," I said, taking the hose from him and quickly pulling them on. From behind came the sound of bare feet shuffling across the stone floor as Anne emerged from the bed.

"I was beginning to think you were going to lay around in bed all day, woman," I remarked as Matthew held up a padded doublet and I slid my arms inside. He closed the row of fabric buttons down the front and then fastened the sets that ran from elbow to cuff on each sleeve.

"I was holding out hope that the room would get warm," Anne said with a laugh. She hurried over to where her maid was waiting with a pair of dresses to choose from. "The green one, Sarah." She knew I would be pleased. It was the color of pale leaves, and it always reminded me of the forest in summer.

"You know, I had so been looking forward to taking Thomas on a successful hunt. Now it appears I won't get the chance before he returns to Beverstone."

"I pray you're not thinking of sending him back there any time soon," Anne replied, grunting every couple of words as Sarah laced up the front of her underdress. "After all that happened yesterday, I would think you would want to keep him here at home, where he's safe."

"Thomas is almost a man now. We can't coddle him any longer. He'll rejoin Sir John's household as expected." I turned to allow Matthew to help me into my scarlet wool coat embroidered with small golden bears.

Waiting for Anne to finish dressing, I pulled up a chair in front of the fireplace and stared into its flames. My thoughts wandered back to the crazed foreigner in the forest.

Where could he have possibly come from and how could a sick man wander all that way so poorly clothed, even on a mild day? More perplexing, if he were a mariner, why would he have left his vessel and traveled here alone? There were so many questions that remained unanswered.

"It is our lot in life, Matthew," I said lowly, glancing back to check on Anne's progress, "that we spend all of our days waiting on our wives. One day you will understand." The varlet's face stretched into a broad grin.

"You'd better not be over there filling that poor boy's head with more of your nonsense," Anne said as Sarah finished binding her golden hair, covering it with a silk lace veil. She then draped a wide fur mantle over my wife's shoulders to keep her warm.

"Ready so soon, my dear?" I said as I offered her my arm. She smiled warmly as she walked over to my side, and together we made our way down to the chapel for our morning prayers.

"Sir Richard," a voice roared from across the courtyard. A stout man wearing a light blue coat gently brushed Edmund aside and moved briskly towards the hall. It was Therry Wode, Guy's younger but much larger brother. The old steward puffed out his chest and cinched up his belt before hurrying to intercept the intruder.

"It is fine, Master Edmund," I said, waving him off. "Therry is obviously here to inquire about his brother's health." Stopping a few feet behind the uninvited guest, Edmund nodded wordlessly as he crossed his arms and glared at the taller man under a furrowed brow.

"I beg your pardon, my lord," Therry said with a bow of his head, "but your man didn't have a mind to let me in to see you just now." The younger Wode brother was a stone mason like his late father, who had once managed my quarry before it ran dry. Therry clutched his brawny hands together at his waist in an expression of humility.

"The entire manor has been on edge since my son and I were assaulted in the woods yesterday."

"I'm glad to see my lord was not harmed." The stone mason offered another quick bow of his head. He had kind eyes framed by a full, dark beard and roughly shorn head.

"Thanks be to your brother, Guy. He bravely placed himself between us and the stranger."

"Please, lord, tell me the truth. How is my brother? A neighbor just came and told me that he's very sick."

"I should have sent word to you earlier. For that I am truly sorry. Your brother is in his quarters under the care of a surgeon from Stony Heath. I was on my way now to check in on him. You are welcome to accompany me." I motioned him back across the courtyard.

"What happened to him, lord?" Therry asked as we made our way to the door in the western wall.

"We encountered a foreigner poaching deer in Colle's Chase. Without warning, he attacked Guy and the other huntsmen when challenged. Your brother was bitten on the arm, and Hugh Eworthe was killed." I opened the door and gestured him to climb the stairs.

"It'll take more than a bite on the arm to kill my brother," Therry replied with a weak smile. At the top of the stairs we turned and entered a hallway; I guided him to the left.

"It was only after the stranger was killed that we learned he had the Pestilence. I am afraid your brother has been infected."

"Pestilence?" The burly stone mason shuddered at the news. I continued to urge him forward as we passed a series of doors along the inner side of the hallway, each representing a single chamber where a servant or guest could reside.

"Brother Phillip?" I spoke through the third door on the left as I knocked softly. "May we come in?" There was no immediate answer, so I knocked again. The only response was the sound of footsteps shuffling across the floor. With a click, the latch slid back and the door creaked open.

"My apologies, Sir Richard," the monk said in a pitched tone. "I was just finishing up." He stood in the doorway fastidiously wiping his hands on a small crimson towel.

"How is he?" I asked, craning my neck to peer over his shoulder into the room.

"I'm afraid there's not much more that can be done for him here. It's in the hands of God now." Brother Phillip stepped aside to give me enough room to enter. As I started to walk past him, I noticed several dark, wet splotches down the front of his robes.

"Is that blood?" I questioned the monk, pointing to his chest. Realizing the towel in his hands had once been white linen, I took a quick step backwards, bumping into the stone mason.

"What the devil have you done to my brother?" Therry growled from behind. Brother Phillip blotted at his robes as if he had only dribbled a bit of wine on his chest at a meal.

"Ah, yes. I should have thought to bring a change of clothes." He gave Therry a sidelong glance before tossing the bloody towel next to the wash basin. "I thought you said you'd seen a man with Plague before, Sir Richard. It might be best if you don't come in." Perhaps sensing my hesitation, the monk flashed a tender smile. "Your man is ill, but I'm certain he won't try to attack you."

"I really must insist," I said halfheartedly. Therry's breath was hot on my neck. It would appear as cowardice if I were to wait outside while he went in. Steeling myself, I slowly walked into the room. The smell of vinegar and vomit was revolting.

"I'm sorry, Sir Richard," Guy said in a graveled voice. He struggled to rise in his bed. His chest was mottled by a dark red rash, and beads of sweat glistened on his pale forehead.

"Lie back, son," the monk chided him. "You'll start to bleed again." On a table next to the bed was a small metal bowl filled with a dark liquid; several bladed instruments sat upon a blood-soaked towel nearby. A mud-like paste had been applied to his right arm where a vein had been pierced a short time before.

"Guy," the stone mason spoke softy as he slid between me and brother Phillip. "It's your brother, Therry. How do you feel?"

"I'm sick, not blind, baby brother," he coughed. "I should've been more careful. I can't believe I've been killed by a bloody foreigner."

"Don't talk like that," Therry argued. "You're in the hands of a skilled surgeon." The monk's face reddened as he looked down at the floor.

"What is the matter, brother Phillip?" I inquired.

"I washed him with vinegar and rose water and then bled him in an attempt to balance his humors, but I fear I haven't really done him any good. He's beginning to bleed underneath the skin. I'm confounded by how fast it's progressing. From all of my reading, it should take at least a few days for the disease to run its course. Your man is—"

"There has to be something you can do," Therry interrupted. "I can't pay much, but I'll give you all I have." Guy coughed loudly into his hand before wiping a bloody handprint on the bed sheet. His face seemed to grow more pale.

"Nonsense," I countered. "He was injured in my service. I will pay his account. Do whatever you must to save him."

"It's not a matter of coin," the monk protested. "I didn't have time to pack when your men arrived. I brought only what few supplies I had in my satchel. If we were back at the priory, the buboes could be lanced and filled with a salve. Brother Stephen also knows how to prepare theriac, a powerful ointment made from the flesh of serpents."

"You mean to tell me that snake meat will cure the Plague?" I could understand placing a poultice on wounds, but it made no sense to give a sick man poison.

"Well, it is said that disease is a divine punishment upon man. The flesh of serpents is proof against venom; it only stands to reason that it would also be a curative for the poisonous effect of sin upon the body." The monk sounded doubtful of his final conclusion. I considered pressing him for other options but chose to leave the debate for another time.

"We're wasting time," Therry interjected. "Begging your pardon, lord, but if something isn't done soon, it'll surely be too late."

"Brother Phillip," I said, turning to the monk. "Would it be better to convey him to Stony Heath or to send a man to fetch the necessary supplies? It could very well take a couple of hours to transport him by horse and cart."

"Brother Stephen is the head of our infirmary. He is a much more skilled physician than I could ever hope to be. If you want to give your man a chance—albeit a small one—to survive, he should be sent to the monastery without delay."

"Very well, at the very least I owe him that." I placed a hand on the shoulder of Guy's brother. "Therry, run and fetch the marshal of the stables. Instruct him to come here at once." Without a word, the stone mason turned and ran down the hall.

"May I ask you a personal question, Sir Richard?" the monk asked as he began to carefully repack his satchel.

"Of course, brother Phillip. What is it?"

"I understand that you were close with our former prior, Prior Thomas?" I had not thought of that name in many years.

"Yes, I respected him greatly. In my first few years as Lord of Colleville, I frequented your monastery to read some of the magnificent tomes contained within its library. Prior Thomas was always very friendly towards me and, in times of need, provided me with good and wise counsel. I named my son after him, and I mourned his passing deeply."

"I had heard as much, but I've never seen you visit the priory in all of my years there. Did you find his successor to be lacking in those traits?"

Prior Gregory, as far as I was concerned at the time, had few of his predecessor's good qualities, and we had barely spoken a word in the past several years. Although the young monk standing before me spoke with sincerity, I could not help but wonder whether it was innocent curiosity that posed the question or something less genuine. As I searched for the words to tactfully relate my longtime disagreement with the prior, William and a pair of lads rushed into the room. Therry filled the doorway behind them.

"You sent for me, Sir Richard?" The stable master panted as he wiped his brow with the cuff of a sleeve. Behind him were his son, John, and a younger lad named Owain Dun; both served as grooms in the stables.

"Master William, have a horse and cart readied. I want Guy taken to the priory."

"You want *me* to take him all the way to Stony Heath, Sir Richard?" The old marshal swallowed hard as he stared at the figure lying on the bloodstained bed.

"You may remain at the manor, Master William. Guy's brother can see that he makes it safely to Stony Heath; however, I want you to personally ensure that all the necessary arrangements are made at once."

"Very well, my lord." He slowly retreated from the room, dragging the two grooms along with him. Several times he loudly hushed the boys as they hurried down the hallway.

"Brother Phillip, I want you to remain here for a few more days to monitor my man Lewys and ensure the disease does not spread any further within my walls." Before he could respond, I added, "I will, of course, have my man secure permission from your prior when Guy is delivered."

30 December

Feast of Saint Sabinus

I WAS AWAKENED BY A LOUD pounding on the door. The latch was quickly pulled, and the door swung open. The golden light of a candle twinkled through the embroidered curtains. A moment later the fabric near my head was pulled back by a shadowy figure.

"My lord, I apologize for the intrusion," Edmund said breathlessly as he touched his candle to the oil lamp next to the bed; the room filled with a soft warm glow.

"What hour is it?" My head was groggy from sleep. The logs in the fireplace had turned to embers.

"It's after Vigils, lord; still a few hours before dawn." The stress in his voice told me that something was seriously wrong, which was all the more troubling as nothing ever seemed to rattle the old steward.

"I trust you have a good reason to disturb my sleep, Master Edmund. What is it that concerns you so?" I slid from the bed and pulled on my old velvet robe. "Help me find my shoes," I said wearily.

"It's about Hugh," he said reluctantly, looking past me to the body beginning to stir on the other side of the bed.

Good. A forester or someone from the village must have come across his corpse, but why would word of it come so late in the night? I only hoped the news would provide a sense of relief. Edmund's demeanor gave me cause to believe his body had been preyed upon.

"Is something the matter, husband?" Anne asked, doing her best to brush back several wild locks.

"All is well, my dear. Go back to sleep." I nudged Edmund towards the door as I rubbed sleep from my eyes. Once outside the chamber, I closed the door and signaled the steward to continue in a low voice.

"All of the doors were barred as you instructed. I checked them myself before retiring. I was awakened in the middle of the night by a loud shrieking and rushed outside to investigate. From what I have gathered, some of the dogs had started barking and acting strangely. John Sorel, William's oldest son, and Michael Burnes were on watch with one of the footmen inside the gatehouse—"

"Master Edmund," I interrupted. "I am too tired for a long story. Just tell me what is the matter."

"Well, by the time I got downstairs and made it out to the courtyard, I found one of the archers along with Adam Stoney hacking at a dark shape on the ground inside the gatehouse. Adam was shouting that Hugh had just killed young Michael."

"Hugh what? That's impossible. Hugh's dead. I saw him die with my own eyes. Wild dogs must have carried off his body."

"That may very well be, lord, but John Sorel told me the same story when I came across him in the courtyard. He was badly hurt but still alive. I pressed him to tell me what had happened and then came straightaway to inform you."

"Matthew! Wake up, boy, and fetch me my sword!" A moment later my varlet shuffled through the door dressed only in his hose and a linen shirt. His eyes were still half-closed as he handed me my longsword. "Now, Master Edmund, let us go deal with this person claiming to be Hugh."

"Husband? What is wrong?" Anne appeared in the doorway behind Matthew.

"Go get the girls and lock yourselves in the upper chamber. Open for no one but me. Matthew, go and watch over them." I slung the sheath to the ground before rushing down the stairs to the great hall. My mind desperately tried to make sense of Edmund's report. I was certain it could not be Hugh. I had seen enough men die in my lifetime to know there was no way that he could have recovered from his wounds. A rage started to build inside me.

I almost tripped over some of the kitchen servants who were sleeping around the hearth. I ran through the screens passage and out into the cold darkness. A thin crescent moon did little more than cast a faint silver sheen across the stone. The noise of dogs barking echoed throughout the courtyard.

"On me!" I shouted at the few men I could see stirring outside the tenements to the left of the gatehouse. The frosty air burned my lungs as I ran.

Nearing the inner doors of the gatehouse tower, I realized that I could hear no sounds of a struggle. There were no discernible shapes within the dark recesses of the passageway, only the faint glimmer of moonlight on a wetness spreading between the cobblestones.

"Torch! Will somebody fetch me a bloody torch? And make those blasted hounds quit their caterwauling?"

Edward Cornwayle appeared behind me, barefoot and bare-chested with a sword in his hand. He offered me a small brass lantern.

"On me, you bunch of swag-bellied louts!" Edward shouted with a tone of authority to the handful of men cautiously keeping their distance. "Rally to your lord!" The 28-year-old esquire had fought against the French in Paris. Knowing that he was behind me bolstered my courage enough to wade into the blackness.

I hoisted the small lantern in front of me; its faint, flickering light made the cobblestones appear to tremble. Tightening the grip on my sword, I took a few measured steps forward. The ground was slick with blood; I almost lost my footing more than once. In the midst of the inky pool lay the first dead body.

God help me. A look of sheer terror was still frozen on Michael's youthful face. He appeared to have been mauled by a large bear. His throat was ripped wide open, and in places the white bones of his chest were visible. A small axe and broken lantern lay at his side.

The second corpse was only a few paces further, though I could not tell to whom it belonged. It had been hacked to pieces; only a shredded green huntsman's tunic gave the torso any semblance of a humanoid shape.

"Forgive me, Sir Richard," a voice groaned to my right. I almost slipped again in the bloody mess under my feet as I jerked the lantern around to find Jack slumped in the dark corner. "I should've never let the boys stand watch with me." Adam was crouched next to him pressing a blood-soaked cloak to the footman's chest. As I stepped towards them, the old porter pulled the dressing back momentarily, revealing dozens of deep gashes down Jack's chest; his red livery jacket was nearly rent in two.

"I got him, Sir Richard," the wounded footman said through gritted teeth, his voice filled with pain. "Nasty bugger killed Michael, though. Nearly did me in, too."

"Hold on, Jack. You're going to be all right." I turned to the growing crowd now huddled just outside the inner gate. Several had half-drawn bows in their hands. "Someone fetch the surgeon. Tell him to hurry."

"Go!" Edward bellowed at a wide-eyed boy standing next to him.

"What the devil happened here?" I asked the footman, but he just shook his head as if he did not have the words to explain. His face was pale from either fear or loss of blood. Desperate for answers, I turned to Leonard Sampson; he carefully stepped around the intruder's corpse to retrieve his bow.

"To be honest, I'm still not sure, lord. I was standing watch atop the gatehouse staring off into the blackness when I suddenly heard the hue and cry come from downstairs. I banged on the porter's door as I ran down the steps. As soon as I arrived, I saw Jack running some poor fool clean through with his spear, taking him all the way to the ground. The whole time Jack kept saying the same thing over and over: 'Hugh killed Michael. Hugh killed Michael.'" I wanted to once again enter a word of protest against the murder's identity, but Leonard's cold dark gaze made me pause.

"My first reaction was to run over and try to help the boy on the ground who looked to be bleeding to death. But as soon as Jack pulled his spear out of the corpse, the blasted thing started getting back up and going after him, so I sunk a pair of bodkins into the devil's back. Can you believe the crazy bugger acted as if he hadn't felt a thing? If anything, it just sent him into a rage, and that's when he turned on me. That's when I saw his face. It was Hugh Eworthe."

"That's simply not possible. You must be mistaken."

"I'm sorry, Sir Richard, but I saw him with my own eyes. It was Hugh; of that fact I am certain. I've seen him a hundred times before. Anyway, I tried to reason with him, but he'd have none of it. He appeared to be seized with some kind of madness. It was all I could do just to keep him away from me. Finally, Jack ran over and skewered him from behind. Hugh went to the ground but kept trying to rise and grab Jack. We just hit him and hit him and hit him again until he stopped moving." I looked back down at the mutilated corpse. I still doubted whether it was Hugh or resembled him in the darkness.

"What the devil's happened?" William Sorel peered cautiously through the open gate, armed with a hayfork and a torch. His eyes flared in horror when he noticed the body of a young boy lying dead on the cobblestones. "Where's my son?" he shouted. "Has anyone seen my son? He was going to help keep watch. John? Where are you?"

"Calm yourself, Master William," I barked. "Your son's still alive. Now step inside and secure that gate." I turned back to the esquire. "Edward, see if you can locate John Sorel. Master Edmund said he spoke with the boy earlier, so he can't be far."

"Aye, lord," he replied, turning to the crowd at his back. "Spread out boys. He can't have gone far."

"Sir Richard?" Leonard called from behind. I turned to see him laying Jack's head down carefully onto the bloody linen rag. "I'm sorry. There was nothing I could do. He's gone."

A few moments later the thin monk cautiously made his way into the gatehouse carrying a small lamp. Perhaps it was the moonlight, but at the sight of the bodies he appeared to become even more pale. He clutched a trembling hand to his mouth as he slowly crept forward.

"Brother Phillip, what do you make of all this?"

"Barbaric," he muttered in a mousy voice before making the sign of the cross. "This man has been butchered like an animal. What, pray tell, do you expect me to examine?" He must have seen a look of anger flash across my face, because he quickly hitched up the hem of his robe and approached the corpses. He knelt and placed his lamp next to the larger body.

"His skin is ashen and his eyes are strangely void of any color," the monk said as he gingerly moved around the folds of blood-soaked material. "There are no outward signs of Plague, if that's what you wanted to know. But, of course, he could have been infected and simply not have developed any of the outward signs yet. Tell me, Sir Richard, why was he attacked? Was this not one of your men?"

"*If* that was Hugh, he was mad with disease. He attacked the men on watch." I shook my head in disbelief. "Look what he did to poor Michael Burnes."

"You say your man did this?" the monk asked as he crouched over the boy's corpse. "It looks like he has been mauled by a wild animal. His throat is nearly gone." He stood and approached Jack. "And your man somehow caused these wounds as well?" he asked as he examined the long, deep gashes down the footman's chest.

"Yes. Even though he knew all these men well, he went for their throats like a beast. What could cause a man to behave so?"

"While I admit your huntsman, Guy, is the first case of Plague I have personally treated, I have never read of it or any other illness afflicting its victim with savage hysteria. In the same way a huntsman can tell what kind of animal has passed along a trail by the tracks it leaves, every disease has predictable signs that can be recognized by a trained physician.

None of these men here bear any sign of Plague. I am at a loss to explain what has infected them."

"Hugh was attacked by a stranger in the forest so savagely we all were certain that he had died. Now he has returned here and attacked others in the same manner. Is it, or is it not, Plague? And more importantly, how do we protect ourselves from it?"

"I cannot say for certain; however, a century ago, those who were affected by the Great Mortality were quarantined. I've read that a few actually survived, but I'm afraid most died within a few days. The corpses were so plentiful that they were either dumped into pits or burned."

"I thought the Church considered cremation to be a sacrilege?"

"An exception can be made for the purpose of preventing the spread of disease," the monk said with a shake of his head.

"So we should isolate the living and burn the dead?"

"That'd be the most prudent course of action."

I dreaded having to give the order to cremate the bodies. All of those men had served me well, some for many years. It seemed so callous to burn their remains, but I must confess that, after all of the chaos and confusion, I was relieved to just have a plan.

"William," I said, turning back to the marshal, "I need you to arrange a detail and have these bodies taken to the church green behind Saint Wystan's. Send a lad to the rectory to summon Sir Denis so that he may pray for their souls." Sir Denis Palmer had been born and raised in Colleville and served as its parish priest. As he had never received a theological degree to warrant an academic title, it was our custom to address him by the honorific *sir*.

"As heartless as it may sound," I continued, "do not allow any mourners to delay you in your task. Burn them immediately and spread their ashes in the graveyard. Is that understood?"

"Yes, lord." He hesitated for a long moment. Worry had carved deep lines across his brow.

"Master William, I need you to carry out your duties. We will find John and see him returned to you."

"It's a miracle!" Adam Stoney suddenly exclaimed from just inside the inner gateway. "Thank the heavens. Look, the boy's not dead." He knelt close to Michael, who was struggling to sit up.

"You men, get me some linens," brother Phillip exclaimed as he darted around me. His earlier caution had been completely discarded. "I need to staunch the bleeding. Hold him still, master porter." He held his small lamp over the opening of his satchel and began rifling through its contents.

"Easy, son," the porter said soothingly as he pressed a hand over Michael's neck. "You need to lie back so that the monk can tend to your wounds." The boy grasped the folds of Adam's long wool coat and tried to pull himself up. He opened his mouth as if to speak, but only a low groan could be heard.

"Let go of my arm, son," Adam appealed, his voice betraying a sudden alarm. "You're starting to hurt me." Only then did I notice the boy's wide, milky-eyed stare.

"Get away from him," I shouted to Adam, but the warning came too late. Michael sank his teeth into the side of the porter's throat with a ferocious bite. Adam only managed a single gurgling sound before he collapsed atop the boy in a violent convulsion.

"Help! Help!" brother Phillip shrieked as he leapt backwards, flailing his arms and dropping his lamp in the process. The baked clay vessel shattered as it hit the ground; a wave of burning oil washed across the bodies of Michael and Adam. Michael continued to rise, effortlessly shoving the heavier corpse of Adam Stoney to one side and completely ignoring the flames climbing up his body. Although I was astonished that he could still be alive, I found it even harder to believe that he had not uttered a single cry of pain.

"He's the devil incarnate!" the monk screeched as he crawled backwards with Michael lumbering after him. "Kill him!"

I held back, hoping the flames would spare me from having the boy's death on my conscience, but it was not meant to be.

"Forgive me, Lord," I muttered as I stepped forward and buried my blade into the back of his skull. He dropped instantly to the ground.

The smell of burnt hair and flesh drove me from the gatehouse in search of fresher air. A crowd had once again gathered around the doorway; terror was chiseled upon their collective faces. For a brief moment, the only sounds were those of the monk's whimpering.

"Sir Richard," Edmund suddenly said. "One of the lads found John Sorel. He's over here."

"Someone see to brother Phillip," I said as I stepped through the ring of men and followed the former soldier. We walked across the courtyard to a dark corner. There, behind an empty butt of ale, sat the missing boy. Two grooms were hovering over him, both appearing to be on the verge of crying.

"I think he's dead," one of them whispered.

"It is okay, lads. Are either of you hurt?" They both shook their heads. "Then stand over there out of the way." I cautiously approached the body of young John. The front of his hose was soaked with blood. From several feet away, I could tell that two or three fingers were missing from his left hand.

"John?" I called softly to him. "John, boy, can you hear me?" There was no response. I knelt a little more than an arm's reach away. *Don't get too close*, I reminded myself. *He could be infected.*

I used the flat side of my sword blade to move his hand away. Suddenly, he raised his head and met my gaze. I almost fell backwards but quickly regained my composure and lowered the tip of my longsword. Instead of a pale, expressionless stare like that of Michael, there were a pair of soft blue eyes filled with tears.

"It hurts, lord," he sobbed. "Where's my father?"

"Wait right there, son. Your father will be along soon. We just need to have you examined by the physician first." I looked back and nodded to Edmund. William was standing directly behind him. Holding up a hand, I instructed the boy's father to keep back. "All right, John. You're a brave lad. Dry those tears and tell me what happened."

"Me and Michael had begged Jack to let us stand guard with him. We just wanted to do our part and help out." He paused to wipe his nose on his sleeve. "I don't remember how long we'd been there, but we all got really sleepy. I remember thinking that I could hear someone moaning outside the gates, so I looked through the porter's squint and saw Hugh just standing there on the bridge."

"Are you sure that it was Hugh?"

"Yes, lord. Michael saw him, too. We went and told Jack—he was asleep on a stool out in the courtyard. He punched me in the arm and told us Hugh was dead and we'd just been dreaming. So we went back and looked again. Hugh appeared sorely hurt and covered in blood and wasn't even able to answer us when we called his name. We both agreed that he must be too injured to speak, so we opened the gate. We almost didn't because Jack had told us not to let anyone in, but we both agreed Hugh weren't no stranger."

Several shouts erupted from the gatehouse. Whirling around, I immediately ran back to the doorway. The throng of servants suddenly parted in front of me an instant before a human head rolled across the cobblestones and came to rest at my feet.

"What the devil have you done, Edward?" I bellowed at the esquire, who was standing over Jack's corpse. My hand instinctively tightened its grip on my sword as a rage began to once again well up inside me.

"He came at me, Sir Richard," Edward protested. "I had no choice. I was trying to get the monk back on his feet when I caught a glimpse of Jack struggling to stand. The next thing I knew he was lunging for me." The situation was rapidly spiraling out of control. I could not help but wonder who might be affected next by the mysterious disease.

"He had the same demonic look on his face as the boy who attacked the porter," brother Phillip added with a reluctant nod. He was pressing a strip of cloth to the back of his head.

"How were you injured?" I demanded. "Tell me you did not come in contact with the footman!" Brother Phillip was the only man in Colleville with the knowledge of how to stop this ghastly epidemic.

"I slipped and bumped my head when your porter was attacked," he said, his face coloring from embarrassment. The esquire nodded in agreement.

"Brother Phillip, would you be so kind as to go and see after the Sorel boy's wounds?" Edward asked in a soothing voice. The monk quietly clutched his satchel to his chest and walked across the courtyard, passing through the throng of murmuring servants. Edward then took a knee and cradled the head of Adam Stoney.

"I was not aware that you and Master Adam were close."

"We weren't," he replied with a shake of his head. Polished metal glimmered in his hand for an instant before he plunged a dagger through the ear of the dead porter. "We have to be sure." He stood and wiped the blade clean on his scarlet hose before wordlessly returning it to its sheath.

For the first time since being dragged from my bed, the knot in my stomach finally relaxed. I slowly walked around the gatehouse, studying the scattered corpses. It was as if the entire world was going mad, and, for the life of me, I had no idea how to respond.

"Sir Richard?" Edward said, placing a hand on my shoulder. "We need to know what you want us to do." With a heavy sigh, I gestured for the gaggle of men to come closer.

"Gather round, lads." I looked at each of their faces as they approached; many of them were unable to hide the terror that filled their hearts. William was among the crowd, his son clutched tightly under one arm. Those closest to him and the boy took several steps away from them. I could not fault them for their cautiousness.

"Master William, as I said before, you are to arrange for a detail to take the bodies to Saint Wystan's. Collect Sir Denis and give him just enough time to say prayers for their souls and then burn them to ashes. Take every precaution."

"Yes, Sir Richard."

"And, Master William, your son must be placed in isolation under the care of brother Phillip." The monk nodded meekly; the marshal of the stables did not.

"But, lord, he's not sick. He was cut across the hand in the fight. He may have lost some fingers, but there's no way he could be infected with the Plague." The boy just looked down at the ground, sobbing quietly with his bandaged hand tucked into the pit of his arm.

"At least let brother Phillip continue to treat his wound."

"That's not necessary. I've tended to many a cut without ever having to call for a fobbing monk—" He clenched his teeth and bowed his head. "Begging your pardon, Sir Richard. I meant no disrespect. I'm just anxious to get my son home."

"See to it, Master William. Then return with a cart to collect the bodies as I instructed. As for the rest of you, go back to your beds. Try and get some sleep. In the morning I want you all to go about your normal duties. We are going to take every necessary precaution to prevent the further spread of this disease. As long as everyone does his part, everything will be fine."

I stood there as the crowd began to shuffle back to their rooms. Slowly, the chill of the night began to creep in and overwhelm the courage I had felt earlier. Eventually, I was left standing in the courtyard alone except for my son.

"Are you all right, Thomas?" He nodded quickly, as though he felt the need to reassure himself as much as he had to convince me. "Come with me then. It is time that you learned one of the more difficult responsibilities that comes with being lord of a household." I turned and walked back to the gatehouse, where a few of the servants had begun working to scrub up the pools of blood.

"Where're we going, Father?"

"Adam Stoney died in our service, leaving behind a widow, Clere, and three sons: Jacob, Luke, and Powlis. It would be improper for another man to deliver the news in my stead." We solemnly climbed the narrow, spiraled stairwell to the upper floor where the porter and his wife had been residing for the better part of two decades.

As I reached the small door, I realized that I still had a sword in my hand but wore no sheath at my side. I passed it back to Thomas before knocking softly on the door.

"Adam?" a voice spoke through the portal as the latch was pulled back with a loud squeak. "What was all the commotion—

" Her words trailed off when she recognized that her husband had not returned. She clutched a hand at the neck of her nightgown as she half-closed the door. "I'm sorry, Sir Richard. I was expecting my husband. What has happened?"

"Mistress Clere, it pains me deeply to tell you this, but your husband has been killed."

"No." She stood there in the doorway for several moments shaking her head in disbelief. "You must be mistaken. He was just here in his bed a few moments ago." Tears slowly began to stream down her cheeks as she realized I had no reason to lie.

"Mum?" a lad called from inside the chamber. It was Adam's youngest son, Powlis, a boy of no more than nine. He came and stood beside Clere in the doorway. "What's wrong? Where's Dad?" She clutched his head tightly to her waist as if trying to shield him from our words.

"How?" she finally demanded.

"Hugh Eworthe attacked the men on watch at the gates. Your husband was killed when he came down to help them. I'm truly sorry, but we fear his body may have been infected with Plague. I have instructed the men to take him and the others to Saint Wystan's, where they will be cremated at first light."

"You mean to *burn* them? Why?! What is to become of them at the Resurrection?" Her spine stiffened with anger as her hands balled into fists.

"Brother Phillip, the physician from the Priory at Stony Heath, has said that it is necessary that we burn the bodies in order to prevent further spread of the disease."

"The devil take brother Phillip," she said through clenched teeth. "My husband served you for twenty good years, he did. You should do right by him and allow him a proper Christian burial." She began to shudder and then to sob.

"Mistress Clere, it has not been an easy decision, but I am certain it is what is best for everyone here."

"Best for us or best for your family?" she wailed. I reached out to comfort her, unsure of what else to say, but she recoiled and fell back onto the floor. "Get away from me. Please!"

"Don't hurt my mother," Luke shouted as he rushed over to her side. Both boys huddled protectively over her.

"I am sorry," I blurted as I stepped back from the doorway. I turned and nudged Thomas towards the stairs, continuing to urge him forward until the sounds of the woman's sobbing faded in the background.

"Wait, Thomas," I said, placing a hand on my son's shoulder as we emerged into the courtyard. "We need to find Master Edmund. He will know where the families of Michael and Jack reside. They, too, must be told of what happened, but first we should go and get dressed properly." Thomas swallowed hard before nodding in agreement.

My mind suddenly turned to Anne and the girls, no doubt still anxiously waiting in the upper chamber. I searched for the words to somehow describe to her the horrors we had all just witnessed. If Thomas recognized the hesitation in my steps, he was gracious enough to keep it to himself. Perhaps he, too, felt a sense of dread. In that moment I would have preferred to face another plague-ridden corpse than be forced to look into my daughters' tear-filled eyes. Little did I know that I would soon have to endure them both.

As the first rays of sunlight cast a faint orange glow over the roof of Colleville Hall, I heard the bell of Saint Wystan's signal the hour of Matins, calling the faithful to their morning prayers. A wooden cart carrying the corpses of Hugh Eworthe, Adam Stoney, Michael Burnes, and the footman Jack rocked lazily across the cobblestones under the direction of William Sorel and two of his grooms. Adam's three sons followed closely behind, doing their best to support their distraught mother. All three boys cast baleful looks in my direction as they passed out of the gates. My rotund, venerable chaplain, Doctor Symond Radclyf, waddled after them.

I had wanted to accompany the bodies out to the graveyard as a demonstration of my good lordship, but I decided against it. The earlier encounter with Clere Stoney and her children still haunted me. I did not want her anger towards me to be a distraction to the other families that might gather in the churchyard. Instead, I returned to my private rooms and did what I could to reassure my wife and daughters that all would be well.

"I think it would be good if we celebrated mass at Saint Wystan's this morning," I explained to Anne. "It could go far towards providing some level of comfort to the villagers."

"What about *my* comfort?" she retorted. Her wrinkled brow and rigid mouth demonstrated her growing anger. "I certainly don't want to go to Saint Wystan's."

"Come now, Anne. It's not that cold out, and it's only a short walk."

"I'm not talking about the walk, Richard. I'm saying I don't feel safe outside anymore. For the last two days, you've said there is no danger of anyone else contracting the disease. Has it somehow already slipped your mind that your man—who you told me was dead—not only contracted the disease, but he also returned here in the middle of the night and murdered three of your servants and nearly killed a fourth? Why the devil would you ask us to leave the manor?"

"Calm down," I said in the most reserved tone I could muster. "I have a duty, as lord of Colleville Manor, to maintain order and keep the peace. I want them to see me with my wife and children to hopefully calm some of their fears."

"Why are their fears more important than those of your family?"

"After all that has happened, Anne, I don't blame you for not wanting to go; however, I feel it is important, and I promise that I wouldn't ask if I felt there were any danger."

"As you wish," she finally said with pursed lips. Although her words were conciliatory, her tone was still full of distress. I knew there was little I could do or say at the moment to alleviate her fears.

"I have asked Edmund to meet me downstairs in half an hour. Together we will conduct a thorough inspection of the entire manor to ensure the safety of you and the children. Rest easy, dear. All will be well."

"Thank you." She arose and left the room without looking back.

"Matthew, be a good lad and fetch my brigandine." The boy jumped up from his stool and ran over to the large wooden trunk along the far wall. A moment later he returned with my armor. As I slid the protective vest over my shoulders, it provided me with a feeling of comfort that I had not felt in a long while. I fondly ran my fingers over its red velvet exterior and hundreds of silver rivets while Matthew buckled the straps down its front. I rarely found need to travel beyond the borders of my estate anymore, so I had few opportunities to feel its security.

Over the brigandine I donned a pleated coat of crimson and gold brocade to conceal the armor and hopefully avoid causing any further alarm amongst the servants. I also pulled on a pair of thigh-length leather boots along with a tall, woolen cap adorned with a gilt silver crest. I intended to address the villagers after services this morning, so I felt it important that I was dressed appropriately for my station.

"Matthew, I want you to burn my old robe and shoes." The boy nodded dutifully. Buckling on my sword and dagger, I went to meet Edmund atop the gatehouse. "And be sure to keep an eye on things here while I am away."

Of course the steward was already waiting for me when I arrived. Resting my arms on the battlements, I looked down at the murky, green waters of the moat. A short, ditch-lined road connected the stone bridge to Churchwell Lane, the main thoroughfare that cut through the center of the village. To the south, it passed the great stone barn and skirted between the lower communal pastures and the fallow fields on its way to the old corn mill and its adjacent pond.

To the north, the road was deeply rutted and led straight to the small stone cross in the center of town a hundred or so yards away. There were about two dozen long, narrow cottages crowded around the market cross, each housing a family that paid me rent. A few had stone walls, but most were timber-framed with thatched roofs. Every plot had some form of hedge around it and a small, seasonal garden, many also with small barns or sheds and animal pens in back.

The parish church lay on the northwest corner of the market, enclosed by a low stone wall. The village smithy was just to the right of it. From the market cross, Churchwell Lane turned west and headed through the upper fields and on towards Stony Heath, no more than four miles away.

"Master Edmund, I do not know if I ever told you, but when I took over the manor, I had been curious to learn as much as I could about its history. An old villager—I cannot recall his name, but he has long since passed away—told me that the entire region used to be farmland, but the previous lord, realizing how lucrative the wool market had become, converted much of it into pastureland. He told me it was then that Colleville went from 'living off the belly of the land to the backs of the sheep.'"

"No, Sir Richard, I don't remember you ever having mentioned it." Despite Edmund's patient response, he was obviously not interested.

"I have decided that we should be prepared in case this epidemic lasts as long as I have read that the previous one did. As soon as the sun is fully risen, I want to personally examine all of the exterior doors and windows. Afterwards, we can inspect the buttery and ensure there is adequate wine and ale as well as have Master Charles inventory the kitchen stores. I also want to visit the barn, granary, and storehouses outside the walls." I could only pray that we would be able to halt the spread of the disease within the walls. "In the meantime, I think we should survey the armory and make certain any spare weapons and armor are serviceable."

The parish church was the oldest building still standing in Colleville. It had been built several centuries ago and was dedicated to a long-dead Saxon king who had purportedly given up his crown to become a monk. I had no idea why it was ever built here or dedicated to Saint Wystan, as his bones were said to rest in another church bearing his name somewhere in the north.

Like he did every Sunday morning, Sir Denis Palmer led the congregation in a procession around the parish church as the bells tolled overhead. Atop his white, priestly robes he had donned a bulky red cloak that was intricately folded to allow him the use of his arms; its color signified that the current

Sunday fell during Christmastide. On his head he wore a white hooded cap that covered his ears.

Ahead of him walked four boys from the village who had been appointed as altar servers. The largest boy led the procession carrying a metal censer suspended by delicate chains, which he swung back and forth as he walked. Another of the acolytes carried an ornate golden crucifix set atop a long pole and was flanked by the smallest two boys, each carrying a large white candle.

Anne and I walked side by side a few feet behind Sir Denis. Even on that dull, overcast day, my wife was radiant in her flowing golden dress and sheer veil lined with pearls. Thomas and James came next, both wearing the kind of tight-fitting silk doublets and woolen hose that were fashionable for young squires to wear but their mothers did not delight in. Lizzie, Ellie, and Bernice trailed their brother, all giggling at some comment one of them must have made. All three were clothed in their finest dresses.

"Are you certain we will be safe, husband?" Anne whispered through an awkward smile. "No one is going to attack us like they did Lewys, are they?"

"I placed a couple of the lads up in the bell tower," I quietly replied, nodding briefly in the direction of the timber belfry that had been added the previous year to the east end of the church. Two men in red jackets were visible peering out of its window.

Standing against the wall of the smithy was John Sadeler, who was tapping his wooden club against his thigh in a rhythm only he could hear. The beadle nodded respectfully as we passed nearby.

"I also have sentries around the village keeping a watchful eye for any sign of danger," I said, returning the nod to John. "We will be fine." The procession snaked around a large black circle in the yellow grass. The acrid smell of burnt hair still hung in the air.

Stealing a backwards glance, I noted Edward and the men close behind us. The grim-faced esquire had his hand on his sword hilt and appeared wary of the villagers who trailed behind him. We all wore our swords to church that day. It was not something we would have normally done, but no one seemed to notice or issued a word of protest.

We followed the priest through a large set of double doors and then a smaller single door on the western facade. The church consisted of a tall, narrow nave that was devoid of any furniture or seating apart from a small wooden pulpit box. At the far end of the room, through an archway, was the square-shaped chancel. Unlike many of the more modern churches, Saint Wystan's did not have any aisles or side chapels.

Filling much of the archway between the nave and the chancel was an intricately carved, wooden rood screen. The congregation followed Sir Denis as far as the screen, where he and his altar servers passed through its small central doorway.

Sir Denis sang groups of verses from the Psalms of David in Latin, and the congregation repeated a refrain between each set. My children had been tutored to speak and write in Latin, but I suspected few, if any, of the villagers truly comprehended the words that they uttered.

After completing the solemn ritual of blessing and partaking of the Eucharist, the priest climbed the steps into the pulpit. He gave the bidding prayer, which was said in English, asking for blessings on practically everyone from Pope Eugenius and King Henry all the way down to the parishioners. The Bede Roll followed, naming those who had recently died and requesting they be commended in the villagers' personal prayers. I had paid the necessary fee to have Hugh, Adam, Michael, and Jack added to the list.

My eyes began to wander around the church's interior. Along either side of the nave and on all three sides of the chancel, the walls were covered in very old and heavily faded frescoes depicting biblical scenes of death and judgment. They seemed even more grotesque than before.

One panel in particular caught my attention: three skeletal men with black, sunken eyes and gray, wrinkled flesh stood atop their graves while an angelic figure in flowing white robes hovered overhead with a long silver trumpet. Small scrolls next to their mouths gave them speech, but the words were too small to read from across the room. To their right was a small chapel from which a monk with tonsured head gazed out a window towards the parted clouds above with hands clasped in fervent prayer. His mousy face reminded me of brother Phillip.

The dead shall rise. Suddenly a chill shot up my spine. Twice I had witnessed a seemingly dead man rise and attack those around him, and I had sent a dying man to a defenseless monastery. *They could all be killed! How could I be so stupid?* I motioned to Edward, who was standing next to my three daughters. He squeezed past a pair of villagers, curtly apologizing when his scabbard thumped across their knees.

"As quietly as you can," I whispered over my shoulder, "have the men make their way outside. Do it quickly." I watched as he began nudging the men-at-arms one at a time and pointing them towards the door in back of the congregation.

"What's the matter, husband?" Anne asked in a hushed tone.

"I must leave right away, but I will have some of the men see you and the girls safely back to the manor." Anne squeezed her delicate fingers around my elbow like a vise. Though she was doing her best not to show her panic, the color in her cheeks began to quickly drain away.

"Why? What has happened?" Several of the villagers behind us began to murmur. Sir Denis raised his voice to drown out the growing commotion as he continued his sermon unabated.

"Forgive me, but I haven't time to explain; I must ride to Stony Heath at once. As I said before, I will leave men to see you safely home."

"Don't you dare leave me here alone." she demanded in a low voice.

"I'm sorry. I don't have a choice." Turning on my heels, I slipped between the two villagers standing behind me.

"Richard!" she hissed, but I did not turn back. I wordlessly made my way through the crowd. I had been so distracted all morning by my encounter with Clere Stoney and trying to quell everyone's fears at Colleville that I had forgotten all about Stony Heath.

I gave the order. Their blood will be on my hands. Glancing back as I neared the door, I saw Thomas and James close behind me, their eyes flushed with excitement. I feared I was about to give my son the experience he so eagerly yearned for.

William Sorel was standing with his wife and younger son near the back of the congregation. I silently grabbed him by the sleeve and pulled him with me to the door.

"Have your grooms ready my horses at once," I instructed him as I flung open the outer doors of the church. My three men-at-arms were already waiting outside with puzzled looks on their faces. "I need to get to Stony Heath as quickly as possible." I released my grip on his doublet and started back to the manor.

"How many horses should I prepare, Sir Richard?"

"Two—four—seven," I quickly counted aloud. "And someone fetch me Master Edmund." I hurried across the church green at something between a walk and a run, not even pausing to explain the situation to the men.

"Is there something I should know?" Edward asked as he hustled alongside me.

"I'll explain on the way. You and the men have until the grooms bring the horses to get yourselves ready. Any longer and I'll leave you behind."

We dashed past Market Cross and down Churchwell Lane. Turning the corner, I half-ran up the road to the manor's stone bridge. An archer atop the gatehouse shouted down for the gates to be opened. By the time I started across the moat, the outer doors were swung open; Therry Wode stepped to one side and allowed me to pass.

"Sir Richard?" Therry mumbled. I sped past him and did not stop until I reached the center of the courtyard. Turning, I began directing the men as they gathered around.

"Matthew, run upstairs and fetch my arms and legs. Do not forget to put on your jack. You will be coming with us." His eyes brightened as he flashed a toothy grin. I would need the varlet to manage our horses.

"At once, Sir Richard," he said as he darted for the hall.

"And what should I bring, Father?" Thomas blurted as he reached my side.

Your mother will be furious, I thought to say but did not. "If you're going, you have until the lads bring around the horses to get yourself in harness." He did not even wait for me to finish before turning and running towards the hall. James hesitated, looking back and forth between me and my son, who disappeared through the door.

"You'll never hear the end of it if Thomas goes and you stay," I goaded him. He opened his mouth to reply but instead only nodded sheepishly. He hurried across the courtyard after Thomas.

"Edward," I addressed the three men-at-arms. "You and Hamond get kitted up. Christopher, I want you to go back to Saint Wystan's and see my family safely home as soon as services are over. Then recall the men I placed around the village and lock down the manor until we return."

"Yes, Sir Richard," they replied as one.

"Andrew," I said to the yeoman as he jogged through the gates. "Who's on watch?" I squinted up at the top of the gatehouse shadowed against an overcast sky.

"Leonard and Gilbert," he responded without looking up.

"Good. They should already be properly arrayed. Get them down here and on a pair of horses. I want them to come with me. Get someone else up there at once to take their place. Afterwards, I want you to go with Christopher and look after my family. Put extra men atop the walls until we get back."

"Yessir." He turned and waved at the two heads peering down through the battlements. "Don't just sit up there like a pair of stupid gargoyles. Get your butts down here now!"

Matthew scurried out of the hall fumbling with an armload of shiny steel. He half-tripped as he hopped off the stairs and nearly dropped my expensive armor; he swore under his breath.

"Calm down, Matthew. You're doing fine." Normally James would be the one to help me into my harness.

"Yessir," he replied, red-faced. Matthew quickly buckled on my leg armor, beginning with the lower legs and working his way upwards, adding a pair of gilded spurs at the end. Owain Dun, the smallest of the grooms, bounded through the gates with my black courser and a chestnut stallion. He practically dangled between the reins.

"Did you double-check those girths?" I asked the lad. He tugged back and forth on each saddle strap a couple of times to show they were tight. "Run back and tell the lads to bring horses for Thomas and James as well." He tossed both sets of reins to Gilbert and took off running.

Matthew helped me remove each arm from my pleated coat through a long slit down the center of the sleeve before fitting it into an articulated piece of armor. He then tucked both sleeves into my belt to keep them out of the way.

"Sir Richard," John Sadeler called as he entered the courtyard. "Has something happened? Do you need my help?"

"We are off to Stony Heath. I really do not have time to explain the particulars. If you could just keep an eye on things here in the village, I will tell you all upon my return."

"Of course, lord." William and his youngest son, Jimme, then arrived, each leading a pair of horses. Following only a few steps behind them, Owain and another boy I did not recognize rushed through the gates with the mounts belonging to my son and my squire.

Moments later Thomas and James practically collided as they both ran through the door at the same time. Laughing, they pushed one another forward across the courtyard. Remarkably, Thomas and James had managed to help each other into their armor; they were completely covered from head to foot. I was impressed.

"I see you've been practicing." They both smiled broadly. "I had thought we would have to leave you behind."

I climbed into the saddle of my jet-black stallion and wheeled him around to face the half-circle of armed men gathered around me. In addition to the brigandine jacket, my arms and legs were fully encased in polished steel that had been masterly crafted to fit me like a second skin. A maille collar was buckled around my throat. The familiar weight of the armor filled me with a youthful fire that melted away the past two decades of relative leisure.

"I fear something dire is about to occur in Stony Heath. You're all aware of what happened here last night. I intend to do my best to keep it from happening again." I had sent Guy to the priory in an attempt to save his life, but I had failed to consider that it might result in the deaths of many more.

"If it's not already too late," I added, looking up at the sundial. It was already past the fourth hour. I searched their faces for doubt; any man who appeared afraid would be left behind to man the gates. I was greatly encouraged that they all were stern and resolute. Thomas and James could not contain their eagerness to take part in a dangerous adventure, their eyes brimming with naive enthusiasm.

Edward and Hamond had managed to throw on their leg armor and maille skirts but only had padded doublets to protect their upper bodies. Leonard Sampson and Gilbert Somercotes wore open-faced helmets and livery jackets made of scarlet wool. Each had a short, cleaver-like sword at his side and carried a yew longbow in his hands. A dozen arrows were tucked into their belts for easy access.

"To horse, men." The small retinue promptly climbed into their saddles. Matthew handed me my gauntlets before mounting his own horse. Likewise, Edward's young varlet, Nicholl, held his master's charger before joining the others on horseback.

Stony Heath lay only a few miles beyond the low ridge west of the manor. A line of ancient oaks spread along the hilltop screened it from our view. It took only a short time for our horses to reach the top of the wooded ridge at a gallop, but in that span, dark and ominous clouds had amassed overhead, carried by a cool northern breeze.

While I would have preferred to charge across the fields with an entire retinue of armored men at my back, it was not warranted, nor was there time. We momentarily curbed our horses as we cleared the last stand of trees. I half-expected to find Stony Heath engulfed in flames.

Instead, in the vale below, just over two dozen beam and wattle houses slumbered around a small, oblong marketplace. The tall wooden spire atop the church of the Holy Trinity, on the far side of town, represented the only prominent structure for as far as the eye could see. On a clear summer's day, the seemingly endless stretch of fertile fields surrounding the village would have been a hive of activity, teeming with as many as a hundred industrious peasants shearing sheep, cutting hay, and driving teams of oxen pulling plows.

The thunder of hoofbeats echoed through the trees behind us. Turning in the saddle, I saw Therry Wode galloping over the crest, furiously whipping his mount down the road in our direction. At the very last moment, he wrestled his horse to a stop, pelting several of the other riders with pebbles.

"You were instructed to guard the manor," Edward scolded him. "Get back to your post." Therry ignored the esquire and instead looked squarely at me.

"No one told me *anything*," he replied coldly. "But I overheard talk of my brother." Therry was wearing a breastplate of blackened steel over a maille shirt, and his thighs and knees were covered by leather armor reinforced with strips of steel. He had a sword strapped to his waist and a short spear in his hand.

"It was a mistake to send Guy to the priory," I said flatly. "We're on our way now to collect him." He glared back at me for a long moment.

"Agreed," he finally said through a clenched jaw. We each nodded in a terse agreement.

"Well, that's a good sign," Thomas commented. "It looks like they all have a fire going down there." A score of small columns of smoke could be counted rising from the maze of thatched roofs, evidence that the cottagers were going about their daily routines.

"We're wasting time here. Leonard, you and Therry lead the way to the village."

"The *village*, Sir Richard?" Leonard questioned.

"I know you all want to get to the priory and out of the cold," I addressed the circle of riders, turning my head left and right. "But we're going to survey the village before rushing in. The Pestilence found its way into the manor easily enough. If it's in the priory, it could have just as easily made it out as well. Be on your guard, men, and keep your distance from everyone. We can't know what to expect."

"Hah!" Therry shouted as he whipped his horse. Leonard wheeled his own mount and charged after him. After a short pause, I spurred Ebon forward, keeping him a few dozen paces behind the lead riders.

"Was it wise to let him come along?" I asked the esquire over the thunder of hooves. Edward looked ahead at Therry before turning to meet my gaze. The corners of his mouth slowly curled downwards. "Speak your mind."

"From what I saw this morning, there's a very real chance Guy may attack others and spread the disease. If he hasn't fully succumbed to the disease, he should be dispatched for the safety of everyone around him. If he has *turned*, for lack of a better word, then he'll have to be dealt with along with possibly anyone who's come in contact with him."

"That didn't really answer my question," I said, glancing back to ensure the others could not overhear us.

"He'd be a devil of a troll to contend with," Edward replied with a grin. "I haven't the slightest notion of how he'll react if it comes down to it. Best to keep an eye on him just in case."

"My thoughts exactly."

Like Colleville Manor, the long strips of farmland around Stony Heath were separated by a network of ditches, and the pasturelands were bordered by hedges and low rock walls to keep in the grazing herds. We made our way across the barren fields and through the communal grazing area on the eastern edge of the village before slowing our horses. Ebon was lathered in sweat and foam. The faint tolling of bells to our backs signaled the end of morning services at Saint Wystan's.

Anne and the girls will soon be safely back to the manor.

Upon entering the village, we rode past the stone walls of the smithy. It appeared dark and lifeless. There were no coals visible in its brick forge. To the left was a low garden hedge surrounding a two-story cottage. Adjacent to the building was a shearing shed and privy hut.

Hamond's horse suddenly reared its head and sidled to the left. Only a few feet in front of him, a pair of geese angrily flapped their wings as they scurried across the road and disappeared through the garden wall, honking the entire way.

"Easy, boy," Hamond crooned, patting the neck of his stallion. "Don't let our dinner scare you."

"Keep moving," Therry said flatly.

Across a narrow lane and beyond a second row of houses, we emerged into the market square. It was encompassed by about two dozen cottages separated by only a few narrow, deeply rutted lanes. The central square was paved with worn, flat stones that made our horses' iron-shod hooves clatter noisily as we trotted along. A number of small wooden booths were folded shut and devoid of any wares.

"Where is everyone?" Thomas wondered aloud.

I'm not sure.

Small plumes of smoke rose from the vents in almost every roof, and the aroma of simmering pottages drifted faintly through the air.

"Likely they are all where we'd like to be right now," I said, doing my best to mask my uncertainty. "Relaxing indoors around the warmth of their fires."

"Shouldn't there be people out?"

"No market today," I replied, shaking my head. "It's Sunday."

"Yeah, but shouldn't there at least be someone outside? It's not that cold."

I dismounted and walked slowly across the market square, stopping at the base of the large stone cross in its center.

"Sir Richard, look over there," Leonard said in a low voice, pointing towards a narrow cottage on the far side of the market. A gaunt figure was peering around the corner of a building. He quickly jerked his head back when he realized he had been noticed.

"You, there." I called out. "Have no fear. We mean you no harm." The man cautiously stepped around the corner and watched us from under the low thatched edge of his roof. He appeared unwilling to leave the relative shelter of his eave.

"Thomas, keep the men back." As I started towards the villager, his eyes quickly darted from side to side, searching for a place to run. I could hardly blame him. I was dressed in hardened steel, while he wore only a simple undershirt and a pair of woolen hose. He had a small wooden cup in one hand.

"Good day," I greeted him as I raised my empty hands. The last action appeared to put him a bit more at ease.

"Lord," he nodded his head in a half-hearted bow. "What brings you'n your men to Stony'eath?"

"We are on our way to speak with Prior Gregory."

"Have the Welsh invaded?" He looked back and forth between me and my heavily armed retinue.

"No, but several of my men have been attacked in recent days. We have business at the priory and did not wish to take any chances." I craned my neck to take a quick glance through his open window. There were a few sheep inside but no other people. "Has something happened here in Stony Heath? Where are the rest of the villagers?"

"Still up at the Holy Trinity, I'd reckon. Seems like the old priest really likes to ramble on and on these days."

Of course they're still at church, you old fool. The bells you heard were from Colleville, not Stony Heath. Stop being so bloody paranoid.

"So why are you here instead of at Sunday service?" The villager flashed a wry smile as he took a hearty drink from his mug.

"Well, y'see, my lord, I got kicked in the leg by a randy goat last spring." When I did not immediately respond, the man sighed and rolled his eyes as if I were too dense to understand. He reached down and patted his thigh before demonstrating a weak limp. "I've a bum leg and nobody's willing to carry me all that way, so I just sits here at home alone." He took another long draw from his cup before wiping his mouth on his sleeve.

"That is a pity," I said, turning and waving for Matthew to bring up my horse. "So the rest of the village is still at the Holy Trinity? That explains why we found no one out of doors. Except, of course, for you."

"You aren't gonna send the churchwarden after me, are you lord?" He retreated a couple of steps in the direction of his door.

"No, but you had best take care of that leg. It would be a shame if it were to become infected and have to be cut off." I grinned broadly as I took the reins from my varlet and climbed back into the saddle.

We turned our mounts west and rode through the other half of the village. The cottages became more spread out the further we got from Market Cross. As we passed the last few houses, the road turned sharply to the left and skirted a low hedge bordering the church green. Dozens of ancient grave markers were visible inside the enclosure.

The stillness was suddenly broken by the clamor of raised voices coming from somewhere near the rear of the column. I quickly curbed Ebon and turned in my saddle to search for the source of the growing din. As bells rang overhead, a large group of villagers hurried through a break in the hedge and emerged into the middle of the street only a few feet behind Thomas and James.

For a brief moment, the mass of cottagers ceased their boisterous chatter and stared in silence at the formation of liveried soldiers. There must have been at least three score men, women, and children; they resembled a small army crowded so close to the ten of us.

"That's Sir Richard de Colleville," a well-dressed but corpulent townsman said, looking in turn over each shoulder at those standing behind him. He brushed the breast of his pale green gown with stubby fingers covered in silver rings. The brim of his wool hat was rolled up on the sides.

"Sent us the Plague, he did," a leather-faced old woman spat.

"Mind your tongue, crone," Thomas barked, his hand quickly finding the hilt of his sword.

"Hold," I said calmly, raising a hand to stay the men while urging Ebon towards the crowd that now filled the street. I carefully wheeled my warhorse to form a barrier between the squires and the mob, ignoring the looks of contempt on many of their faces. Their cheeks and noses were red from the cold, but none had any outward sign of disease. "Return to your homes. We have no intention of breaching the peace. We are here to collect our man from the priory and then be on our way."

"Did his lordship bring another sickly corpse to dump on our doorstep?" a tall, bony farmer shouted from the back of the group. Several others around him murmured their discontent.

"Enough already, Yon," a young man dressed in a scarlet wool cloak chided him. "We're all sick and tired of you running your mouth. I don't know about the rest of you folks, but I for one am about to starve to death. Come on, Moll, let's go home and eat our dinner." He turned and started down the road with his wife in tow. Several others in the crowd chuckled and followed after him.

"It's not right, I tell you," the leathery old woman grumbled loudly. "None of you can see it, but he's trying to kill us all."

"We can make them leave," a voice called out. A large man in the front sneered and shook his fist in the air.

"We're not afraid of you," Thomas countered.

"That's right," added James.

"Are you so eager to spill blood?" I barked at the squires.

"But, Father, they—"

"But nothing. Their words are empty and meaningless." I wheeled Ebon around to face my son, dismissing the mob of villagers. "They are not fools. They can see you have swords, and they know their hands are as empty as their words."

The sun was climbing steadily higher into the gray sky. "We are wasting valuable time here. It is nigh the fifth hour already." I spurred my courser past my retinue and down the muddy lane. After about fifty paces, the road curved right and bordered the low stone wall that enclosed the priory's courtyard.

"Not even tall enough to keep a lazy goat inside," Leonard grumbled. He stood in his stirrups and craned his neck to see over the wall. "It looks empty."

Set into the center of the courtyard wall were a pair of wooden gates. A small porter's door was cut into the right-hand gate. I reined Ebon close to the entrance and pounded a gauntleted fist upon the heavy door.

There was no response from inside. Instead, the sounds of raised voices once again erupted from back down the road. I hammered on the door much harder twice more as the crowd of villagers rounded the corner and started in our direction.

"Yes. Yes," a youthful voice replied at last. "Don't be so impatient." After a series of metallic clicks, the small door swung open, revealing a pair of bookish men dressed in black robes. One was tall and thin and carried a large wicker basket while the other was much younger and appeared very well fed.

"Well, don't just loiter there," the elder man said coldly. "State your business."

"Sir Richard Colleville to see Prior Gregory."

"Prior Gregory is at chapel and would not wish to be disturbed," the bony old monk stated.

"I assure you, the prior will want to hear what I have to say. It is in regards to the sick man you recently received from my household."

"I told you he is busy." The younger monk tapped the shoulder of his companion and gestured at the nearly two dozen villagers approaching from his left. "For heaven's sake, Peter. They don't look very happy, do they?"

"No, brother James," the young monk replied. "I wonder what set them off?" They shrugged at one another.

"Perhaps you were unable to hear me, brothers." I used a spur to sidle my horse closer to the bony monk. "I asked you ever so kindly to run and fetch your superior." Ebon stomped a hoof impatiently. "If you do not go now, I will have my men pull down these gates and I will search for him myself."

"Very well," the thin monk groaned loudly. He shoved his basket into the chest of his companion. "Here. I'll be back in a moment." He quickly disappeared through the small door, slamming it shut behind him. The inner lock clicked loudly.

I reined my horse to one side to give the younger monk a little more space. He looked down and fidgeted with the empty basket, awkwardly trying to avoid making any eye contact with me or my men. The raised voices grew steadily closer.

"I'd wager that old monk didn't even go to fetch his prior," Thomas said with a smirk. "He's probably waiting on the other side of the gate laughing." The younger monk glanced once more at the approaching crowd before pressing his back tightly against the door.

"If you want, Sir Richard, we can run off and find some ropes," Hamond said with a grin.

"No," I said forcefully. "I think the time has come for us to deal with this rabble." The old crone ignored my threat and led her small company ever closer. Although their numbers had dissolved into fewer than two dozen, they were still unarmed, and a handful of women and a couple of children trailed closely behind the men.

"Archers, place an arrow in the leg of the man who takes another step forward.

"With pleasure," Leonard growled as he and Gilbert quickly hopped from their saddles and nocked an arrow onto their strings. The mob stopped dead in its tracks.

"Brother Peter, was it?" I questioned the young monk who slowly wilted under my stare.

"Not brother Peter, actually," he gulped. "I mean, I'm not a brother yet. I'm still a novice."

"Novice Peter, I am growing impatient. Are you going to let us in to see your prior or not?" The young man's face turned white as he did his best to melt into the doorway.

"Speak of the devil," Christopher blurted out. He was standing tall in his saddle to peer over the top of the wall. "Here comes that skinny old monk, and he's following an older and angrier monk." Peter sighed heavily as two agitated voices soon approached the other side of the gate.

"I know. I know. I told him as much," the voice of brother James grumbled. The porter's door once again swung open, and, an instant later, a man with dark, sunken eyes and only tufts of gray hair for a tonsure line appeared in its opening. He clenched his jaw in anger at the sight of my armed retinue.

"Prior Gregory," I said with a polite nod. "Thank you for seeing me." The elder monk did little to hide his annoyance.

"Sir Richard," he said, addressing me by my title; his tone, however, unmistakably screamed *Cur Richard* whenever he spoke. We shared a mutual indifference towards one another which had begun many years before. He ran his eyes up and down my frame several times with a curl in his upper lip. "It is most unusual for you to appear here, on my lands, in armor no less. Is there a tournament nearby and so late in the year? If so, I was unaware of it. What is it that you require of me?" A few of my men chuckled at his surliness.

There's the condescending Prior Gregory I remember. I decided not to dismount. *If you wish to speak down to me, you will have to look up to do so.*

"I assure you, Prior Gregory, my precautions are warranted. There have been several murders in Colleville in the past few days, and they all appear to be directly linked to the diseased stranger I sent to you on Friday." The other two monks gasped at my mention of murder and disease.

"See! I told you he's been forcing his dead and dying upon us," the old crone cackled. She started to step forward but stopped abruptly as Leonard half-drew his bow. "Order him to leave, good prior, and make him take his diseased men with him."

"Please, *Cur* Richard," Prior Gregory said, waving a hand in front of him as if a gnat were in his face. "Stop spreading all this discontent throughout my village. Death and disease are nothing new to this sinful world, but that doesn't mean you should go on antagonizing these poor villagers. Besides, your man is not the only sickly person under our care; we have nigh a dozen others who are bed-ridden with the bloody flux."

"How can you be so sure they have the flux and not the Plague?"

"I was unaware that your knightly training included the diagnosing of diseases, *Cur Richard*. I am so fortunate that you were able to come here and instruct my physicians."

I did not give him the satisfaction of a rebuttal. "Where exactly are the sick villagers being kept?"

"In the infirmary, of course," the prior replied, shaking his head in exasperation.

"Please tell me you have not put them in the same room that you placed Guy in."

"Where else would they go? The scriptorium? Brother Stephen has taken every necessary precaution to prevent the further spread of *the illness* affecting your man. The woodcutter is in a separate bed on the far side of the room."

"I am sure brother Stephen is a very capable surgeon; however, I must insist on seeing Guy with my own eyes. I could say more, but perhaps it would be best if we were to discuss it in private."

"Very well, you and you alone may enter. Your soldiers must remain outside." The prior crossed his arms and pushed out his chin with smug satisfaction.

"Leave them out here unsupervised? I think you trust my men more than I, especially considering the warmth your villagers have shown them thus far." Edward and Hamond laughed wickedly. "Perhaps it would be better if the two groups were at least separated?" The old monk wrinkled his face for a moment as if he had tasted something awful. He opened his mouth as if to argue, but instead a wry smile crept across his face.

"Open the gates," he turned and barked at the other two monks, giving them an agitated wave of his arms. "Let them in. Let the *villagers* in, and instruct brother Philemon to open another butt of ale for our guests." He glanced back at me as he started into the courtyard. "When you've finished instructing your men, I'll be waiting for you inside."

The old crone triumphantly led her procession through the midst of my men, sneering at Leonard and Gilbert as she passed.

"Sir Richard," she said with an exaggerated bow as she slid past my horse. Counting her mob as they passed, I tallied fourteen men, five women, and three children; the last was a young girl with ruddy cheeks and sparkling green eyes who reminded me of Lizzie.

"Edward," I called to the esquire as I dismounted and passed my reins to Matthew. "Stay here with the men and keep everyone on alert. Do not forget that the disease is here in the priory. If we are fortunate, it has not yet made it outside the walls. Do not let any strangers come within an arm's reach of you, unless you are certain they are not afflicted. Thomas and I are going to accompany the prior inside and see to Guy." I clasped a hand to his shoulder before giving him one last instruction in a low voice: "Keep a close watch on Therry."

"Yessir," he replied with a quick nod.

"All right, Thomas. It is time we go and find out how bad things really are." I turned and walked across the courtyard to where the prior was standing. He was shaking his fist in irritation while he spoke to his young novice.

"Thank you for your patience, Prior Gregory. It truly is urgent that we visit your infirmary now."

"By all means, *Cur* Richard. You begin by having me turn my priory into a public house, and now you treat me as if I were one of your retainers to command."

"Good Prior," I addressed him through a forced smile. *If you do not shut your mouth, I will grab you and do my very best to shake some sense into you*, I desperately wanted to say but did not. "I only wish to ensure that no harm comes to you or your fellow monks. Brother Phillip told me that you had personally sent him in haste to my home when you determined the stranger in the woods was infected with Plague. I have not properly thanked you for your kindness. For that I am sorry." The prior nodded and then sighed as if the verbal grappling had finally grown too wearisome to keep up.

"Come with me," he replied, waving his young novice forward. The boy scurried ahead and held open a wide door at the far end of the courtyard. Prior Gregory passed through first, followed by myself and then Thomas.

The parish church at Stony Heath, dedicated to the Holy Trinity, had been built several centuries ago. Much later, a quadrangle of buildings was added onto its western side, creating a central wooded cloister.

We emerged onto a square arcade of arched columns supporting an upper floor and surrounding the wooded garth. The parish church's belfry was visible high over the eastern roof.

"I'm Peter," the young novice said quietly to Thomas as he passed through the door. "I'm still only a novice."

"So I heard," my son replied with a chuckle. "My name is Thomas, and I'm still only a squire."

"This here is the cloister. It's where we come to read or to work or sometimes just to relax."

"It looks peaceful, but where are all of the other monks?"

"They are in the refectory having dinner," the novice said as he pointed ahead. Thomas and I followed the prior around the cloister walk. "It's not far." The sun had finally broken through the clouds above and was casting rays of light through the bare branches of the fruit trees in the garth.

"Prior Gregory, it occurs to me that the stranger appeared to be wearing the clothes of a sailor. Did you find any evidence as to where he might have come from?"

"The Lord only knows," he shook his head. "Despite the fact that he appeared to have died a gruesome death from any number of deep puncture wounds, we were able to determine that he would have soon died from the Plague anyway. We removed a few personal effects from his corpse before cremating him. The first was a set of rosary beads; that is how we knew he was of the Catholic faith. The second item was what appeared to be a personal letter, but it was written in a foreign tongue that none of us was able to read."

"And Guy? How is he doing?" The old monk suddenly stopped and bowed his head.

"I'm afraid that he is not long for this world. Brother Stephen said he doubted your man would make it through the night. Regretfully, there is nothing more that can be done for him." He turned and continued around the covered walkway. To our left was the lavatorium where the monks would wash themselves. I recalled from my visits years ago that the scriptorium lay above it. Depending on the hour, there could be several monks up there working diligently to translate texts and copy important manuscripts.

"Tell me," I continued to press. "Have you witnessed anything out of the ordinary about this Pestilence? Despite his illness, the stranger in the woods attacked several of my men as fiercely as a wild sow guarding her brood. And, while he showed all the signs of Plague as brother Phillip has explained to me, he also had milky eyes devoid of any color, not unlike a blind man."

"That's very odd indeed." His tone made it clear that he doubted the veracity of my account.

"That is not the half of it. One of the men he attacked we were certain bled to death, so we left him in the woods until we could return with a cart. He was gone by the time my men returned, but he showed up at the gates early this morning and attacked several more of my men as equally savage as the stranger had. It seems that the disease somehow conveys upon its victims an unnatural hunger." The prior once again stopped in his tracks and turned to face me. The corners of his mouth curled downwards with a look of disapproval.

"Our Savior alone has the power to raise the dead; it would be heretical for anyone to imply otherwise. You say your man was dead, so you brought him back to the manor where he went mad and killed more of your servants? Was he dead, or was he alive?"

"No." I was growing impatient with him. "I am saying that we only thought he was dead. Somehow, my huntsman just got up and *walked* back."

"You're not making any sense, Sir Richard." He started for the doorway in the corner of the cloister.

"Actually, it makes perfect sense," I replied, placing a hand on the elder monk's shoulder to slow his pace. "Don't you see, Prior? That is why they found no trace of him. The lads were looking for a dead man and, not finding a body, must have only searched for what might have carried it off. Finding neither animal tracks nor ruts from a cart, they returned to the manor and reported that he had vanished without a trace."

"It sounds, *Cur* Richard, as if your men make as poor of huntsmen as they do surgeons. It makes no difference, though. Plainly speaking, your man will be dead soon. He'll be cremated like the other corpse, and, Lord willing, that'll be the end of it."

"No, Prior Gregory, that is exactly what I am worried about. The stranger we encountered in the woods was very violent, and my men were only afflicted after being physically bitten by him. You say that Guy is close to death? That is exactly what we have thought about every other victim just before he got up and attacked everyone around him. I fear that your monks working in the infirmary and the villagers they are caring for are in mortal danger."

Prior Gregory stared blankly at me for a long moment before nudging his young novice. "Come along, Peter. Let's show these men to the infirmary. Perhaps brother Stephen will be able to make sense of their story."

Following the prior through the door, we entered a large, rectangular room that had stone benches built into all four of its walls. It had a high ceiling and walls richly decorated with painted scenes from the Bible.

"This is the chapter room. We use it for meetings," Peter explained to Thomas as he followed us into the room. The novice hustled to the left and moved to open another doorway. Prior Gregory placed a hand on the door, preventing the novice from opening it.

"Sir Richard, through this door is the refectory," the prior said in a low voice. "The brothers will be eating in silence, so you are asked to refrain from talking." Prior Gregory removed his hand and allowed Peter to open the door. We entered a long, narrow room with a row of tables to either side. It was pleasantly lit by windows along the entire northern wall. The dining hall had the capacity to feed thirty to forty men, though at the moment there were only eight monks sitting on the left side of the room eating a simple dinner of bread and fish. The only sounds came from a young monk standing atop a stool behind a tall lectern at the far end of the room. He was reading from the Scriptures in a hymn-like voice but paused and looked up as we entered the room.

"Read. Read," the prior chastised the young monk in a loud whisper. We followed Peter around a large wash basin and between the two rows of tables to a small door on the far wall behind the lectern. The clattering of our armor was thunderous in the still room.

Peter approached the door and knocked gently. "Brother Stephen," he said in a low voice, "you have visitors." For a moment I thought I could hear the faint sound of whimpering as the monk behind us paused to turn a page.

"Wait!" I shouted to Peter, but it was too late. The door swung open to reveal two men crouched over the quivering body of a monk, his black robes rent apart, revealing a horrific sight.

"Will!" Peter cried out, gaping at the mangled figure on the floor. The novice started to rush into the room, so I grabbed him by his habit before he could pass through the door. The two creatures raised their heads and stared at the boy with white, emotionless eyes; bright red blood ran from their mouths.

A ghastly pale woman clad in a bloodstained white gown suddenly appeared in the doorway and violently seized ahold of Peter. He wailed as she wrestled him from my grasp and dragged him down to the ground. Prior Gregory let out an ear-piercing scream as he turned to flee.

Before I could react, Guy Wode streaked past with lightning speed and tackled the prior. The chamber echoed with his painful screams. Turning, I grabbed the hair of my former woodward with my left hand and, in a single motion, drew my sword and decapitated him with a back-handed cut.

Tossing the head to the ground, I rushed over and dragged Prior Gregory to his feet. He stood frozen in place, slowly looking around the room as if in a trance.

"Run!" I shouted at him. The prior stared blankly at my face. "I said run!" I hollered again, slapping him hard across his cheek. Suddenly, a blood-soaked monster streaked past us, and, a heartbeat later, we heard a loud crash followed by the scraping of metal across the stone floor.

"Thomas!" I bellowed, turning to the left. A black-robed figure was crouched atop my son. Its head was savagely thrashing around upon his neck. With all my might I kicked the devil in its rib cage, sending it rolling across the room and into the back of the lectern; the young monk who had been standing petrified atop the stool fell helplessly into the fiend's arms.

I grasped Thomas's arm and pulled him to his feet. Ignoring the frightful screams that filled the air, I pulled my son into the corner of the room to look him over.

"I'm fine, Father." The armor protecting his neck was smeared with dark blood.

"Are you sure?" I asked, rubbing a hand over the bloodstained metal plate. "Did it bite you?"

"I said I'm fine. My bevor saved me." Thomas suddenly shoved me to one side. "Look out!"

Two corpselike men rushed through the door towards us. As I turned, the first devil was already too close for a lethal blow, so I punched it in the face with a gauntleted fist. Its teeth exploded across the floor as its body careened past me to land under the dining table. Thomas skewered the second one in the heart with his longsword, but its speed carried it forward, impaling itself all the way to the hilt. It chomped at his face with voracious jaws. With a deep groan, Thomas quickly pivoted to his side and flung the creature across the room, losing his grip of his sword in the process.

"Saints preserve us!" a high pitched voice squealed from somewhere behind us. Several of the monks had climbed atop the tables and were shrieking with horror. Their howls sent the devils into a frenzy. The creature that Thomas impaled jumped to its feet and chased after a monk running for the exit, the blade of my son's sword still sticking out its back.

"Run, you fools!" I shouted at the panic-stricken monks. They jumped from the table and ran towards the chapter room.

The monster whose face I had smashed was atop a crying monk at the foot of the table. I hacked it across the back with two powerful blows, the second almost completely severing its arm. The monk, freed, scrambled to his feet and ran for the exit screaming. The one-armed devil clamored under the table and chased after its prey.

"Let's go, Thomas." He started towards the chapter room. "Not that way." I led him in the opposite direction, entering the adjacent room. The stone floor was covered in pools of blood. In the center of the room was the mangled corpse of a young monk. Small beds lined two sides of the long, narrow chamber. A torn canopy hung loosely around a bed on the far wall.

A foul stench filled the room. There were no visible exits. "Who builds an infirmary without an outside door? Come on, Thomas, we have no choice but to go back the way we came. Stay behind me."

Together we hurried through the refectory and into the chapter room. The floor was slick with blood around the bodies of two dead monks. Another, in a far corner, faintly cried for his mother with pale lips, a crimson pool rapidly growing beneath his trembling frame. Outside in the cloister, the sounds of pandemonium grew increasingly louder as we neared the exit. I quickly pulled the door shut and turned to address my son. Strangely, he smiled when I met his gaze.

"All right, son. We move slowly and carefully. Keep your wits about you and we'll be fine." Thomas hoisted his dagger and gave a single nod of understanding.

Throwing open the door, I quickly glanced to either side for threats. Across the arcade, a monk attempted to climb a tree in the garth only to be pulled down by a bloodthirsty ghoul that savaged him on the ground for the span of a heartbeat before rising and chasing after another shrieking victim. To the right, a young monk ran through the door to the lavatorium screaming for help.

I grabbed Thomas and pulled him along the covered walk to the left, keeping my sword raised defensively before us. In the far corner, the prior stumbled his way through the door to the courtyard; three creatures in white robes streaked after him. A moment later, the entire outer area erupted in the shrill screams of women and children.

"Come on. We've got to get to the men. To Arms!" I shouted the last command into the air. "To Arms!" I hoped Edward and the rest of the men would hear the call and react in time. There was nothing to be done for the dead or dying monks in the cloister.

"Watch our backs," I told my son as we cautiously made our way down the covered walk. Pulling Thomas through the door, I abruptly crashed into a large, black-faced figure, my sword becoming trapped in the press. I tried to back up but could not as Thomas was pushing from behind.

"It's me, Sir Richard," Therry exclaimed. "Where's my brother?"

"Go!" I ordered him, but the burly footman refused to budge. "He's dead, Therry, now run." The footman shook his head and pushed me effortlessly to one side. As I turned to scold him, Therry leveled his spear and skewered a ravenous monk under the chin as it rushed through the doorway. In a single, fluid motion, he twisted to the side and slung the creature across the flagstones.

"I'll be right behind you," Therry said calmly.

The courtyard was a scene of horror and mayhem. Some townsmen were trying to run for the gates while others even tried to claw their way over the eight-foot wall. A few mothers dashed after them, one with a babe clutched to her chest, while another lost all reason and left her child to fend for herself. I quickly scanned the large rectangular field looking for familiar faces.

"Hurry up and open the blasted gates," Edward shouted from outside the courtyard. Nicholl had somehow managed to get inside and was fumbling with the lock while at least a dozen villagers pounded on the gates around him. A few yards to the right of the entrance, Gilbert scrambled over the top of the wall and dropped to the ground. A moment later, his bow was tipped over the wall after him.

"This way," the archer called before putting two arrows in the back of a black-robed demon that was atop a shrieking woman; it did not appear to feel the bodkins pierce its rib cage.

"Aim for their bloody heads," I shouted at him as I led Thomas and Therry towards the exit, scanning back and forth for approaching danger. Three other ghouls were wrestling on the ground with men from the village.

"Got it," Nicholl finally exclaimed. A moment later the gates were dragged open, revealing Edward and Hamond with swords drawn. Leonard and James stood immediately to their backs.

"This way," the esquire called to the cottagers, who frantically rushed past him.

"Father, behind us." As I turned, a figure rushed forward, the hilt of a sword swaying in front of its chest. At the last moment I shouldered Thomas aside and slashed down with my sword, cleaving its leg just above the knee. The monster collapsed onto the cobblestones. Rushing over before it could rise, I hacked down onto the nape of its neck with my blade and then kicked the creature over to expose the handle of my son's sword.

"Get your bloody sword, and don't lose it again." I scooped up a small girl who was standing dumbfounded in the middle of the chaos; she never uttered a sound as I slung her over my shoulder and headed for the open gates.

"Sir Richard," Matthew called from the courtyard exit. He was somehow leading four horses in a dead run. James was atop his own horse, sword drawn, leading the way.

"Come on, lads. Keep coming." I threw the girl over Ebon's neck and climbed into the saddle. Edward ran over and handed up a young boy to Thomas as soon as he had mounted. He then slapped the horse's flanks with the flat of his sword. As soon as Therry took his reins from Matthew, Edward grabbed the young varlet by the back of his doublet and hurled him up into the last saddle.

"Hold the gate and protect the commons," I ordered them. "Nicholl, bring up the rest of the horses." The two archers promptly rushed to either side of the gates and continued shooting arrows into the monsters, giving the villagers time to flee. The young varlet rushed back through the gates leading a trio of horses.

"Get out of the way!" Gilbert yelled to Nicholl as a pale woman trailing the remains of a bloody linen sheet charged towards them. The bowman jumped to one side and loosed a bodkin into her chest, but it barely slowed her down. An instant later, she collided with poor Gilbert, and he wailed as her teeth tore into his flesh.

"Help!" the bowman screamed. "Save me!"

"Get off him, you stinking harpy!" Leonard bellowed as he drew his sword and rushed to his companion's side. He hacked the ghoul repeatedly until she stopped twitching. Kicking her off, Leonard grimaced and turned away when he saw the mutilated body of Gilbert. He started slowly backing his way towards the gates.

Over the incessant screaming of terrified villagers, the bells in the church tower began to ring out in alarm. Thomas, James, and Matthew galloped through the gates.

Keep your horse moving on the battlefield, I reminded myself. "Everyone still alive has already fled. The rest of you get clear of this place." Holding the girl with my reining hand, I circled my stallion in front of the retreating men, scanning the field for oncoming attackers.

"Don't leave me," cried a young lass of not more than seven or eight. She darted from behind a cart on the far side of the courtyard and started running for the exit. "Please, don't leave me."

A blood-drenched creature heard her panicked screams and abandoned the corpse it had been gnawing on. Before I could react or call out, a dark horse galloped past, its hooves clattering on the cobblestone. Edward veered his stallion in the direction of a second monster that had raised its head to leer hungrily at the girl; he trampled the ghoul under his heavy mount.

"Get down," Edward shouted as he thundered directly towards the girl. She quickly flopped to the ground and covered her head in terror. An instant later, Edward's stallion hurdled her tiny frame and careened into the second creature, sending it sprawling across the courtyard. The esquire then spurred his way back towards the gates, reaching way down and somehow snatching the child off her knees as he rushed by her.

"Withdraw and shut the gates," I ordered, shifting Ebon to one side to allow Edward to exit. Thomas and James waited just outside the gateway. "Go, Thomas. I'm right behind you."

As Edward galloped by them, Thomas and James spurred their horses away from the priory. I took one last look across the courtyard; it was littered with the mutilated bodies of a dozen or more villagers. The white-eyed monk that Edward had trampled began to rise again.

Madness!

Hamond pulled the gates closed and then vaulted into his saddle. Large clods of earth flew through the air as we spurred our horses into the fallow field. The rest of my retinue were waiting about forty yards south of the priory gates. The fear upon the faces of the men and women standing behind them was palpable. I counted only twelve villagers and two monks, one of those being Prior Gregory.

"Easy, lass," Edward said soothingly to the young girl squirming uncomfortably in front of his saddle. He did his best to reposition her behind him. "You're safe now. Just hold tight to my saddle." He wheeled his mount around to face me. "What the devil just happened in there, Sir Richard?"

"Yeah, it was crazier than a French bath house," Hamond said with an evil grin.

"Whatever infected Hugh and Adam and Michael has now spread throughout the priory. Is anyone injured?"

"Just don't tell me we have to go back in there," Leonard blurted, shaking his head. A few others murmured in agreement.

"Is this all that made it out?" I asked no one in particular. "There were at least three times this many inside the priory an hour ago." Before anyone could answer, a new wave of terrified screams pierced the incessant clamor of church bells. Turning in my saddle, I saw a ghoulish monk chasing a woman down the road in front of the church and into the midst of several villagers who were responding to the cries for help. The creature savagely slashed and chomped at any and all within its reach.

"Here," I said to the teary-eyed woman standing nearest to my horse. "Take her."

"But, lord, she's not mine." The woman started to back away, waving her hands.

"I said take the blasted child," I bellowed as I lifted the girl from Ebon's neck. The woman reached out and accepted the orphan without further protest. "Therry and Leonard, take the varlets and lead these people away from here. The rest of you, follow me."

I galloped towards the melee as fast as I could; Thomas and my men-at-arms struggled to keep pace with my charger. More of the devil creatures swarmed out of the priory, drawn to the cries of pain like ravens to the stench of carrion. One ghoul scrambled through an open window and across the graveyard; two others tore their way through a low hedge. I lopped off the pale head of the rearmost creature as I overtook him.

"Get back in your homes!" I called ahead to those in the crowd still alive. I cleaved the skull of another as I galloped past him and then trampled a third.

"Come on, Rachel," a man hollered as he pulled his wife across the road and into the closest house, immediately slamming the door shut. An instant later, a dark shape leapt through the cottage's open shutters; a loud shriek rang out. Another ghoul charged into the adjacent home eliciting more frantic calls for help.

What the devil are you doing, Richard? You can't hold the village with so few men. I glanced back over my shoulder; Thomas was close behind. *Is it worth your son's life?*

"Hold," I commanded my men, jerking back on my reins. "The village is lost. We save those we can and make our escape." Thomas and Edward both skidded their horses to a halt next to mine. Grimly, they nodded in agreement.

"This way," I shouted to the few commons still visible in the town. "The village isn't safe. Run this way." The men-at-arms echoed my calls, and we did our best to protect the handful who fled through the fields in our direction. We hacked down several more of the corpse-like monsters, one of which looked like the young monk who had been reading at the lectern.

"Prepare to move," I directed my men once we had regrouped some distance from the priory. I counted an additional nineteen villagers, mostly women and children. They were all sobbing breathlessly.

Two men-at-arms, two squires, a footman, an archer, and two young varlets. Nowhere near enough to defend all these people.

"We have to move. Thomas, you and James lead us back to the manor. Make a wide arc around the village. Take us several hundred yards due south before turning east to Colleville. The rest of you, protect the left flank."

Prior Gregory plopped heavily down onto the earth. He was pale and trembling. A second monk was compelling him to stand.

"I can't go on," he panted. He held a bloody hand to his left shoulder; a large wetness was slowly spreading down the front of his black robes. I dismounted and cut a large swathe off the bottom of his habit, pressing it to his wound.

"Keep that pressed tightly to your shoulder, Prior, and get on my horse." I lifted him to his feet and positioned Ebon in front of him. The old monk pitifully kicked his spindly white legs, trying to pull himself atop the warhorse. The second monk hurried over and gave his superior a push to help him into the saddle.

"Sir Richard," Edward protested. "I won't ride while you walk. Please, take my horse." He dismounted and led his stallion over towards me.

"We don't have time for this, Edward," I said, waving him off. Instead, he grabbed one of the children and placed her into his saddle before handing the reins to his varlet.

"Ballocks," grumbled Hamond, as he, Leonard, and Therry followed suit. My son, too, started to slide from his own saddle.

"No, Thomas. We need you and James to find us a safe path back. It'll be dark soon, and we have many in our midst who can't fight. Get moving."

It had been several years since I wore my harness for anything other than show, so I was not used to walking or running under its weight for long periods of time. The two-mile march to the base of the ridge had not taken too much of a toll on me, but I was dreading the sharp incline in the road ahead. The only saving grace was the fact that many of the women were exhausted and were slowing the pace of the group. The fat merchant in the pale green gown painfully waddled down the path; one of his shoes had been lost somewhere along the way.

James and Thomas rode perhaps fifty yards ahead of everyone else. My son's head continually turned back and forth, searching the trees ahead for any sign of danger. He had a young boy from the village seated behind him. Apart from a faint scream far off in the distance, everything was eerily quiet. The thirty or so townsfolk, some afoot and some mounted, trudged along silently behind squires. Even the wind had forsaken the vale.

My small retinue formed a thin wall along the left side of the villagers. If an attack were to come, that would be the most likely direction. In front, Edward walked with his sword propped over his shoulder. Behind him was Leonard, an arrow nocked on his bowstring. In back, Hamond carried his sword by the blade in his off-hand while he chatted up the young woman sitting astride his horse. Therry brought up the rear. Although he occasionally glanced backwards, his spear was resting leisurely on his shoulder.

"Sir Richard?" Prior Gregory called out to me, his insolent tone completely gone. Matthew was leading the prior on my horse as well as a mother and child atop his own. The second monk walked just behind his superior, his black habit hitched up to his knees to keep it out of the muck. He had large, owl-like eyes that seemed to follow me with an uneasy stare. I did my best to simply ignore him.

"Yes, Prior Gregory," I replied as I slowed my pace to allow Matthew to overtake me.

"You must know by now that these are the End Times. '*Et dedit mare mortuos, qui in eo erant: et mors et infernos dederunt mortuos suos, qui in ipsis erant: et judicatum est de singulis secundum opera ipsorum.*'"

"The sea will give up its dead and death and hell will give up the dead in them and then something about judgment?" The second monk smirked and appeared eager to correct me.

"The dead have risen, my son," the prior intoned. "That's all you need to know. It's the Second Coming. You should have your confession heard before it's too late." The mother and young girl atop Matthew's palfrey both began to cry again.

"Come now, Prior. You cannot tell me that you believe this disease is a sign of the Judgment." I was curious to hear his rationale, but a commotion up ahead cut short our discussion.

"Left! Look to your left!" Thomas called out. Turning back towards Stony Heath, we saw a man and a woman scrambling across the muddy field towards our position. Not far behind them were two additional figures, both covered in bright red blood. The woman kept falling as she tried to hurry across the broken ground.

"Ha," shouted Thomas as he spurred his mount.

"Ballocks! Thomas, get back here." My breath was wasted. He galloped headlong across the furrows to intercept the ghastly pursuers. Before I could even turn to give the orders, a goose-feathered arrow whizzed past my head and struck the earth a stride beyond its target; a second quickly followed and struck deep into the lead monster's thigh. The devil staggered briefly but continued racing forward undeterred.

As soon as Thomas cleared the first villager, he jerked his stallion to a halt and dumped the boy to the ground at the feet of the woman. He swore as she darted past the child now sprawled on the ground. In that moment I knew exactly what my fool-born son was about to do.

"On me," I shouted as I started across the fifty yards of open field towards him. Thomas wheeled his horse to the side, forming a barrier a few steps in front of the boy, bracing himself for the attack with his sword held high at the ready.

Forty yards. Thomas swung but missed as the first creature leapt atop his stallion's flank and began clawing at his armor. I was already too breathless to call out to him. Three arrows struck the demon's back in quick succession but to no effect. The monster was too close for Thomas to bring his sword around, so he smashed in its teeth with an armored elbow.

Thirty yards. The second ghoul attacked, biting a chunk out of the courser's throat and causing it to panic.

Twenty yards. I screamed out a hoarse challenge to the devil as my son's stallion reared up and collapsed on its side. Thomas instantly cried out in pain, and I, God help me, tripped and fell flat on my face.

"No!" I bellowed, furious with rage. Scrambling to my feet, I once again started running as fast as I could. Thomas did not give up; he slammed another elbow down onto the first monster's head.

"Argh!" Thomas cried as the stallion thrashed around on its side. He continued to slam elbow after elbow into the face of the creature until its skull finally cratered.

Ten yards. The other devil scampered over the flailing stallion and climbed atop Thomas, who was still unable to free his trapped leg. My heart almost burst as I realized I would not reach him in time.

Sprinting past me, Edward lowered his shoulder and barreled through the demon like an angry bull. The two rolled over and over several times, locked in a deadly embrace before the man-at-arms pulled back an arm and thrust a dagger through his opponent's temple.

"Fool of a boy," I wheezed at my son moments later, desperately trying to catch my breath. "What the devil were you thinking?" It was all I could do not to collapse onto the ground. I motioned for some of the men to help free my son; it took three of them to push the dying horse off of him.

"I couldn't just watch them die," Thomas said as he raised his visor. I was so proud of him in that moment as I helped him to his feet. But I tried to maintain an angry scowl.

"Were you bitten?" He shook his head, his eyes still wide with excitement. "Are you certain?" I asked as I looked him over. He nodded. "How bad is your leg? Are you able to stand?"

"I'll be fine, Father," Thomas said before wincing and nearly falling down as he tried to take a step. "I'm sorry," he said with a grimace.

I waved over Hamond and Therry, who helped him limp back to the caravan while Leonard carried the boy who had been riding behind Thomas. I paused to look down at the two creatures: the devil whose skull had been crushed resembled one of the patients from the infirmary while the other was dressed like a merchant.

"He couldn't have been infected more than half an hour ago," Edward said, pointing his sword at the ghastly merchant. "If the disease can spread that quickly, how many others might now be infected?"

"I fear we might soon find out."

"What do we do with the bodies?"

"We should burn them, but we have neither the oil nor the time to waste." I motioned far across the vale to the west. "The sun's already beginning to set. We must get home before it gets too dark."

It was twilight by the time we entered the stand of trees atop the ridge about a mile from Colleville Manor. We had no torches, and the rising moon was concealed behind a bank of clouds, so a blanket of darkness fell over us. We simply trudged forward, focusing on the faint lights of torches atop the manor's distant walls.

Every bird that fluttered or rodent that scurried in the night caused women to scream and children to cry. My retinue did its best to keep the villagers moving and tightly grouped. As we neared the manor, the muscles in my hand ached from nervously gripping my sword.

It's the ghost you can't see that terrifies you more than the devil standing before you.

"Sir Richard returns," a voice called down from atop the gatehouse. "Open the gates!" The heavy doors swung outward as Bartholomew and Gyles, armed with torches and spears, stepped forward to hold them open. Passing through the inner gates, I signaled my men to encircle the villagers as they filed into the courtyard. Grooms ran forward and took control of the horses, helping the riders dismount and nudging them in the direction of the others.

"Good people of Stony Heath," I addressed the huddled crowd. "I welcome you to Colleville. You are now secure within my walls and are welcome to remain here, under my protection, until such time as it is safe to return to your homes. Let it be known, however, that you will all be expected to contribute. Those who are not willing to work should not expect to eat.

"I know that you have already experienced unimaginable terrors, but I must ask you to be patient for a short while longer. For the safety of everyone, you must each be examined for any sign of Plague. You who have been in physical contact with a diseased person will be isolated until such time as it is determined that you are free of infection. There will be no exceptions."

I expected there to be quite a bit of grumbling, but my words were met only with blank stares. The events of the last few hours had taken their toll upon everyone.

"Master Edmund?" I called to my steward.

"Yes, Sir Richard."

"Summon Mary and the rest of the maids. Instruct them to examine the women. Give them use of the great hall."

"Yes, lord." He waved at one of the two lads standing behind him; the boy dutifully took off across the courtyard.

"Thomas," I said in a low voice, turning to my son now at my side. He was using Matthew as a crutch. "Tell me the truth. How badly are you hurt?"

"I'll mend. With a bit of time." Thomas would not admit to being in pain, but he would wince whenever he shifted his weight. I stuffed my gauntlets inside my helmet and handed them over to my varlet.

"Go see to your mother and sisters. Ensure they are well and that all of the shutters remain closed. I will be along when I can." He and Matthew walked arm in arm slowly across the courtyard.

"Edward, once the womenfolk have been shown to the hall, the men of Stony Heath are to be examined here in the courtyard. I will allow you to handle the particulars, but it is cold, so do what you can to make it quick."

"Yessir." The esquire started directing the villagers to form a single rank across the center of the yard. Mary and three of the maids arrived a short while later with folded linen sheets under their arms and began ushering all of the women, young and old, towards the hall.

"Master Edmund," I said, turning and placing an arm around the steward's shoulders to guide him off to one side. "How many unused rooms do we have here at the manor?"

"If memory serves me correctly, taking into account the recent arrival of your retainers, there should be nineteen rooms along the walls and three guest rooms on the interior." The rooms inside the hall were normally reserved for important visitors; those outside along the walls were much more spartan and were provided for the use of servants.

"Move the men-at-arms inside as well as Andrew Fowler; have him send for his family at once. After the examinations are completed, group the villagers as best you can and place them in the other vacant rooms. Supply blankets to the remainder and invite them to sleep on the floor in the great hall." Edmund nodded with each item as if it were already completed in his mind.

"I am sure our guests are famished from their ordeal. Please see that they are all given something to eat before the tables are removed from the hall."

"Yes, Sir Richard." As the old steward left my side, I finally recognized that one of the guards flanking the gatehouse was

William Sorel. There were dark circles under his eyes and his shoulders were slumped forward.

"How is your son, Master William?" I asked, waving the marshal over.

"He's been better, lord," William replied with a heavy sigh.

"Did you not send for brother Phillip?"

"After the way I spoke of him this morning, I didn't think he would respond. Besides, Agnes made a poultice to help rid him of infection. I'm sure he'll be fine in a few days."

"Nonsense. I plan to visit brother Phillip shortly. I will ask him to visit your son first thing in the morning."

"That's very kind of you, lord, but it's not necessary to trouble the monk." He nodded to Edmund as the steward walked up. Without another word, William turned and walked back to the gatehouse.

"Sir Richard," Edmund said with a furrowed brow. "The prior has a deep wound to his shoulder where he said he was bitten. A man from the village has several gashes on his forearms that he said he got when he jumped through a shuttered window. None of the others had any visible marks on them except for a couple of boils and cankers, but those men claimed to have had them for a number of years."

"Thank you, Master Edmund. I am on my way to see brother Phillip. I want Prior Gregory lodged in the room next door."

"Very good, my lord. I will see to the others."

Across the courtyard, the frail old prior wearily adjusted his black habit. On either side of him stood the pudgy townsman with one shoe and the other monk. The latter nudged his fat companion into silence as I approached and watched me with a hawklike glare.

I am so sorry, I wanted to tell the prior. *It is my fault that you were attacked and all of your monks are dead.*

"Prior Gregory, would you like to go see brother Phillip?" I asked, motioning him towards the door in the western wall that led to the dormitories. He nodded weakly and started across the courtyard. The other two men turned to follow; I held up a hand to stop them.

"Perhaps you would care to join the others in the great hall while I see to Prior Gregory's accommodations?"

"My name is brother Philemon," the monk stated, "and I am the subprior at the Holy Trinity. I will not be requiring a meal this evening." He wagged his chin as he spoke as if I should be overawed by his presence before motioning to the large man standing next to him. "And this is Alexander Ducworthe, a well-respected member of the community."

Alexander smiled at the mention of his name, flashing a set of yellowed teeth. His silver rings glimmered as he curled his fingers around the lapels of his plush gown.

"Sir Richard," the townsman said with an almost imperceptible bow of his head. "I am at your service."

"Master Alexander, I invite you to join the others in the great hall and take your ease. I am sure you will be more comfortable in the warmth of the hearth than standing here on these cold stones." I nodded towards the large pink toe visible through the rend in his hose. He opened his mouth to argue, but the subprior waved him off.

"Please excuse Alexander," the monk intoned as the heavyset townsman reluctantly shuffled off, more than once stealing a glance back over his shoulder. "As the reeve of Stony Heath, he is not accustomed to being dismissed. We have come to rely greatly upon him. Alexander is highly esteemed by his fellow villagers." His words were flat and unconvincing.

"I am sure you are right, brother Philemon. Now, you should join Master Alexander in the hall while I see to your prior." His mouth immediately curled downward.

"As I said earlier, Sir Richard, I will not be having supper. I think it best that I stay close to Prior Gregory."

"Allow me to make myself clear, brother Philemon. You will not be residing with Prior Gregory. You may either join the others in the warmth of the hall or remain here in the cold. That is your choice." I once again motioned the prior towards the door; he patted brother Philemon on the shoulder as he turned and walked in the direction of the servants' quarters.

"Prior Gregory, what can you tell me about how the last Great Plague spread?" I motioned him up the stairs, leaving the other monk to grumble loudly as he stomped across the courtyard to the great hall.

"We have in our library a book brought back from Paris by brother Stephen, God rest his soul. It says the Pestilence was the result of noxious vapors created by the conjunction of certain planets—I forget now which ones—but those vapors were blown by the winds across the world. That miasma, or bad air, entered into men's bodies through their pores and disrupted their humors, which in turn led to sickness."

"Forgive me, Prior, but I am more skilled in the use of a sword than an astrolabe. Have the planets once again come into that same alignment?"

"I—I do not believe so. But disease itself is a divine judgment upon man, and the planets are merely signs in the heavens that enable us to predict when such judgments might be inflicted upon us."

"Only now it seems to spread from bites, like rabies in dogs, and turn dead men into cannibals." I guided him down the hall to the left. "This way."

"There are diseases that are transmitted by one's breath. Leprosy is an example."

"So you think Guy only had to breathe on the villagers in the infirmary in order to infect them?"

"Yes, perhaps. That is how some diseases are spread."

"But he was bedridden, and, if a sick person only has to breathe on someone else to spread the disease, how is it that not everyone is already ill?"

"As I have said," he sighed, "it is in the hands of God who becomes sick and who doesn't. That is how the Lord tempers our souls; if we entrust our care to Him, His Grace will allow us to recover." I was not convinced. Still, I kept a few feet away from the prior.

"Brother Phillip is in the last room on the left," I said, pointing towards the end of the hall, lit only by the soft glow of a wall lamp. "Tell me, Prior, what are the usual symptoms of someone infected with Plague?"

"The disease is almost always preceded by a fever and chills. Often there appear a number of small red bumps not unlike bug bites but with pinkish halos around them. Then swelling and tenderness in the armpits and around the neck and groin. Some begin coughing up blood, and their health obviously declines very quickly after that. In the latter stages there will be ugly black tumors that are filled with blood. The fingers blacken, causing the skin to pull back from around the nails. If they survive long enough, there may be hideous black spots all over their bodies." His description painted a gruesome mental image.

"Here we are." I stepped past Prior Gregory and listened at the door. Only a faint murmuring sound could be heard coming from within. "I think Brother Phillip may be praying," I whispered as I knocked softly on the door. Almost immediately there was a heavy thud followed by a groan as something crashed to the floor inside. My chest tightened as a bumping sound grew steadily louder in the room.

The monk's been infected as well!

My heart almost leapt from my chest as something crashed violently against the other side of the door; my hand reached for the hilt of my sword.

"Oh, heavens!" Prior Gregory exclaimed as he jumped backwards.

"Stand back, Prior." I hooked him with my left arm and gently shoved him back. Listening breathlessly for a moment, I contemplated whether to force my way in or turn and lead the old man to safety. The latch clicked loudly and the door slowly creaked open. The room beyond was cloaked in darkness.

I lurched backwards as a dark shape came through the shadowy doorway. It was brother Phillip, though his hands were black and fresh blood trickled from his nose.

"My apologies, Sir Richard," he whimpered. "I didn't mean to startle you."

"What the devil happened?" I demanded. His face turned pink with embarrassment.

"You scared the daylights out of me, Sir Richard. I was recording some of my observations about the Plague when you knocked on the door. In my panic, I overturned my ink and knocked my candle to the floor." He shrugged and wiggled his ink-covered fingers in front of him. "To make matters worse, I tripped over a chair in the dark and, well, tried to open the door with my nose." I could not contain a hearty laugh.

"I have brought your prior to see you," I said, still grinning broadly. "He will be staying in the room adjacent to yours for the time being. I want you to see to his wound." I paused for a moment to carefully phrase my next statement, the smile quickly disappearing from my face. "Let me know at once if there are any complications."

"Yes, Sir Richard. It will be my pleasure."

"Prior," I said, turning to the old monk, "please take your ease in the next room. I will have some supper brought up to you as soon as it can be arranged." As I started down the hallway, I turned and gave him one final instruction. "I am sure you will understand, but I must ask you to remain in your room."

Crossing the courtyard, I made my way through the great hall and up the stairs to my private chambers. My body ached to finally shrug off the heavy weight of my plate armor. Anne met me at the door, her eyes and cheeks bright red from tears.

"I am still angry with you," she said softly, laying her head against the cold steel of my breastplate. "I was so furious when you left me and the girls alone in the church this morning." She lifted her head to gaze at me with her soft green eyes. "But I'm glad you're safe."

"We were too late," I sighed heavily. "They're all dead, Anne."

"All?"

"Only Prior Gregory and one of his monks remain from the monastery. Of the villagers, we were able to save maybe thirty. There were more than a hundred in the village." I unbuckled my sword belt and tossed it aside. "Their blood is on my hands."

"It wasn't your fault, Richard."

"It was, Anne. I never should have sent Guy to the priory."

"You only did what you thought best to help your man. That has always been your way." She wrapped her narrow arms around my steel frame in a gentle embrace. It felt strange. I was usually the one consoling my wife, not the other way around. After a brief moment she led me over to a chair next to the fire. "How did they die?"

"Guy. He infected several monks and villagers in the infirmary, and from there the disease spread so quickly that all we could do was flee." She would eventually overhear soldiers telling gruesome tales in the hall, but I did my best to spare her the horrifying details. "Thomas was so very brave today.

He charged into the fray single-handedly to rescue a pair of villagers. I was so angry with him, yet so very proud."

"Why do you men always feel the need to prove yourselves?" She managed a half-smile. "Thomas came here earlier and forbade me from going downstairs. I could tell his leg was bothering him from the way he leaned on the door, but all he would say is that he'll be fine by the morrow.

Part Two:
War

31 December

Feast of Saint Sylvester

THE BELLS OF SAINT WYSTAN'S echoed through the window to mark the first hour of the day. Every muscle in my body cried out in pain as I sat up and willed my legs over the side of the bed.

"Good morning, husband," Anne said cheerfully. She was already dressed and carried her book of hours in one hand; it had been my wedding present to her almost twenty years before. As I pulled on my robe, Anne gracefully walked over and gave me a warm kiss on the head. "I trust you slept well," she smirked, taking a seat on the bed next to me. "If not for the snoring, I would have thought you were dead."

If you only knew, I thought but did not say. I had lain awake half the night contemplating all of the things I should have done differently.

"Did I really sleep through Matins? I can see you went to morning prayers without me."

"I didn't think Doctor Symond would fault you just this once," she replied with a warm smile. "Besides, you and Thomas could use the extra sleep after all you went through." I felt a tinge of guilt for agreeing with her.

"How is Thomas?"

"Still abed, I hope."

"Good. Keep him there. He needs to give his knee time to mend."

"That's not going to be easy." She smiled wryly. "He inherited much of his father's willfulness." We both laughed and, for a brief moment, sat together in comfortable silence.

"I'm just glad you're safe," she finally blurted out, reaching out to embrace me. "I can't tell you how afraid I was when night fell and you hadn't returned."

"Anne, darling, I promised you everything would be all right, didn't I? Nothing on earth could prevent me from returning home to you." Sometimes a man feels compelled to make promises that he knows he may not be able to keep. Fortunately, it was enough to put Anne at ease.

"What're your plans for the day?" she asked.

"I must see to our many new guests. I can't help but feel responsible for the fact that they're here. It's only right that I ensure they're well treated." Anne nodded with a forced smile.

She peered deep into my eyes as if gazing through a window to my thoughts.

"Well, I best get to it, dear," I said as I rose and walked over to the corner of the room, where my varlet sat furiously scouring my breastplate. It should have been James's responsibility, but my feckless squire had a knack for getting others to do his work for him.

"Matthew, what are you doing to my harness, lad?"

"Polishing the rust off, lord," the boy replied with barely an upward glance.

"The armor looks good," I said, turning to take a seat in front of the fireplace. The young varlet raised his head and smiled broadly at the compliment; his hand never ceased its circular motion. "You know you shouldn't let James talk you into doing his chores for him."

"I don't mind, lord. Truly."

"Tell me, what excuse did he give you this time?" Matthew's cheeks colored at the question.

"James said I was the one who armed you, so I'm the one who has to clean your armor."

"Very well, Matthew," I said with a soft chuckle. "If you have your heart set on doing everyone else's work for them, I am not going to tell you otherwise, but I had better not hear of you falling behind in your personal duties. Understood?" The varlet returned a quick nod.

"Then why are you still sitting there, lad? Do you expect me to dress myself?" Matthew jumped to his feet and hurried over with my brigandine, which he once again concealed under a fur-trimmed coat. Buckling on sword and dagger, I made my way downstairs and through the great hall. Morys Hopton, the butler, was giving an earful to a handful of villagers unfortunate enough to have been discovered still trying to sleep around the hearth.

"Can't lay around all morning. There's work to be done." He waved and clapped his hands at them as if he were chasing chickens out of the roost. "No one's going to eat a bite until the floors are swept and the tables are set up."

Emerging from the hall, I saw that the courtyard was filled with dozens of men, women, and children, some of whom were laughing and talking amongst themselves while others simply sat along the walls with bewildered looks on their faces. A blustery wind whipped over the northern wall to sting my cheeks.

Standing to the right of the gatehouse, brother Philemon had his back pressed tightly against the wall; a large man in a dirty green gown hovered only inches in front of him. The monk's eyes narrowed as he slowly nodded his head. Though the other man's back was turned, I knew the heavyset frame belonged to Alexander Ducworthe. He leaned forward and clasped a large hand onto brother Philemon's shoulder, causing the subprior to wince in pain.

"Sir Richard," Edmund called from behind as I started across the courtyard. Brother Philemon's eyes suddenly widened at the sound of my name, causing Alexander to turn around.

"Master Charles says three of his scullions haven't shown up for work this morning," Edmund explained as he hurried to my side. His jovial face was bright red from the cold. "He says there's no way he can cook for so many extra mouths without any help in the kitchens." The steward gestured at the dozens of villagers milling around the courtyard. Alexander smiled awkwardly and doffed his cap as we approached; brother Philemon's eyes fell to the ground.

"Send a lad to their quarters and tell them their jobs will be given to boys from Stony Heath if they do not wish to work. Come to think of it, I want you to start assigning all of them some kind of work to do."

"It also appears that Master William hasn't been seen either. Owain Dun said neither he nor his sons were in the stables. Should I send someone to check on him?"

"No," I replied, pausing at the door to the servants' quarters. "He did not look well when I spoke to him last night. I am sure that he is busy tending to his son. I was just about to stop in and check on Prior Gregory. If Master William does not show up soon, I will ask brother Phillip to call on him."

"How are you feeling this morning, Prior?" I asked the venerable monk. He was slouched on the side of his bed, his habit pulled open, leaving him bare down to the waist.

"Much improved, Sir Richard," he rasped. "I should offer a prayer to Saint Sylvester for my recovery. As you know, today is, after all, his feast day." Brother Phillip knelt in front of him, delicately examining his superior's bony frame. The skin around the bite was a blackish-red color, and dark splotches had spread across his torso. His body trembled despite a blazing fire only a few feet away.

"That is very good news," I replied. Brother Phillip smiled in gratitude as he completed his examination.

"You should lie back down, Prior," he instructed. "You need to recover your strength. Let's get you covered up now." Brother Phillip pulled a heavy blanket over the prior before gesturing me towards the hallway. "I'll be back shortly with something to help with the pain."

"How bad is it?" I asked the monk as he closed the door behind him.

"It's the same as with your man, Guy. The prior is infected with Plague." Upon entering his room next door, he poured water into a basin and pulled back the sleeves of his robes. "It is progressing faster than anything I've ever read about." He gave a slight nod to the large book resting atop his bed.

"Do you mind?" I asked, reverently lifting the heavy tome and running a hand over its leather-bound cover.

"By all means, Sir Richard," he replied as he dried his hands on a linen towel. I gently opened the book; it contained hundreds of pages made from very fine vellum. The title was elegantly inscribed on the first leaf in large, gothic letters: *Liber Medicinarum.*

"You asked me earlier why I no longer visited the monastery."

"Yes; you said Prior Thomas had been your friend, and you mentioned that you used to come frequently to read."

"Upon the death of Prior Thomas, God rest his soul, Prior Gregory, who was at that time subprior, was elected as his successor. Everything quickly changed. A few weeks later, I had an occasion to visit your library, and a monk was directed to follow me around as if I were going to steal a book. It did not take long for the enjoyment of reading in the monastery to sour, as did my opinion of Prior Gregory. Have you ever tried to read with someone standing over your shoulder?"

"Try translating a manuscript from Greek with someone looking over your shoulder," the monk replied with a soft smile before shaking his head. "That is unfortunate. I'm sorry. Prior Gregory is still very protective of his library."

"What can be done to avoid the Plague?" I asked, continuing to flip through the delicate pages. The entire volume was penned in Latin and filled with colorful illustrations showing the movements of the planets, the elements of the world, and the humors of the body.

"First and foremost, you should flee the area in search of healthier air."

"You make it sound so simple. I cannot just drag my family across the countryside. Besides, we live more than a dozen miles from the nearest town. There is nowhere more remote than Colleville." Without the manorial rents, there would also be no income to sustain us.

"Barring that, it is recommended that you wash with vinegar and avoid filth, southerly winds, baths, and rotting things in general."

"Baths? Really? How can a man be expected to avoid filth and foul odors and yet not bathe himself?" I closed the book and placed it back on his bed.

"Why, yes, baths open the pores through which corrupted air can enter and infect the body."

"The prior mentioned something about poisonous gases from distant planets as a cause of the Plague. If that is the case, is there nothing that can be done to clear the air?"

"Fumigating the air with aromatic herbs is believed to help eliminate the vapors, and merry living can help keep the humors in balance." He allowed himself a thin smile before tossing his linen towel into the basin. "Much of what we know comes from the writings of the ancient Greeks. In truth, we understand little more now than we did a thousand years ago."

"You do not sound very optimistic," I stated flatly. The monk could only shrug in return. "Brother Phillip, would you be willing to accompany me as I check in on my marshal of the stables? You may remember his son was injured during the fight with Hugh early yesterday morning."

"Certainly. I just need a moment to gather my things."

Stepping into the courtyard, we were met by a man with a dark beard and round belly; a short woman and a young boy stood a few steps behind him.

"Sir Richard?" he said with a bow, quickly removing his wool cap to expose a balding head. His voice was deep but humble.

"Pardon the interruption, but my name is Piers Smythe and this is my wife, Rebecca, and my son, Piers, and we wanted to personally thank you for saving our lives." He wore a thick leather apron and had large hands covered in burn marks.

"I would imagine that you are the blacksmith at Stony Heath, are you not?"

"Yes, m'lord, and I'm at your service." His eyes continued to dart between me and the monk.

"Tell me, Master Piers, if you had use of a forge and the necessary tools, would you be able to fashion barding for a horse?" The loss of Thomas's expensive stallion had left me contemplating how to better fend off the monsters if it came to another fight. I had paid more coin for that charger than any one of my men had earned in a month's fighting across the English Sea.

"I'm afraid not, Sir Richard. At least not of the kind of quality you'd be wanting. Would that I were able, but I've spent my life fashioning tools for farming, nails for building, and the like. I could, though, remove the dents from your armor or repair the edge of your sword."

"Thank you, Master Piers," I said, patting him on the shoulder as I moved past him and started towards the gatehouse. "I will have to think of something else."

"Tell him," Rebecca chided her husband from behind.

"Sir Richard?" the blacksmith called.

"What is troubling you, Master Piers?" I replied, turning back to meet him. "Please be quick of it. I really am in something of a hurry."

"Of course, my lord. It's just that—" He bit his lip as he looked at the monk standing to my side.

"Out with it, man. Brother Phillip is not going to bite you." The blacksmith reddened as his wife nudged him in the back.

"It's not that, Sir Richard," Piers stammered in a low voice, glancing around the courtyard. "It's just that I thought you should know that someone has been saying you conspired to send the Pestilence to Stony Heath so you could have the land for yourself." With a heavy sigh, he allowed his body to slump as if he had just let go of a heavy burden.

"Who would make such an outlandish claim?" I demanded.

"Our reeve, Alexander Ducworthe." His gaze remained locked to the ground in front of me.

"Thank you for telling me, Master Piers," I said, forcing myself to gently smile. "You have no cause for concern. You and your family are safe here. I am confident that I can handle a village reeve no matter how large of a shadow he may cast." The blacksmith could not hold back a small grin.

"Of course, my lord." Piers bowed his head briefly before turning and ushering his family back across the courtyard.

"Brother Phillip, what can you tell me of this Ducworthe fellow?"

"He earns—or, I should say, earned—his trade as a fuller. His father gave generously to the Holy Trinity during his lifetime, which, I understand, led to his son's appointment as village reeve. In my short time at Stony Heath, Prior Gregory has entrusted him with a growing list of administrative duties in and around the village."

"I see," I replied, guiding the monk towards the gatehouse. It was odd that a man as distrusting as Prior Gregory would put a weasel in charge of the hen house. "I suspect your prior felt it was better to keep him busy than constantly under watch."

"Idle hands *are* the Devil's workshop," the monk said with a chuckle.

"Perhaps I should do the same and find him something to do. In the meantime, I would appreciate it if you did not mention this to anyone else."

"Of course. I won't say a word."

Crossing the stone bridge, we turned north along the edge of the moat towards the stables. A lone groom stood outside rasping the hooves of a roan palfrey. Two other riding horses were tied to a nearby rail awaiting their turn. Though his words could not be made out, he was obviously having a pleasant conversation with his four-legged companion.

"Master William lives in the cottage next to the stables," I said, pointing to the two-story timber-framed house situated between the paddocks and the hay barn. The monk nodded in acknowledgment, but his tonsured head was turned back to the west.

"What is troubling you, brother Phillip?"

"I'm just being paranoid," he responded with a nervous laugh. "I keep thinking about how quickly the disease has spread and how—" he paused momentarily. "How Stony Heath is just up the road."

"You have nothing to fret about. I have posted guards all about the manor keeping a watchful eye for anyone approaching from the west." Several chickens squawked noisily as we made our way around a small stack of firewood in front of the house.

"Master William," I said, knocking on the door. There was no immediate answer. "I have the physician here to see your son." I knocked again, but there was no response.

"Perhaps he stepped out?"

"Doubtful." I pounded on the door even harder. A muffled cry came from somewhere inside.

"Did you hear that?" brother Phillip gasped.

"Help!" the voice called; it was weak and hard to make out. "Please, help!"

"Go fetch the men." I grabbed the monk by his robes and shoved him in the direction of the manor. "Go!"

He hitched up his habit and took off running towards the stables. The brood of hens scattered in his wake. Drawing my sword, I raised a leg and kicked hard at the door; it did not budge. "If you can hear me, come and unbar the door."

"They're going to get me! Help!" came the voice again faintly. I took several steps back, lowered a shoulder, and barreled straight into the door. With a loud crack, the latch broke and the door swung wide open. Unable to slow my momentum, I stumbled and fell heavily to the floor; my sword skittered into the shadows.

"Ballocks," I groaned, quickly climbing to my feet. The room was cloaked in darkness, the shudders still closed from the night. A single column of light from the doorway cast long shadows against the far wall.

Where's my blasted sword?

Scanning the room, my eyes slowly adjusted to the darkness. It had been several years since my last visit to William's home. The stairwell to the upper floor was somewhere in a back corner.

A black shape, quick and silent, suddenly rushed out of the shadows. Instinctively, I drew my dagger and retreated backwards. The figure surged towards the doorway after me, revealing a bloodstained dress and a hideous face amid a wild mess of hair; its ashen skin glowed in the sunlight.

She charged forward faster than I could retreat. As her arms reached up to grasp my throat, I quickly stepped to the side, ducking her outstretched hands, and embedded my dagger in the base of her neck. With all the force I could muster, I flung her to the earth. The ghoulish hag rolled across the ground and crashed through the stacked firewood.

An axe! Stuck in a large round stump was a forester's axe. I let the dagger fall to the ground and lunged forward to jerk the axe free. The gruesome figure sprung to her feet and turned to face me. Her long, thin fingers were blackened and curled like the talons of a falcon.

I hefted the axe over my shoulder as the creature bared its blackened teeth and once again lunged for my throat. I unleashed a powerful swing, and the axe struck her across the jaw so hard that she was spun completely around, sending her teeth flying across the wood pile. I took a step back as the corpse flopped to the ground.

Impossible! She slowly raised her shaggy head and glared with emotionless white eyes. A mangled jaw hung precariously from the bottom of the dark, bloody face. Within a heartbeat, the monster was once again back on her feet.

"Die, you she-devil," I grunted as I plunged the axe into the top of her head. With a brief shudder, she collapsed to her knees and slumped to the ground when I released my grip on the axe.

"Oh my Lord," I heard brother Phillip squeak. The monk was frozen in place by the stables with a hand over his mouth.

"Where are my men? I sent you to bring back help."

"I—I sent the groom to fetch them," he stammered.

"Then make yourself useful and grab that axe," I told him as I snatched up my dagger.

"What am I supposed to do with it?" He stood motionless.

"Defend yourself, man." He slowly walked over and stood next to the corpse.

"Who is—was she? Did you know her?"

"Agnes Sorel, William's wife. Now stop wasting time and pick up that axe." I turned and approached the open doorway. "Hello!" I called into the darkness.

"Help me! Please hurry!" the voice came from somewhere off to the right. It sounded like the faint cries of a child. Steeling my nerves, I strode across the room to where a piece of metal glinted on the floor. Sheathing my dagger, I quickly scooped up my sword and turned to face the direction of the voice.

"I'm here, Sir Richard," a silhouette spoke from the doorway; it was wielding an axe with both hands.

"Open the shutters," I ordered the monk. "I can't see a thing in here." Brother Phillip worked his way down the wall, pausing before each window to unlatch its shutters. Within a few moments, the sunlight had overpowered most of the shadows.

Following the sounds of sobbing, I moved across the room to the right, ducking a small iron pot hung from a rafter and slipping around a table littered with small jars of spices.

"No! Get back!" The cries echoed from the cold, dead fireplace in the center of the wall ahead. A large cauldron hung from a hook in the center of the black opening.

"Are you in there?" I called into the dark shaft, slowly easing my head past the cooking pot to look up.

"Help!" the voiced echoed far up the chimney. "They're going to get me!"

"Aaagh!" Brother Phillip shrieked from behind. Recoiling, I struck my head against the edge of the fireplace, causing my knees to wobble and small lights to dance in front of my eyes.

"Are you all right, Sir Richard?" The voice belonged to Edward.

"Yes, yes. Find the stairs." As I blinked away the stars, Edward stood in the center of the room dressed in full armor. Christopher and Hamond were at his back; all three brandished swords.

"I'm sorry," squeaked brother Phillip. "They startled me when they rushed in."

"Edward, there's a child in danger somewhere upstairs, perhaps hiding in the chimney. He sounds desperate." The esquire nodded and moved across the room. The other two men-at-arms followed closely behind him.

"I found the stairs," Hamond said a moment later, pointing his sword at the far corner. He kicked a chair aside and skirted around a long table adorned with four wooden porridge bowls. "Mind your step," he grumbled as he reached the back wall. "It looks awful bloody dark up there." The old stairs creaked loudly with every footstep as he started his slow climb. Edward and Christopher rushed into the cavernous darkness behind him.

"See if you can find a candle or something," I instructed brother Phillip. The monk had already discarded the axe.

"There's a partially open door up here atop a small landing," Hamond said in a hushed voice. The dim light glimmered off their dark steel frames.

"Be careful," I warned him as he slowly pushed open the door. The stairs groaned loudly as Edward, Christopher and I climbed up the narrow passage.

"Seven hells!" Hamond suddenly exclaimed as he jumped back and jerked the door shut. An instant later there was a loud thud against the other side of the door. The burly man-at-arms grabbed the handle and held it tightly closed.

"What was that?" Edward asked. All three of us crowded around Hamond at the top of the stairs.

"Someone charged at me."

"Who was it?" I demanded, trying to push past Edward and Christopher. A heavy scratching sound grew steadily louder against the back of the door.

"I'm not sure," Hamond replied, tightening his grip on the latch, "but it sounds like a bear's trying to come through that door to get at us."

"Where's that light?" I called down. The clawing noise grew even more intense. "Brother Phillip?" The door shuddered with another heavy blow.

"Coming," shouted the monk. A moment later he rushed up the stairwell, a fluttering candle shielded behind his cupped hand. Hamond had both hands on the door latch to keep it tightly closed while the rest of us were huddled around him.

"You'd better wait out here," I instructed brother Phillip. The candle in his hand was shaking, causing our mass of shadows to tremble against the wall.

"Sir Richard," Christopher said. "You should allow us to handle this. After all, that's what you pay us for." Reluctantly, I took a step back. They were in full harness while I only wore my brigandine. Christopher stepped past Hamond to stand on one side of the door while Edward moved to the other.

"You boys better know what to do when this door opens," Hamond said with a quick glance over each shoulder. As he placed his shoulder firmly against the door, the noise inside grew instantly louder.

"Ready," Edward said, placing a hand on Hamond's shoulder. With a growl, Hamond jerked the latch and shoved the door open, slamming into whatever was behind it and smashing it against the wall behind. He continued to grunt as he used the heavy oak door like a vise to pin the creature into the corner; a single small arm flailed around the edge of the door, clawing at the air in front of Hamond's chest.

"Any day now, ladies," he croaked, the pitch of his voice rising as the door began to slowly push him backwards. "He's strong as an ox." Edward darted around his companion and slashed down on the exposed arm with his sword, cleaving through bone and flesh. The esquire's sword never slowed as he quickly brought the blade around and thrust it behind the door, creating a wet crunching sound.

Hamond took a step back and a small, ghoulish figure flopped to the floor. He and Edward both looked down and grimaced with disgust.

"It was young John Sorel, all right," Edward said. The boy's pale skin was covered in dark, bulbous tumors and bright red blood glistened down the front of his linen nightshirt. Small tips of bone were visible through the ends of his fingers, the nails having been sheared completely off; they were deeply embedded into the back of the blood-streaked door.

"Savage little devil, wasn't he?" Hamond chuckled grimly. He used the tip of his sword to flick the clawlike hand away.

"Look out!" Christopher shouted as he leapt backwards through the doorway. He careened off Edward to fall at my feet, nearly sending me down the stairs. In the center of the dark room was Master William, slowly clawing his way across the floor; much of his thighs had been torn away.

"Wretched troll!" Hamond spat as he sidestepped the corpse, placed a mailed foot square on its back, and then buried his sword through the base of its skull. "Have you ever seen the likes of this before? He looks as if he's been gnawed on by a pack of wild dogs."

"Follow me," I instructed the monk before cautiously moving around Christopher and Edward to enter the room. An oil lamp flickered atop a small table nestled between a pair of low beds against the left wall. One set of the bed linens was heavily stained with blood, and a pungent odor hung thick in the air.

"Please try and keep the candle still, brother Phillip." I was busy studying the body of the former marshal: his eyes were milky white and his skin ashen, but there were no outward signs of Plague.

"Is it safe?" a voice called from across the room.

"Yes, it's safe," Edward responded. "You can come out now." A moment later, two small legs appeared dangling from the fireplace in the middle of the far wall. With a grunt, a young boy wriggled his way down and crawled out of the flue. He was covered in soot from head to toe; his eyes were wide with fear and remained locked upon the corpse in the center of the room.

"Come with me, son," brother Phillip said soothingly as he walked over to the boy, sidestepping a pool of congealed blood in the center of the room. The monk placed an arm around him and steered him back towards the stairwell. "What's your name?"

"James," he replied meekly.

"Aren't you one of Sir Richard's grooms?" Brother Phillip used the cuff of his habit to wipe away some of the grime on the boy's face.

"Uh huh," he nodded.

"I'd wager you're a bit hungry right now. Come on and we'll see what we can find to eat." The monk led the boy past Edward and Christopher to the stairwell.

"Brother Phillip," I called to the monk. "Give your candle to Christopher before you leave." He reluctantly surrendered the light before turning and leading the boy down the stairs.

"Search the rest of the house," I instructed the men. "Make sure there's no one else lurking about." There were two doors along the right wall; Edward used the tip of his sword to push the first one open.

"It's pretty dark in here, but it looks like a bedchamber," he said, peering through the doorway. Christopher joined his side and stuck the candle into the room. "Empty."

Hamond walked over to the bedside lamp and picked it up.

"The oil's pretty much all gone," he said with a shrug.

"Open the windows then," I chided him, crossing the room to the second doorway. Hamond threw open the shutters and filled the room with sunlight.

"So what the devil happened here?" I asked over my shoulder as I crouched in front of John's small corpse. I used a dagger to carefully cut away the blood-soaked bandages around his hand. Three fingers had been severed at the knuckles, and the flesh of the arm was covered in a hideous rash.

"We knew the boy was sick," Edward noted. "But the marshal made it sound like it was just an infection from the cut to his hand, and he didn't mention anything about his wife being infected either."

"Do you think the boy was actually bitten by Hugh and not cut by Jack?" Christopher inquired.

"If so," I wondered aloud, "either John lied to his father, or William lied to us all. But why would William have lied about his son instead of asking brother Phillip for help?

"What would the monk have been able to do for him?" Hamond asked, shaking his head. "Pray?" He stood over the corpse of the marshal. There were large hunks of meat missing from his upper legs and pelvis. "And just look at William's corpse. It looks as if something has been feasting on his legs."

"From what we saw at Stony Heath," I explained, "a man is transformed into a living corpse shortly after he's bitten and is consumed with a ravenous desire to attack others. But I never witnessed two of them eating each other."

"No," Edward said grimly. "Me neither. That means the marshal must have been attacked by his wife and son."

"While he was still alive?" Christopher shuddered. "Wouldn't someone have heard him screaming?" The idea of a man being eaten alive by his family caused my stomach to turn.

"The boy'll be able to tell us more," I sighed. "Come on, we should get back to the manor."

Like any other Monday morning, a number of villagers were mingling outside their homes, greeting one another, some cheerfully exchanging eggs for milk or butter or cheese. They took no notice of their lord and his men-at-arms walking briskly along the moat towards the manor bridge.

"Stranger in the distance!" a watchman shouted down from the gatehouse, frantically pointing over our heads to the west. I hurried through the gates and up the spiral stairs to the rooftop. Edward, Christopher, and Hamond were never more than a few steps behind.

"Where?" I demanded, scanning the horizon for movement.

"There, lord. Coming through that far stand of trees." Following the line of his finger towards Stony Heath, I spotted a filthy villein staggering out of the woods and into the wide, fallow field leading to the manor. As he drew closer, the dirt on his face began to look more like blackened tumors.

"He's diseased!" the guard shouted over his shoulder. A number of the women in the courtyard below became hysterical. I wanted to hit him in the back of the head.

"Are you daft, man? Why further terrorize the refugees?" I had intended to reprimand him further but his warning created quite a different effect on the cottagers living around Colleville Manor. Hearing the watchman's cry, they began casually walking down the lane searching for a better view beyond the hedged cottages.

"Get back in your homes, you bunch of lackwits!" I shouted. "That man could be carrying the Pestilence." Reluctantly, they began making their way back down the road, still pausing to look for the stranger through gaps in the hedges.

The creature craned its head towards the village, sniffing the air like a hungry predator. Suddenly, it began running swiftly across the final two hundred yards of pasture towards Colleville.

"Archers," I called down into the courtyard. "Come put an arrow in his brain."

Bertram emerged from the stairwell a few moments later. Pausing just long enough to gauge the wind, the skinny lad nocked an arrow onto his string, pulled it back to his ear, and promptly let it fly. The bodkin cut a high arc through the air before striking the figure in the center of its chest. The creature half-spun from the impact but never slowed its deliberate pace towards the manor.

"Stinking wretch," he hissed before sending a second arrow that dropped at the last minute to imbed in the figure's groin. Bertram cursed under his breath as the monster continued to run unhindered.

"Step aside," Aleyn said as he trotted up to the battlements to stand next to his companion. He drew and released a quick shot that hit the monster high in the shoulder. I glanced down to see several heads sticking out of open windows to the left and right of the gatehouse, all jeering at the two competitors.

The bell of Saint Wystan's began to ring out in alarm. A few villagers darted from their homes and through the gate into the churchyard.

"Look," Andrew pointed with an arrow. "All the bell ringing's just making it even madder." The creature scrambled over a rock wall and ran through the garden behind an outlying cottage; there were no less than six goose-fletched arrow shafts sticking out of its body.

"Huzzah!" a chorus of cheers rang out when an arrow struck the monster through one of its eyes. Aleyn danced a small circle to celebrate his winning shot.

"Seven arrows to kill one attacker?" I asked, quenching their enthusiasm. "That's hardly cause for excitement. And before you get too carried away with your revelries, it'd be good for you to remember that whoever—or *whatever*—that was, I'd wager that someone down there in the courtyard shared an affinity with him." Their smiles quickly melted away.

"Good. It's time that you all let the seriousness of our situation sink in. We expended a few dozen arrows in the village melee yesterday. We've no idea how far the infection has spread or how long it may last, so we must begin conserving our resources immediately. A few more of these kinds of competitions and there will be no arrows left."

"I'd only like to point out," Andrew finally commented, "that, at the very least, we didn't put any of the men at risk."

"Not good enough. You and your men are supposed to be the best bowmen in Colleville. At least, that is what I was told when you signed your indentures. Make every arrow count. In the meantime, have the loser run and fetch those arrows." Turning for the stairs, I was met by the household steward.

"Sir Richard," Edmund said breathlessly. Beads of sweat rolled down his red face. "Is it true? Have William Sorel and his family all been killed?" The archers began to grumble.

"Regretfully so," I replied, placing a hand on his shoulder and guiding him down the stairs. Edward, Hamond, and

Christopher followed close behind. "I take it you saw brother Phillip?"

"Aye, lord. He was walking with young James. He said that you and the lads had to—"

"We did what had to be done," I interjected. "Now, as grim as it may sound, we must consider finding a replacement at once. The manor cannot very well operate without a marshal of the stables."

"Perhaps Lewys Massy would be up to the task?"

"I could not agree more. Send him to me if he is willing. In the meantime, young James will need time to recover from his ordeal. See what you can do about picking out a few of the boys from Stony Heath to serve as grooms. I will be needing the horses prepared to ride out in a couple of hours. I plan to take the men-at-arms and footmen along with me."

"Where to, my lord?"

"If there is one, there will likely be more. It is imperative that we ready the villagers for whatever may come. Get word to John Sadeler that he is to muster every able-bodied man in Colleville and drill them into the ground." The steward nodded his head.

"Edward, ready the men."

After a quick dinner of salted beef and Lombard pasties, I led my small retinue out through the gatehouse. My three men-at-arms were, like myself, armored from head to toe in steel harness. Behind them rode my three remaining footmen.

"Will the archers be joining us later?" Edward asked, glancing back over his shoulder.

"No point wasting the arrows," I replied with a shake of the head. "You were at Stony Heath yesterday. You saw the crazed devils charge headlong through a hail of bodkins as if they could feel no pain. If they find their way here, it's going to take a block of armed men to defeat them out in the open. Today I just want to see if the levy is worth its salt."

The midday sun was no more than a pale glow behind the dark bank of gray clouds. As we cantered down the muddy road west of Colleville, there were about forty men milling around in the large pasture. A dozen carried longbows, but the vast majority leaned on their polearms or had them awkwardly propped over their shoulders. The men were passing around loaves of coarse bread and drinking from small canteens made from boiled leather, likely filled with home-brewed ale. A handful of their wives had gathered and were standing far back from their husbands, talking and laughing amongst themselves as if it were a normal Monday afternoon. Most held baskets or large sacks in their hands.

John Sadeler was standing near the back of the crowd. He wore an open-faced helm and had a breastplate strapped over his maille shirt, all of which were painted black to prevent rust. A thin red sash across his chest distinguished him from the rest of the men.

"In array, you sorry lot," he shouted when he caught sight of the approaching riders. John had a wooden baton in his hand that he shook menacingly at whomever was nearby. Serving in the role of the levy's vintner, he was the officer in charge of the mustered villagers. "In array, I said. In array."

The two dozen or so footmen hastily took the last bites of their dinner as they bunched into a block of three rows. They were all armed with billhooks. The six-foot-long implements were good for pruning branches in the orchards, but they were also effective at snagging an opponent's armor in combat or slicing the reins of a horse.

"Bills at the ready," the vintner shouted. The front rank lowered their weapons so that the top spikes were pointing forward, forming a steel hedge. The second rank dipped theirs about halfway to the ground and the third kept their shafts almost vertical.

We rode down the short line; the mustered footmen ranged in age from young boys to gray-haired men, most wearing padded jacks likely sewn by their wives or mothers. Some had simple helmets and small, steel bucklers hung from the pommels of crude swords at their hips. Deep lines of worry were carved across their collective faces.

"Be of good hearts, men," I addressed them as I rode back down the line. "I seem to recall your previous musters being much more lively events." A few of them allowed themselves a tiny smile. "You have trained for battle many times before. You know full well what to do: work together as one body, and all will be well." Despite the words of encouragement, there was still a feeling of foreboding in the air that was almost palpable. Circling around, I reined Ebon alongside my retinue several yards in front of the levy.

"Gentlemen," I said to my men-at-arms, "see what you can do to get these men ready for battle."

"Yessir," Edward replied with a grin, dismounting and tossing his reins to his varlet. "It's about time we had a little fun." The esquire elicited several laughs as he sauntered across the field towards the center of the formation. Picking out a man in the front rank, Edward paused about a foot in front of the villager's extended billhook.

"What's your name?" Edward asked the man as if he had seen him a hundred times before but had somehow forgotten his name.

"George," the billman responded. A wide grin crept across his face.

"Hit me, George," Edward growled, suddenly turning serious. George's eyebrow went up as he stared blankly at the esquire. "I didn't stutter, man, and you're not here to pick apples with that thing. I said hit me, or so help me I'm going to come over there and smack you with the working end of my sword." George glanced to the man on either side of him as if looking for approval; both men just shrugged.

George grimaced as he tightened his grip, lowered his stance, and then thrust his weapon at the smirking esquire. Edward quickly half-stepped to one side, grabbed the shaft of the weapon, and yanked it towards himself, pulling its wielder to the ground. With amazing swiftness, the esquire slid between the adjacent billhooks and rushed forward, giving George a ringing slap across the back of the helmet as he struggled to rise from his knees.

"Dead," he said coldly. George's face reddened with embarrassment as Edward helped him back to his feet.

"What're you laughing at?" Edward demanded of the villager standing to George's right. He glared at the man as he walked backwards several steps to just beyond the steel hedge. "Care to try and do better?"

"My pleasure," the villager remarked as he started to coil his body for a powerful thrust. Edward quickly reached for the shaft once again, but the man anticipated the move and jerked back on his billhook. Instead of trying to pull his opponent down, Edward gripped the weapon tightly and shoved it straight back with all of his might. The billman stumbled and fell into the man behind him. Once again, Edward streaked through the opening and pantomimed a sword thrust at his prone victim as well as follow-up strikes at the men to either side.

"Dead. Dead. And dead," he said icily. "Let that be a lesson to you all. Don't get cocky. It could cost you your life, not to mention the lives of those to your left and right." He helped the prostrate villager to his feet. It was easy to see why all the men respected Edward Cornewayle and his fiery countenance.

"Therry," I said, turning back to my three footmen, "would you, Bartholomew, and Gyles be so good as to show these men how to defend against a wily man-at-arms?" All three slid from their saddles and walked to the center of the formation.

"Make a hole," Therry barked at the villagers as the three footmen wedged their way into their midst, forming a new column. Bartholomew stood in the front rank followed by Therry and then Gyles in the back. "At the ready," he said as all three locked their halberds into fighting positions. Edward responded by drawing his sword and gripping it with one hand on the hilt and the other on the center of the blade.

"Are you sure you're all ready?" Edward asked casually. Without awaiting a response, the esquire hooked the back of Bartholomew's halberd with his hilt, dragging it down and stepping forward. He then pivoted the point around as he prepared to deliver a thrust. With a loud clang, the side of Therry's axe blade reverberated off Edward's helm with a quick but powerful chop.

Both men laughed heartily as they resumed their starting positions. After a couple more demonstrations, Hamond and Christopher joined Edward in front of the formation. The three men-at-arms took turns giving the villagers a chance to counter their attacks. I took the opportunity to ride around and speak with John Sadeler, who was standing behind the masse of men.

"What have you heard about the disease?" I asked him.

"Only that it turns men into monsters that can't be killed by normal weapons." He looked grim as he pushed his helmet back on his brow to peer up at me. "Even if I have to get Sir Denis down here to bless every single blade, I'll have the men ready to march on Stony Heath and put an end to it all. You can count on it, lord." I smiled broadly at his confidence.

"Monsters or not, they can still be killed. If you cleave in their skulls, I assure you they will go down. An arrow in the head will do the trick just as well. Either way, it means you will have to let them get close."

"Understood, lord. Should we practice the volley?"

"By all means," I said with a nod as I reined my horse to one side. "Let's see what they are capable of." Edward and the others joined me on horseback to the left of the formation while the vintner began calling up the village archers, who had been lazily watching the entire spectacle with some amusement.

"Archers, form a line." John used his baton to shepherd them into place a few paces behind the billmen. Each one of them pulled several arrows from his belt and stuck them in the ground at his feet. "At the ready." The footmen all assumed a defensive posture and held it while John paced up and down the line behind them, nodding in approval.

"Kneel," the vintner commanded. All three ranks took a knee. A few of the men took their time and were rewarded with a whack across the back of their skulls. "Bodkin in the brain," John said with each blow as he walked down the line, never forgetting which men had been slack. He repeated the commands several times to ensure they had learned the lesson well before signaling the archers to prepare themselves.

"Ready your bows." Each archer plucked an arrow from the ground. "Nock." They placed a shaft on their strings. "Kneel." The billmen quickly dropped to a knee. "Mark." Each archer focused on one of the straw targets that had been placed in front of the dirt mound a hundred yards away. "Draw." They pulled the strings back to their ears, their wooden staves creaking under the strain. "Loose." With a single loud twang, a dozen arrows streaked across the pasture and stuck in and around the targets.

"Have them tighten up their aim, Master John. Not a single one of those would have been a killing shot."

"Ready your bows," he once began again. They continued the exercise until most of their arrows were exhausted. It was readily apparent that they were only wasting arrows.

"Master John, I think it might be more effective if you march your men closer to the archery butts and repeat the exercise."

"Yes, Sir Richard," he replied with an exaggerated nod. "Prepare to advance." Each footman raised the shaft of his billhook to his right shoulder while the archers gathered up their remaining arrows and stuffed the points into their belts. "March," the vintner at last commanded.

The formation walked slowly forward, keeping a roughly square shape as it crossed the uneven pastureland. John Sadeler continued to bark orders and harangue any man by name who stepped out of line. Following closely behind on our horses, my retinue evaluated the levy's progress. Edward reined his stallion alongside mine and watched me intently.

"Your thoughts, Edward?" I asked him quietly.

"They seem capable of walking without falling down. There's something to be said in that. However, if you're asking if I think they can stand up to an attack of the snarling devils, I have my doubts."

"They don't have to withstand a charge of mounted knights."

"No, my lord. They face something far more terrifying." I started to laugh but quickly stopped when it became clear he was not joking.

Edward's right, whether you want to admit it or not, I chided myself. *There's no way to know how they'll respond if faced with the horror of living corpses.*

"Well, we can't just tell everyone to hole up in their cottages and hope for the best. Who knows how many may have been infected from Stony Heath or how likely they are to seek us out here. With any luck, there'll only be a few and we'll eliminate them just as easily as the one this morning."

"But there could be scores of them," Edward said, reading my thoughts. "We all saw how quickly the madness spread throughout Stony Heath." He paused for several moments. "Do you think we can win?"

"I assure you, Edward, I wouldn't be out here if I didn't think so. We either face them out here on our own terms, or we hide in our homes and wait for them to pick us off a few at a time. It's not really much of a choice."

"Halt," the vintner called out. "Billmen at the ready. Archers, ready your bows. Nock. Kneel. Mark. Draw. Loose." The second round of volleys almost all landed on target. As more and more white fletchings could be seen sticking out of the straw figures, the spirits of the villagers seemed to swell. After the archers had expended the last of their arrows, I spurred my charger forward and addressed the formation.

"Men of Colleville, the enemy we face does not await us on some foreign shore but is instead coming here, to our very doorsteps. We cannot know whether it will be today or tomorrow, or next week, so you must be ready at a moment's notice. There can be no retreat and no surrender. I tell you we fight for all we hold dear. If Colleville falls, so does our entire world. Keep your weapons sharpened and never far from reach.

"I wish to commend each and every one of you today. You have all performed admirably. I have every confidence that you will do your duty. Now return to your homes and enjoy a hot supper with your families. We will muster again at midday tomorrow." I turned Ebon towards the manor and led my men homeward.

As we rode back across the pasture, my thoughts drifted to that muddy field in France some twenty years ago when I had been all but certain that Death whispered in my ear. Pages had led our horses to the rear as our captains marshaled us into position; knights and men-at-arms alike had been directed to stand amongst the archers and footmen there in the muck and mire. Far in the distance, the enemy's side of the battlefield had seemed too small to hold even the French vanguard of mounted knights poised ready to trample us into the sodden ground.

I recalled how my heart had swelled when King Harry rode down our lines, shouting words of encouragement to us. We had somehow forgotten our exhaustion, and our thoughts of death and despair had been expelled. We had fought like lions that day and had overcome the seemingly insurmountable odds.

As we passed Market Cross and turned south on Churchwell Lane, I took note of how close together the houses were.

Perhaps it would be better to put all the men to work building a defensive bulwark around the town than trying to turn them into a small army.

"Look at ole Drew," Hamond blurted, pointing to the yeoman archer atop the gatehouse; Bertram was at his side. We were just shy of fifty paces from the gates. "You'd think he's the new lord of the manor up there. Begging your pardon, of course, Sir Richard." The men all laughed.

"What the devil's he pointing at?" Christopher asked, turning in his saddle. Andrew was pointing back towards the west where the orange sun was beginning to slip below the cloud bank and edge closer to the horizon. A moment later the bell in Saint Wystan's started ringing an alarm. All of us looking towards the belfry, Aleyn Gifford was hanging out a window, frantically gesturing in the direction we had just come from.

Has a fight broken out between some of the villagers?

From our location on Churchwell Lane, there were simply too many cottages and hedgerows to see where we had left the villagers at the archery butts. I signaled with outstretched arms that I could not understand what they were alarmed about.

"Figures!" Aleyn hollered. "At least a dozen of them. Coming out of the far tree line."

So it begins!

"On me!" I shouted, wheeling Ebon around and thundering back down the road. As we neared the pasture, I hurdled its hedge border and galloped towards a gaggle of men casually strolling back to the village. Far across the field, more and more dark silhouettes continued to pour out of the woods; the tolling bells behind us only sent them into more of a frenzy.

"In array! In array!" I ordered as I wrestled my stallion to a halt and leapt from the saddle. It would be up to the two varlets to lead our mounts to the rear. "Get your men in formation," I shouted at John Sadeler, grabbing him by the shoulder strap on his breastplate and pulling him along with me. My stomach lurched as the horizon was darkened by a wave of the creatures. "Place your archers on the flanks. Tell them not to waste their arrows."

"In array, men! In array! Archers to the flanks!" The vintner shouted orders at the men near him and frantically called back those who had almost made it to the village.

"Make haste, men." I pushed my way through the forming ranks with Edward, Hamond, and Christopher close on my heels. We drew our swords and took up positions between columns of footmen. Therry, Gyles, and Bartholomew likewise elbowed their way into the formation and did their best to hastily prepare the men around them for what was about to come.

"Maintain your spacing," Edward chided the billmen lining up behind us. "Use your spearpoints to keep them back as best you can. Hack them down when you see an opening, and, whatever you do, don't bloody well hit one of us."

The enemy was charging directly at us, driven forward by the ringing bells and the terror-filled shrieks of women and children far to our backs. The low sun only made it doubly impossible to gauge the size of the host coming against us.

The closest ghoul was at least sixty paces away when the arrows began to fly. One missile struck the figure in its chest, but several more littered the ground around its shoeless feet. Closely behind it were a black-robed monk and a woman in a bloodstained dress, both with dull white eyes and expressionless faces.

"Save your blasted arrows," I bellowed in vain as arrows continued to fall short of their mark. Turning, I quickly addressed every villager within earshot. "We can wipe them out here and now, men. They are in total disarray. Just hold your ground and cut them down as they come." I reached up and closed my visor. The world grew instantly darker as the sky above and ground below were obscured by steel plate. The sound of my ragged breathing drowned out many of the distant noises.

"Billmen, at the ready," the vintner ordered as the first creature came within two dozen paces. Steel-tipped poles were lowered into position to either side. An instant later, a billhook came down in a savage chop, cutting deep into the base of the first ghoul's neck, knocking it to the ground. I rushed forward and stabbed a sword point through its skull before jumping back into position.

Out of the corner of my visor slit, I saw that another ghastly monk was struck by a billhook, severing its arm at the shoulder and causing it to stumble and roll across the earth beyond my field of vision. An instant later, a series of painful screams erupted from nearby.

Keep your wits about you, man. It was all I could do not to turn and look at the growing commotion. *Edward has your right. Focus on your front.* I tightened the grip on my sword. Just then a diseased old man dressed in tattered rags streaked across the broken ground as nimbly as a young boy. His mouth was opened wide, exposing a jagged row of rotted teeth.

The footman to my left thrust his heavy billhook at the monster's head, shearing the flesh from the side of its skull but barely slowing the creature's charge. Stepping diagonally forward out of the creature's path, I hacked down into the exposed bone with the blade of my sword, removing much of its head in the process. More agonizing screams rang out from somewhere far down the left side of the line.

"Hold the line!" the vintner shouted from behind.

There were so many figures surging forward that it became hard to keep track of them all. Arrows continued to fly in from the sides while heavy billhooks chopped down at the growing mound of bodies to the front. A dark corpse in bloody rags lunged at me before I could bring my sword around. Instinctively, I put up my off-hand to block its attack, but it kept charging forward. With a quick step back, I sliced down, taking its leg off at the knee before shoving it down and thrusting a sharp point through its face.

I quickly scanned from side to side; Edward was close on the right and Hamond was not far to the left. I thrust a sword point into the head of a feral boy who was missing half of his face. A moment later, something hit my right leg. Looking down, I saw two villeins thrashing atop a prone man-at-arms, his sword stuck in the mire next to his head.

"Do your worst, you wretched dogs!" Edward bellowed a challenge to them both. An instant later, the thin point of a dagger broke through the back of one skull. I grabbed the long brown hair of the second and separated it from its shoulders in a backhanded slash. I offered Edward a hand and quickly jerked him to his feet.

As we glanced up, a monster barreled directly towards us with arms outstretched and yellow teeth bared. A villager shouldered between me and Edward to thrust his bill deep into the corpse's chest. The heavy shaft quivered as the creature continued to savagely claw at the air, shoving the footman further back into the ranks.

"Hold him still," I shouted as I stepped forward to deliver the killing blow. I cleaved in his skull and took several steps to the rear. A chorus of shrieks rang out from behind as several billhooks fell to the ground to either side of my feet. Turning and throwing open my visor, I saw John Sadeler desperately trying to halt the tide of villagers discarding their weapons and fleeing for their homes.

"John! Look out!" I shouted a heartbeat before a feral boy leapt atop his shoulders and began clawing at his face. I started to rush to his aid, but there were at least a half-dozen other ghastly creatures circling around the broken formation like a swarm of bees, mindlessly attacking anything that caught their attention, their bloodlust being driven by cries of terror and screams of pain.

Edward, Hamond, and Christopher were still at my side, but only a single archer and three or four footmen remained to our backs. The terror in the remaining villagers' wide eyes meant they, too, were about to flee. A billman struggled to rise from the ground near my feet, the pale linen of his padded jack red with blood.

"Here. Take my hand," I said, trying to help him up, but I instantly jumped back as he lifted his head and focused a pair of colorless eyes on my outstretched hand. With a thrust of my sword, I dispatched him and turned again to check my rear.

"The disease is already spreading! To horse! To horse!" I shouted, before slamming my visor shut to deal with an ashen-faced shepherdess charging forward. Pivoting again, I hastily scanned the field for Matthew's location.

"Horses!" Christopher shouted. "Bring up the blasted horses!"

I finally caught sight of my young varlet, who was about twenty paces behind us. He was desperately kicking his nervous horse forward while wrestling with the four other stallions tied to his saddlebow; the incessant cries of fleeing and dying men were doing nothing to ease his task.

Nicholl was also mounted and struggling to lead the other three horses to our position. My heart sank when he stopped well short of us; the color drained from his face.

"Craven tosspot," Hamond blurted as he, Edward, and Therry together rushed forward to claim their horses. I started towards Matthew before being struck from behind by a violent blow. Blackened fingers groped around the side of my sallet, wrenching my head back to one side. I reached over my shoulder, seized the monster by the black folds of its garments, and then hurled it to the ground with all my might.

"Aaaaaagh!" Matthew cried as a filthy villein pulled him from his horse. Gyles darted over and almost cleaved the monster's head in two from behind. I ran as fast as I could in Matthew's direction as the horses began to kick and rear up. The stupid boy refused to let go of the reins even after his horse began dragging him backwards across the field.

"Get the horses!" I barked at Gyles and Therry; they had a better chance of catching them. Another creature lunged from out of nowhere. I ducked its grasp and threw a shoulder into its abdomen, toppling it to the ground. I followed up with a powerful chop to the back of the head.

"Sir Richard," Hamond called as he and Edward started to circle back. Gyles had given up the chase and was rushing back to my aid. Matthew was face down in the dirt a few dozen paces away, his horse cantering across the field towards the manor with Ebon still tied to its saddle.

"Just get the horses!" I shouted, waving Edward off. His stallion could not bear the weight of three men. To the west, three more ghouls charged our position.

"Look out!" Gyles warned as he brought his halberd down in a powerful stroke. It cleaved deep into the first one's hip, causing the creature to crumple to the ground and begin flailing around wildly. I bounded forward and delivered an upward slash to the second monster, cutting through its jaw and the front of its skull.

Gyles brought his halberd around for another strike, but the third ghoul was moving too fast. It tackled him to the earth. Rushing over, I lopped off its head before kicking the corpse off of the footman. Blood spurted from a deep gash to the side of Gyles's neck.

"You're not dead yet," I grunted as I dragged him backwards by the collar. "Staunch the wound with your hand." From the side, a living corpse clad in a mud-stained black habit reached out. I slashed at the monster defensively, my blade striking the front of its knee, causing the leg to fold back and collapse under its weight. I broke off the attack to continue dragging the wounded footman back to where a few remaining villagers were making a bold stand.

"On me!" I shouted to them. "If you run, you're dead." I slammed my visor shut and decapitated a ghoul charging from the left. A moment later a man shrieked to my right. A bloody corpse thrashed atop a levied footman. An archer darted forward and shot his last arrow into the back of the monster's skull. He threw his bow to the ground and drew a short sword.

"Your horse, Sir Richard," a voice shouted from behind. Hamond had my black courser in hand. Dragging Gyles over, I expended my last bit of energy heaving him over the saddle.

"You too! Get on!" I ordered the archer. I slapped Hamond's stallion across its flanks with the flat of my blade as soon as the villager had scrambled atop Ebon.

"Go!" I shouted. Hamond's mount shot forward into a gallop, nearly unseating the burly warrior.

Turning back, I saw Edward racing forward with one of the hackneys in tow. As soon as I had taken the reins from him, the esquire hastily circled around to defend our escape.

"Hold still, you wretched nag!" I cursed as the animal kicked and threw its head. I nearly fell underneath the panicked horse as my foot slipped out of the stirrup. Once I finally managed to drag myself into the saddle, I wheeled the mount over to the closest footman and hauled him off the ground. The other ran over and jumped on the back of Christopher's stallion.

"Let's go!" I shouted to the men. Edward hacked off the helmeted head of a milky-eyed villager that had risen a few feet from Ebon. An instant later, we wheeled our horses and thundered back across the corpse-littered pasture in the direction of Colleville Manor.

"Open the gates!" Christopher called ahead as he, Therry, and Nicholl tore past Market Cross and through the village. Hamond was only a short distance behind them, dragging my black charger in tow. I continued to furiously spur the roan hackney all the way past the parish church and around the large stone cross. Edward was not far behind me.

"Open the gates!" a sentry shouted down from the gatehouse. "Sir Richard returns! Open the gates!" Large clods of earth cascaded through the air as we made the sharp turn off Churchwell Lane and galloped the last fifty yards to the front of the manor. Thomas and James Berkeley held the heavy doors ajar as we sped across the bridge and into the courtyard; a sea of terrified faces was crowded within its walls. The gates slammed shut and were barred as soon as Edward raced through them.

"Where're the rest?" Lewys asked as he placed a hand on my horse's bridle.

"There are no more," I responded grimly, sliding from the saddle. Rivulets of blood dripped from the hackney's side where it had been gouged by spurs. Several young lads rushed forward and took control of the other stallions. "They are dead. They are *all* dead."

"He's dead, too, I'm afraid," the archer said as he hopped down from Ebon. Walking over to the courser's side, I gently lifted Gyles's head; his face was ashen and stained with blood. I stood there frozen for several moments, unable to escape the unfocused gaze of his pale blue eyes.

He's going to turn soon, I reminded myself. *Act now before he can infect the whole manor. Think of your children.*

"I'm truly sorry," I muttered to him as I drew my dagger and plunged it into the base of his skull. Withdrawing the bright red blade, I wiped it clean on his sleeve before sheathing it.

At least Anne was not here to witness this.

Unbuckling my sallet, I flung it down onto the cobblestones and kicked it across the courtyard in a fit of anger. A collective gasp passed over the crowd. My face burned with embarrassment as hundreds of teary eyes bore down upon me. A young boy picked up the helmet and solemnly carried it over.

"Thank you, lad." I said, tucking the sallet under an arm and playfully bristling his hair. *They're all looking to you, Richard. You've got to hold it together.*

"Husband?" a familiar voice called. I looked over to see my wife standing on the steps of the hall, our three daughters desperately clinging to her sides, their cheeks red with tears. "Are you wounded?" she asked as I walked briskly to her.

"What? No, I am fine." Glancing down at my breastplate, I realized there were countless streaks of dark red running down its smooth metal surface. "It's not my blood."

All I could do was shake my head with frustration at the thought of Matthew Scoffe, Gyles Sterlyn, Bartholomew Grene, John Sadeler, and dozens of villagers whose names I did not even know. "We lost so many men today."

As I looked around again, the countless faces seemed to gravitate even closer. There had to be a hundred in total, most belonging to frightened mothers with young children clutched to their skirts. One woman wore a dress freshly stained with mud.

"Anne, did anyone from the village seek refuge in the manor after the fighting broke out?" I asked in the calmest voice I could manage.

"The courtyard has been a madhouse for much of the last half hour. I have no idea who may have come in or gone. Why? Is something wrong?" Ellie slipped around behind her mother to be hidden from view.

"Take the girls inside. I will come for you when I feel that it is safe." Anne started to protest but relented when Lizzie tightened her grip around my wife's waist.

"Very well. Come along, girls." She turned and ushered them through the doors into the great hall.

"Did anyone see what happened to Bartholomew?" I asked, turning back to what remained of my retinue. Of the fighting men I had taken with me to the muster, only Edward, Hamond, Christopher and Therry had returned alive. "Did he flee the field?"

"I saw him fall," Christopher replied grimly. "Had half his face bitten off early on in the press."

"I should have been there," Thomas said as he limped over to stand at my side. His eyes were downcast. He still felt slighted that I had instructed him to remain at home and recover while the rest of the men went with me to muster the villagers.

"No one doubts your courage, Thomas. I would have made the same decision even if you were not my son." He thought for a moment before nodding reluctantly.

"How is your knee?"

"The swelling has mostly gone," he said, gingerly shifting his weight to the injured leg. "I'll be ready the next time you ride out."

"You more than proved yourself at Stony Heath yesterday," Edward added, placing a hand on Thomas's shoulder. "But you were lucky that someone was there to save your backside. If your leg's not ready, you'll not only place your own life at risk but all those around you as well."

"I couldn't agree more," I added. Unfortunately, there were only a handful of fighting men left within the walls of the manor. I doubted I would have the luxury of leaving anyone behind if we were forced into another battle.

"You men come here," I called out to the archer and two footmen from the village who had stood their ground until the end. One of them was embracing a young woman and an infant in the crowd. He quickly left their side and hustled to join the other two men in front of me.

"The three of you performed bravely, and I will see that you are rewarded for it. What are your names?"

"George Blythe," replied the first footman. He was the man who had first gone up against Edward. I was glad that he had survived.

"Miles Dirikson," the archer answered. He could not have been any older than Thomas; he had no helmet upon his head and wore only a crudely made jack.

"Robert Asheley," said the second footman.

"Is that your wife, Robert?" I nodded towards the woman and child.

"Yes, lord, and my son, Robyn. Mary ran here as soon as the bells started ringing."

"And you men," I said, turning to the other two members of the levy. "Are your families here as well?"

"No, Sir Richard," George replied with a furrowed brow. "We live on the far side of the village. My wife and children would have made for the church. I can only pray that they made it there in time."

"I am sure they are well, George, and that you will see them again soon. I fear we cannot go to their aid right now as it is already much too dark, but you have my word we will go and fetch them when we are able."

"Sir Richard," Lewys interrupted, "where do you want us to take the horses?"

"The stables, of course. Where else would you take them? Can no one else make even the simplest decision?"

"Begging your pardon, but I thought you might want to keep them inside the walls"

"Ballocks!" I blurted out. "They'll kill all the horses." I shoved Lewys abruptly towards the gates and began signaling to the grooms. "Everyone, go! Fetch as many of the horses as possible and lock the rest in the great barn. The stone walls should keep the buggers out until we can figure out what else to do." I spun around to face my men-at-arms. "Mount up and guard their flanks."

I raced up the gatehouse stairwell hoping to gain a better perspective of the manor green and any approaching danger. There were at least two dozen good riding horses in the stables just outside the northern wall; they would have very little protection from the bloodthirsty creatures. My legs were burning by the time I emerged onto the upper roof. Andrew was there with Leonard and Bertram, their faces as pale as ghosts.

"What are you all standing around here for?" I demanded breathlessly. "Did you not hear what is going on? Where is the enemy?" Bertram made a wide sweeping motion in the direction of Stony Heath with his yew bow and swallowed hard. Shouldering past Leonard, I stepped to the edge of the battlements.

For the briefest of moments, the world was so very warm and peaceful. The sun had begun to set behind the horizon, bathing the fields in an amber glow. The bell in Saint Wystan's had finally ceased its clamoring, and, for the first time I could ever remember, not a single cow was lowing or sheep bleating or rooster crowing in the village below. The eerie silence was only broken by the sounds of men and boys running along the outer edge of the moat in the direction of the stables.

"By the saints," Andrew mumbled. "The dead are walking!" For a long while, the four of us stood together mesmerized as scores of men, only moments before lying dead on the field, were slowly rising and beginning to move about.

"Eighty-two," Leonard groaned.

"What did you say?" I asked.

"I counted eighty-two. That's one for every man, woman, and child within these walls." A blood-curdling scream suddenly echoed from a small cottage near Market Cross.

"Get everyone back inside!" I shouted down to Lewys and his grooms, who were each leading two horses back from the stables; Edward and Hamond were riding alongside them, vigilantly looking for any sign of danger.

"Hurry up! The diseased are within the village. Get back inside and bar the gates."

"Look, lord, over there," Andrew said, pointing towards the church belfry. Two archers dressed in my red livery were hanging out of the upper windows and firing arrows down at several ghoulish figures creeping around the church walls. "It's Aleyn and Raulfe. I should've sent their relief over an hour ago, but I got sidetracked watching the battle unfold."

"Do you have any idea how many cottagers made it inside the church? Did you see any of the routed billmen make it that far?"

"I haven't a clue. I saw quite a few women and children running all over the place shortly after the bells started ringing, but I don't recall seeing anyone with weapons. What do you intend to do?"

For the first time in my life, I had no answer to give. A hundred different scenarios quickly ran through my head, but every single one of them ended very badly.

"It's almost dark. There's nothing we can do to help them right now. We'd lose every man sent to rescue them. We can only hope that those walls will be sufficient to keep the devils out until morning. I want you to join me in the upper hall within the hour. We can discuss our options. See if you can find Alexander Ducworthe. Tell him that I want him to speak for the villagers of Stony Heath."

"Thank you for joining me this evening," I addressed the nine men seated in the upper hall. The servants had erected three short tables in the shape of a horseshoe. Thomas and James Berkeley sat to either side of me, but Anne and the girls were being served in the solar; everyone else had crowded into the great hall to have their supper.

"For those of you who have not had the pleasure of making his acquaintance," I said, gesturing to the large figure seated at the far end of the table to my right, "Alexander Ducworthe is the reeve from Stony Heath."

"Please," he said, placing both hands on the edge of the table and pulling himself to his feet. "The honor is all mine." Alexander flashed a toothy grin as he looked around the room. With a loud groan, he plopped back into his seat.

"Master Alexander, allow me to introduce you to the members of my household." I placed a hand on Thomas's shoulder. "This is my son, Thomas. And this," I said, looking to my left, "is my squire, James Berkeley, the son of Sir John Berkeley of Beverstone." Turning, I gestured to each man seated at my right hand:

"My steward, Edmund Bromeley, has diligently administered my household for the past two decades. Master Lewys Massy, although only recently named marshal of the stables, has served me faithfully since our days in France together some twenty years ago. My beloved Doctor Symond Radclyf has long ministered to me and my family as our chaplain here at Colleville Manor." Turning to my left, I introduced the fighting men:

"My good esquire, Edward Cornwayle, and my trusted yeoman, Andrew Fowler, have both kept a watchful eye over me and my family for many years. Hamond Benstede and Christopher More are my men-at-arms who each possess invaluable battlefield experience." I took my seat.

"You are all here because I require your counsel. It seems we have found ourselves in an impossible situation, and it will take all of us working together to keep this disease out of our midst." Several of the men nodded in assent. Like me, none of the men had touched his plate.

"What about the villagers in the churchyard?" Thomas asked. "How can we sit here and eat when there are people out there being killed?" His words cut deeply.

"Let me remind you all," I said, standing and looking directly at my son, "that we have been soundly defeated twice now, both times during daylight and in the open. It would be suicide to face these devils in the black of night. It must be agreed here and now that our priority is to ensure for the defense of the manor house and only afterwards turn our attention to aiding those outside of it. I will not tolerate dissent by anyone." I continued to stare at Thomas for a moment.

"You are quite right, Sir Richard," Alexander said before noisily sipping from his wine goblet and then wiping his mouth with his sleeve. "We have a responsibility to protect those poor souls who have been forced to seek refuge here, myself counted least among them." He placed a hand on his breast and solemnly bowed his head.

"Speaking of which, Master Edmund, how many people do we now have inside the walls showing any sign of the disease?"

"At most, three," he responded. "Brother Phillip has informed me that the prior's condition has worsened. There are also two women from Stony Heath who have complained of a fever, but I am of the opinion that their fevers are benign and caused only by the cold air. Nevertheless, I had them quarantined after a group of villagers threatened to throw them over the walls." Alexander forced a wet cough as he slapped an empty goblet onto the table. He tapped his pudgy forefinger on the rim of his glass and waited for a lad to come and refill it.

"Sir Richard," he finally said in a solemn tone. "I can assure you that whatever your steward *thought* he heard, he was obviously mistaken. They all know that I won't stand for any foolishness. Most likely, it was just a coarse jest between friends."

"Master Edmund, where are those women now?"

"In a room adjacent to Prior Gregory."

"I want a guard placed outside their rooms. No one is to enter or leave without my permission. We must prevent the disease from spreading any further inside the manor. What about the rest of the villagers? Were you able to accommodate everyone?"

"I'm afraid not," Alexander interjected, sucking grease off the ends of his fingers between each word. "There are simply not enough rooms. Many are being forced to sleep on the floor of the great hall." The reeve leaned over the table and looked squarely at Edmund as he took another drink from his cup.

"By my count," the steward responded without bothering to look at Alexander, "you have added sixteen to your personal retinue, if you include Andrew Fowler's wife and children; add to that two monks from the priory, thirty-three cottagers from Stony Heath and fifteen more from Colleville, and you actually have seventy-six additional mouths to feed. You have doubled the size of your household in the last three days. I have done what I can to accommodate them."

"No one doubts your efforts, Master Edmund," I said soothingly. "What of our food stores? How long can we support so many people?" The steward paused for a moment as Alexander chewed loudly on a fried pasty, eliciting a boisterous laugh from Hamond.

"Your guests downstairs have already consumed as much meat and spiced ale as was served at the Christmas banquet, and there are still six nights remaining in Christmastide. I asked Master Charles to start cutting way back on the courses. Otherwise, it looked as though there would be nothing left but bread and ale by Epiphany. As for the fish, if consumption is limited to Fridays and saints' days, the stores should last another four or five weeks, but certainly not enough to see us through the Lenten season."

So much for noblesse oblige. I lowered my gaze to the table and nodded thoughtfully as the steward finished speaking; his grim report had dealt a painful blow to my pride. How much worse that it should occur during one of the most hallowed times of the year.

"Let us not forget to count our blessings," Doctor Symond offered. "This is the eve of the Feast of the Circumcision, when our Lord shed His blood. We should all consider ourselves fortunate enough to fast on such a solemn day."

"Thank you for your wisdom, Doctor. We still have almost a week until Twelfth Night, more than enough time to procure additional resources." I turned to address the marshal of the stables. "Master Lewys, what is the condition of the horses?"

"Well, Sir Richard, me and the grooms were able to rescue eight of your finer horses from the stables before you called for the gates to be barred. We've built them a makeshift corral in one corner of the courtyard."

"What about the rest?"

"We herded them into the great barn."

"How long do you think they can survive in there?"

"Not too long, I'm afraid. One end is filled with hay, and its stone walls should keep the devils out, but we didn't have enough time to give them any water to drink. I'm also concerned the horses in the courtyard may eventually develop lameness from standing day and night on the cobblestones."

"See what you can find to put down as bedding. Otherwise, you may have to put the grooms to work digging up the stones within the corral." Lewys nodded in agreement.

"Andrew, how are your archers holding up?"

"For all I know, Aleyn and Raulfe are both still safe in the belfry. Leonard and Bert have spent most of the day on watch atop the gatehouse but will do whatever is required of them. In the last half hour or so before I left to come here, they had dispatched a handful of the dead skirting the edge of the moat. I instructed them to stay out of sight as much as possible and avoid brandishing torches as the monsters appear to be attracted to both noise and movement."

"Well done. Make sure your men are properly fed as soon as we are done here."

"Yes, Sir Richard."

"Very well. If there are no other reports to be given, let us consider what can be done for those outside the walls. We counted eighty-two of the foul creatures out in the grazing field before it got too dark to see. Every one of them could already be stalking outside the manor and the church as we speak. It must also be assumed that most, if not all, of the villagers holed up in the churchyard are unarmed women and children and therefore incapable of fighting their way out. So what are our options?"

"We should have the archers cover us from the gatehouse while we cut a path straight to the church," Thomas declared. "It's shameful to cower behind stone walls while the village is under attack." I slammed my cup down on the table, ready to berate my son.

"While I agree that we could probably make it to the church," Edward calmly interjected, "there's no way we'd make it back here with more than a handful of the villagers still in one piece."

"And everyone we lose to the hungry devils," Hamond added with a smirk, "will eventually come back to bite us in the butt—or somewhere equally tender." A few of the men chuckled at his comment.

"Don't mistake my caution for cowardice," Christopher said. "But why don't we just have the archers take care of the ones closest to the manor walls? Once they have cleared those out, we could make noise to attract more of the buggers from the village and take care of them as well. Eventually, we could thin out their ranks enough to make it more of a fair fight."

"That's all well and good," Andrew remarked, "but we have less than a hundred arrows now, and keep in mind that it takes a perfectly aimed shot to the skull to actually take one of these monsters down. A bodkin stuck anywhere else doesn't even seem to slow them."

"So make more arrows, yeoman," Hamond jibed. "Sir Richard wants to hear solutions, not your personal problems."

"Without access to a smithy to forge more arrowheads or a lathe to form more shafts, we can't make any more arrows, you big dumb ox. Use your head for something other than a helmet peg."

"Sir Richard," Christopher said humbly, interrupting his two colleagues. "I fully understand that you must place a higher priority upon the safety of the manor house as opposed to that of the village, but my mother and father live with my sister and her husband north of the village. While I hope they made it to the church in time, they are old and it is a long way to run. With your permission, I would like to ride out and try to locate them."

"With all that has been going on, I have not thought to ask about your families. I am truly sorry for that." As I looked around the room, many of the men had somber expressions. "Who else has family outside the walls? Hamond?"

"My wife and daughters are downstairs in the great hall. She had sense enough to come here once the church bells started ringing."

"Edward?"

"No, my parents sold all their holdings last year and now live near Gloucester. That's not to say that there's not a pretty face or two that I'm hoping to rescue from the churchyard the first chance I get." Several of the men smiled.

"Leonard has a wife and two young sons," Andrew added. "And Bertram, Aleyn, and Raulfe all have parents and brothers or sisters living in the village. Raulfe is stuck up in the belfry with Aleyn, so I haven't spoken to him about his family, but I did talk to Bert. He said his family would have likely made for the church—if they are not out there on the battlefield."

The last comment was a punch in the gut. Some of the men had remained at their posts even though their loved ones were outside the protective walls of the manor. Any attempt to reward them for their loyalty would only be an empty gesture.

"Christopher, I am truly sorry, but I cannot allow you to travel outside the walls by yourself. You heard Edmund's report. Apart from those of us in this room and the men stationed on the walls, there is no one else capable of defending the manor and all of those within. I assure you that we will do everything possible to reach those trapped in Saint Wystan's."

"And what of those who weren't able to reach the church in time?" Christopher countered.

Then they're already lost, I wanted to shout at him but held back. "First, we must get aid to those barricaded inside the churchyard. After that, as soon as we are able, every effort will be made to recover those hiding elsewhere around the village. Tomorrow morning we should be able to get a better look at our enemy. Hopefully it will provide us with some insight as to how to best counter the threat. We will need to get word to those trapped in Saint Wystan's. Perhaps we can discover how many people there are inside and their current state of health."

"If you were to write a message onto a small piece of parchment," Andrew said, "I could bind it onto the shaft of an arrow and shoot it into the belfry."

"You will have it first thing in the morning. Is there anything else?" Several of the men collectively shook their heads. I could see the pain on Christopher's face. A feeling of guilt gnawed at my stomach. My family was safe inside the manor walls while he, no doubt, was imagining the worst.

"Master Edmund, can anything be done to accommodate more people here in the upper rooms?"

"I'm afraid not, lord. There is only the solar and a few storerooms not already in use for men's bedding."

"Do whatever is necessary to make space in the storerooms so that these men can be reunited with their families; their wives and children should not be forced to sleep downstairs with everyone else. Also, move the archers up into the private chambers as well. If nothing else, they can bed down here in the upper hall during the night. I think we will all sleep more soundly having them close by."

"I will see what can be done."

"And what of me, Sir Richard?" the reeve from Stony Heath said, wiping his chin with his sleeve. "Where are my wife and I to be lodged?"

"I am sorry, Master Alexander. Have you not been given a room above the wall?" As I turned to Edmund, the steward cocked his head back and gave me a look of extreme annoyance.

"Well, yes," he sputtered. "Your steward *did* show us to a small room, but it is very small and right next to—"

"To some of your fellow villagers?" I cut him off. "I am sure Master Edmund has heard how greatly you are admired by them, not to mention how protective you are of them. But if you would rather be moved inside Colleville Hall where it is more spacious—" His eyes widened at the prospect of receiving a much larger chamber. "—I am sure Master Edmund could accommodate two more in the great hall reasonably close to the hearth fire." The steward's faced brightened.

"No. No. No," he stammered, waving his hands before him. "I will remain, as you say, with my fellow villagers."

"Very well. Thank you all for attending to me this evening. I will expect to see each of you at dinner tomorrow." I rose from my chair, signaling that the meal had come to an end.

"Father?" Bernice said, tugging on my sleeve as I exited the upper hall. There were dark circles under her eyes as if she had not slept in days. "Please don't make James go out and fight against the monsters. I'll do anything you ask; just please don't make him go."

"Did he put you up to this?" I looked down the hallway for my squire; he and Thomas had already turned the corner to the stairway.

"No. He would never ask that of you, and I fear he'll never speak to me again if he learns that I came to you, but I have no choice. I love him." Her eyes filled with tears. Taking her into my arms, I held her for a long moment.

"So it's all right if Thomas and I go, but not James?" I smiled down at her head still buried in my chest.

"No! That's not what I meant. I don't want any of you to get hurt. It's just that I'd die if something were to happen to him."

"My dear, sometimes men have to do dangerous things. That is just the way of things, but do not fret over it. If we have to go out, I will bring him home safe. I promise. Agreed?"

Bernice wiped away her tears as she slowly nodded her head. She did her best to force the tiniest of smiles.

"Now get you off to bed."

I ascended to the top of the gatehouse one last time to look out over the village. With the exception of a flickering torch visible through the window of the belfry, everything was black as pitch. A shriek suddenly pierced the cold, quiet night, sending a shudder down my spine. Down in the courtyard, the dogs in the kennel began to bay frantically until the master of hounds came and scolded them to silence.

As I stared at the twinkling light that seemed miles away, the image of dozens of cold and hungry villagers shivering together in the dark was lodged in the forefront of my mind. The rectory and tithing barns were both located outside the church walls; they would have nothing to eat or drink without outside assistance.

"If anything changes," I whispered to the sentry leaning quietly against the battlements, "I want to be alerted immediately. Do you understand? Anything at all."

"Aye, lord." With a deep sigh, I turned and made my way back to the hall.

1 January

Feast of the Circumsicion

N ICY WIND HOWLED THROUGH the fireplace across the room making the bed curtains gently sway with every moan.

"Get up, Matthew, and get a fire going." I called twice for the young varlet before realizing that his bed was empty. It was the first time in three years that it had been vacant.

"I'm so sorry, Richard," Anne said as she placed a hand on my arm. "I know you really liked the boy."

"He was a good lad. Matthew was never slack in his duties. He certainly didn't deserve to die the way he did." Her tender green eyes softly traced the lines of my face. "It'll be hard to find another like him."

"Have you thought about the oldest Stoney boy?" she asked over a shoulder as she slid from the bed, rubbing her arms from the cold.

"Jacob? His is not the first name that comes to mind." Donning my robe and slippers, I walked briskly over to the fireplace. "He's more than old enough, though, and his family will be relying on him to put food on the table. I'll have Edmund go and fetch him first thing." I made a small mound of wood shavings and stacked a few small logs over top.

"How long do you intend to let them stay in the gatehouse?" Anne held up her arms as Sarah helped her slip into her dress.

"Well, since I haven't gotten around to naming a new porter, I don't see a reason to ask them to leave just yet." I touched a candle to the kindling, which slowly began to glow and crackle with flame.

"Please hurry, Richard. It's cold in here." As if her words had sucked the air from the room, the small blaze sputtered and died.

"I'm trying," I pleaded, piling up a larger mound of the kindling. "It's been a while since I had to make a fire." A pillar of gray smoke slowly began to rise from inside the wood shavings before it suddenly spit out a bright orange flame. "There!" I triumphantly exclaimed. "You asked for fire; I give you fire."

"Well done, my dear," Anne spoke over my shoulder. I had not heard her approach. Turning, I saw she was already dressed in a red brocade dress trimmed with black fur.

"Well, I see that I had better hurry and get dressed," I said with a chuckle. "I can't very well have you getting dressed before me." I quickly pulled on my woolen hose. "It might sully my reputation as a man."

Sarah began the tedious process of pulling Anne's hair up before covering it with a headpiece and veil. That gave me several minutes to throw on a shirt and doublet and then add my brigandine and waistcoat.

"Here," Anne said with a smirk as I fidgeted with my belt. "Allow me to help you get ready." She stooped in front of me and used her delicate fingers to straighten the pleats on my jacket. Standing, she placed both hands on her hips and flashed a broad smile. "Now you look presentable. And, don't worry, your reputation is still intact. Sarah and I will keep your dirty little secret."

"That is so kind of you, good wife," I said as I crossed the room and picked up a small wooden box.

"What do you need a pen for?" Anne asked, gesturing to the scribe's case in my hand.

"I have an important message to send this morning." She raised an eyebrow at my enigmatic answer but did not press for additional details.

"Shall we go?" I asked, tucking the box under one arm and presenting the other to Anne. She wrapped her small hand around my elbow, and we walked leisurely down to the chapel.

After our morning prayers, I sent Anne back to our private chambers while I went out to meet Andrew Fowler atop the gatehouse.

Let's find out how bad things are inside Saint Wystan's. The cold air stung my face as I pulled open the heavy door to the courtyard and stepped into a living nightmare.

The thunderous *Cah! Cah!* from scores of carrion crows left me standing dumbfounded in the doorway. A dark, hungry cloud swirled low overhead, encircling the walls of the manor and driving the hounds in the kennel mad. I had to force my legs to carry me across the courtyard.

While most of the refugees had remained inside the warmth of the great hall, insulated from the eerie noise by thick stone walls, the few who had ventured out were staring up at the sky with mouths agape. Their faces were as stark white as bleached linen.

The noise was almost deafening by the time I stepped out onto the gatehouse. A few of the birds flew so close they could have been batted down out of the air with a spade. Andrew and Leonard were both already there. They were practically crouching together behind the battlements.

"Have you ever seen the likes of this, Sir Richard?" Andrew asked in a loud voice, tilting his head upwards.

"Never in my life. What the devil has brought this on?"

"See for yourself," Leonard growled, thrusting a large thumb over his shoulder to gesture over the wall. I slowly walked forward and peered over the edge of the gatehouse. Shuffling around on the manor green, there were at least two score figures with ashen skin and eyes void of color or emotion. Their heads were craned towards the sky like cats watching a piece of string dangled overhead. Five or six more lay in a heap on the stone bridge with the goose-fletched arrows sticking out of their skulls.

"How long has it been like this?" I asked over my shoulder. My voice, raised to be heard over the noise of the ravens, carried much further than I intended. With a guttural moan through bared teeth, one of the creatures locked its milky gaze upon me and began moving briskly towards the bridge. Several others quickly followed suit.

The ghastly creatures scrambled over the small pile of corpses and crashed against the outer gates, their clawlike fingers digging into the oaken doors. More and more of the rancid devils added their weight to the press until the entire bridge was a shambling heap of stinking flesh.

"You seem to really have a way with them, lord," Leonard cracked as he peered from the battlements. He drew his bow back to his ear and took aim at a creature below. An instant later, his arrow cut through the air and struck the ghoul in its shoulder. The devil spun and toppled over the side of the bridge.

"The buggers won't hold still," he grumbled, nocking another arrow.

"Hold," I said, raising a hand to reiterate the command. The ghastly mob continued to pound against the outer gates. "Leonard, get down there and ensure both sets of gates are properly secured. I want the outer one reinforced with a cart wedged in front of it."

"Yessir," he grumbled before hustling downstairs. Looking back over the edge, the injured creature bobbed a couple of times before slowly sinking below the surface of the moat. For several minutes, its arms continued flailing around helplessly under the gentle waves.

Apparently, the dead can't be drowned.

"Andrew, see if you can clear some of them off the bridge." The yeoman drew back his bow and let an arrow fly. Its bodkin pierced the skull of a ghastly woman who immediately crumpled to the ground. A second shaft embedded itself deep into a tonsured head; the blood-covered monk splashed into the murky waters next to his companion. A third arrow noisily ricocheted off the steel helm of a footman before becoming stuck into the chest of a filthy merchant. But for every creature that fell, two more were soon added to the press as more and more gravitated to the front of the manor.

"That's enough for now," I said. "It looks as though we won't have any problem luring them in. Let's step back out of sight and see how they react. In the meantime, I would like to know how things are going inside Saint Wystan's."

"Do you have a message you want to send?" Andrew inquired. I handed him a scrap of parchment that he bound to an arrow with waxed linen thread. Once he had finished, he twirled it in front of me for approval.

"Looks good to me."

"I hope you brought more than one note," the yeoman said with a smirk as he walked over to the back corner of the gatehouse. "It's not going to be the easiest shot I've ever had to make."

"Don't start wasting my arrows now," I replied with a smile. "Nothing would put you on my bad side any quicker." Andrew carefully nocked the arrow on his bowstring, pulled it back to his ear with a sharp intake of breath, and then let it fly. It cut a gentle arc underneath the dark squawking cloud before embedding itself in the wooden frame of the belfry window.

"Ballocks!" a shrill voice exclaimed from inside the church tower. The top of a head slowly peeked out and looked around. Andrew waved cheerfully to his friend, Aleyn, who only shrugged and shook his head. Andrew pointed first to his eye and then in the general direction of the arrow. Aleyn reached up and wriggled the arrow free before disappearing back inside the tower. A few moments later he emerged once again and signaled for us to wait.

"He probably has to go find someone who can read it to him." The yeoman chuckled at his own joke.

"I'm sure he just needs to find something to write with. I only hope Sir Denis keeps a supply of ink inside the church as his rectory is outside the walls."

As if he had overhead the conversation, Raulfe reappeared in the window and waved to get our attention. He pointed down into the churchyard and made a scrolling gesture with his hand. Andrew responded with an exaggerated nod of his head.

"I guess you're right."

Raulfe then made a show of rubbing his belly.

"They're hungry," Andrew said grimly. "Too bad we can't launch a couple of pork loins over there as easily as that message."

"The gates are secure, Sir Richard," Leonard reported as he emerged from the stairwell. "Any word?"

"None so far," Andrew replied. "Knowing Aleyn, he probably had to stop and ask for directions on his way back up the belfry." All three of us laughed heartily at the thought.

"Look there," Leonard blurted as he pointed to a spot between the two cottages closest to the manor. A dark figure was struggling its way through a garden hedge. "Isn't that Gilbert?"

As the creature emerged from the shrubbery, its torn red livery coat was dark with dried blood but still recognizable. There was still a single arrow tucked into the belt at its waistline. Long gray shapes resembling sausage links hung from a large wound to the monster's abdomen, causing it to stumble every few steps.

"He's only half the man he used to be," Leonard snorted as he elbowed Andrew in the arm.

"You're so not right in the head," Andrew replied with a shake of his head. I started to reprimand him for his dark humor when a whistling sound suddenly sent me sprawling to the ground. An instant later, an arrow struck the open door to the stairwell only a few feet away.

"That little bugger did that on purpose," Leonard growled. Both he and Andrew had instinctively ducked behind battlements at the sound of an incoming arrow. Standing and brushing myself off, I glared towards the archer sticking out of the belfry window. The broad grin quickly fled from Aleyn's face.

"What does it say?" Leonard asked as I turned and plucked the scrap of parchment from the arrow. The message was written in a very florid script.

"It's from Sir Denis. He says:

'*Nothing to eat or drink inside.*

Few wounded from levy with weapons.

But most women, children, old men.

When are you sending help?'"

"Are they daft?" Andrew choked. "Does he mean to say that they let in some who were bitten in the attack? Won't they all be infected?"

"Let's pray that's not the case," I replied, turning the parchment over. I placed it atop the wall and began to pen a response.

"Isolate the sick and wounded," I spoke aloud as I scrawled my reply. "Do not let the disease spread. Keep door to the belfry locked. Will send aid as soon as possible. May take a few days."

Aleyn leveled his bow and let fly the arrow carrying their written reply. This time the bodkin struck the stone wall of the gatehouse.

"Did anyone see where it went?" Leonard inquired.

"There it is," Andrew replied, peering over the edge. "It's on the roof of the wall." The arrow had deflected off the gatehouse and become lodged between the slate tiles atop the wall.

"I'm too heavy to climb down there for it," Leonard said as he leveled his gaze directly at the yeoman.

"Fine," Andrew sighed. "I'll go get it, fatty." He descended the stairs and climbed out through a lower window onto the roof over the servants' quarters. He delicately paced across the shingles to retrieve the arrow before crawling back inside. A few moments later, he returned with the broken shaft. Sliding the parchment scrap off the end of the arrow, I read aloud their grim report:

No way to lock belfry door.
Nowhere to isolate sick.
Too cold in churchyard.
Monsters at every window.
Everyone scared to death.

"Sir Richard," Piers called out. Although he was wringing his hands to warm them in the cold, he was almost beside himself with excitement as he ran towards me from across the courtyard. "I think I may've solved your problem of having no barding for your horses." With those last few words, he had my full attention. I nodded and motioned for him to continue. "You see, I once had a mug of ale with a Flemish merchant in Bristol."

"Please, Master Piers, get to your point. I have much to do this morning."

"Oh, yes. Sorry. A merchant once told me that they've got war dogs in his country that wear cloth armor." I gave him a dubious look.

"Explain."

"Well, I forget what he said it was called—everything the Flemish say sounds like a drunken rant to me. But from the way he described it, it was really nothing more than several layers of linen quilted tightly together—not unlike the padded jacks your archers wear. If you think of it, something intended as proof against sword or arrow should be more than enough for teeth and claws. You could start with the heraldic trappings you cover your warhorse in at tournaments—"

"They are called caparisons. Please go on." I did still have a number of decorative saddle cloths embroidered with my crest and arms in storage somewhere; I rarely found use for them anymore.

"Yes, lord. As you say, the caparisons are already sized to fit your horse from chest to flanks. All you'd need to do is have some of the women quilt additional layers underneath."

"Come with me, Master Piers," I said, wrapping an arm around his shoulders. "Let me introduce you to Mary, the laundress. I want you to explain your idea to her and some of the maids and entrust you to oversee their production. We have several horses and likely a limited supply of cloth. Do you have any idea how much fabric each mount will need?"

"I'm not sure, Sir Richard. The man never said anything about how thick they had to be."

"Well, if five layers does not seem to be sufficient, have them stuffed with horsehair or scrap cloth. I want enough for at least six mounts." For the first time in several days, I had finally received some good news.

"I am sorry for your loss, Jacob," I said to the boy standing in front of me in the upper hall. His jaw was clenched tightly, turning the corners of his mouth down into a look of contempt. "Your father died bravely trying to save another's life."

"My mother says you're a harsh lord who does not care for those who do your bidding and you were wrong to burn my father's body." Edmund moved towards him to give him a thrashing, but I shook my head.

Adam Stoney isn't here to rebuke his son, I reminded myself. *Don't go too harshly on him.*

"Mistress Clere, I believe, spoke those words in anguish, and I am certain she would not be very happy with the fact that you have confessed them here." I walked around the table to stand next to the boy. His face slowly softened as his eyes began to well up with tears. "Take this back to your mother," I said gently as I pressed a shilling into his palm. "Tell her it is an advance on your wages."

"Yessir," he replied, looking down at the silver coin in his upturned hand.

"I will expect you back here in time for supper this evening." I placed a hand on his shoulder and directed him to the door. "Now run along, and we will hear no more of what your mother says to you in confidence." Jacob hurried down the hall.

"He sure is a surly little imp," Edmund said after the boy had disappeared into the stairwell. "He refused to speak to me. His mother had to force him to come."

"The boy is hurting, Edmund. And, I must confess, I feel at least partly responsible for his father's horrible death. Give him some time. I am sure he will come around. Or I will have you find a replacement."

"I'm sure you're right, Sir Richard."

"I want to meet with the men after dinner to plan the rescue. See what you can find in the way of a map of Colleville. In the meantime, I will be in the solar with Anne and the children." I turned and started down the hall.

"Yessir," Edmund replied, a few steps behind. "My lord, if I may, I was wondering if you've considered how you will feed all of those additional people? I had to open another butt of ale this morning."

"Once we have dealt with the situation in Saint Wystan's, we will see what can be done about our increasing food stores here in the manor. The great barn is filled with more than enough corn and beans."

As I descended the stairs, a voice echoed up the passage intermittent with Anne's sweet laughter. It was high-pitched but nasal. As I neared the landing, a well-dressed woman stepped through the door to exit the solar with a bundle of clothing tucked under one arm. She was pale and bony and had dark eyes that were set close together. The woman flashed a thin smile under her long, pointed nose. Something about her ill-fitting dress looked strangely familiar. With barely a curtsy, she whirled around and rushed down the stairs.

"Who the devil was that?" I asked Edmund.

"I believe that was Alyce Ducworthe, wife of Alexander Ducworthe, the reeve from Stony Heath."

"I know who the devil *he* is," I growled, still descending the stairs. Anne's head suddenly appeared in the doorway. "What was she doing here, and why was she wearing one of my wife's dresses?" I had spoken as much to Anne as to Edmund.

"Oh, Richard, I should have thought to introduce her to you."

"Why on earth would you give her one of your dresses to wear?"

"She happened by when I was walking through the great hall. She seemed horrified to even speak to me. When I asked her what was wrong, she explained that her best dress had been ruined when she fled Stony Heath. I felt sorry for her, so I offered her one of mine."

"One?" I said, crossing my arms in disbelief. "It looked as though she had a pile of dresses under her arm." Her cheeks reddened.

"Those weren't dresses. I sent her some of your old clothes for her husband." I gritted my teeth to hold back a fiery outburst.

"Oh come now, Richard, they were old and you never wear them anymore. Besides, she told me how embarrassed he was yesterday evening to be in your presence and so poorly dressed." My anger melted under her tender gaze.

"Please tell me you're not going to give the rest of your dresses away." It was not hard to imagine Anne passing out clothing to a line of women stretching down the stairs.

"I thought it important that the Ducworthes be properly dressed. They're well thought of by the people of Stony Heath. The way Alyce tells it, her husband practically ran the village on behalf of the prior."

"I've heard that line before," I said dryly. "The funny thing is, it came from Alexander himself and the monks who invested him with some semblance of authority. I have yet to hear it from anyone who actually *lived* in the village. To be clear, I don't trust anything that man has to say. He's a bootlicking coxcomb, and I believe he is doing his best to stir up trouble here in the manor."

"This is the best that I could find," Edmund said as he unrolled a large piece of parchment on the table in the upper hall. He used a cup and several carving knives to hold down the edges. "I think it is from around the time you were granted the estate. Most of the new structures not reflected on the map should be on the outer edges of the village."

"Very well," I said as I craned over the worn document. "Gather around, men. Let's see what we can come up with."

"The hedges between these cottages are worthless," Andrew offered, tracing his finger along a row of small, black squares that lined an empty pathway labeled *Churchwell Lane*. "As we have already seen, they obscure our line of sight but barely even slow the creatures down."

"Yeah," snarled Hamond. "We'd be right up on it before we could even tell if the devils were lurking behind it. Better we fight our way down the road." He ran a thick finger from the front of the manor down to Churchwell and sideways down the road and past Market Cross to Saint Wystan's.

"That sure is a long ways to run," Thomas interjected with a wry smile. "Especially for an older man in full armor." He gave me a sidelong glance before continuing. "Perhaps a mounted charge would be better?"

"Do we have enough horses?" I asked no one in particular as I looked at the circle of men.

"Only seven horses came back from the battle yesterday," Lewys said flatly.

"What about the eight you brought in from the stables?" I replied. "Fifteen horses is enough for everyone here with a few to spare." The new master of the stables wrinkled his brow.

"We didn't have time to grab any tack. Won't make it very far without a saddle and reins."

"Thomas is right," I said, studying the tiny black squares. "The distance to the church is too great to travel on foot, in armor and surrounded by those blood-crazed monsters. We've no choice but to go for the horses first." I jabbed a finger at the black rectangle labeled *Great Barn*.

"At least it's closer," Thomas added. "We could send out mounted riders first to cut a path and then follow with the men on foot."

"No," I said, shaking my head. My son deflated like a burst wineskin. "Anyone on horseback would have to dismount to open and close the doors. They would be left vulnerable for far too long. It's better if we all move in tight formation."

Edward, Hamond, and Christopher quickly glanced around the press of men before looking at one another. Their furrowed brows showed their concern. The cause of it was obvious. Apart from the yeoman archer and two squires, the rest were administrators, all at least forty years of age. Worse yet, none of them had brandished a sword in anger in more than a decade, if ever.

So who can I count on? I asked myself over and over. *Most of the servants downstairs are women or smooth-faced boys.*

"Master Edmund, how many men can I call on from here inside the manor?" His eyes rose to the ceiling as he began to tally them.

"Beginning with your retinue, you have three men-at-arms, two squires, a footman, and five archers, though two are stranded in the church belfry. Add to that the three men of the levy. That gives you twelve men capable of bearing arms, not counting the household officials and servants. As for those you brought from Stony Heath—"

"Do not count them," I interjected. "As far as I can tell, there is only one man down there with any salt, and I have already given him an important job to do. The rest are all either monks or the kind of men who run at the first sign of danger."

It was a harsh statement, but I was not willing to gamble my men's lives on the likes of Alexander Ducworthe or his cronies.

The men-at-arms all nodded in agreement.

"If you temporarily pull the archers from the walls, Sir Richard," Edward said confidently, moving his finger back and forth between the manor and the barn, "and we keep it tight, twelve will be enough." He looked at Hamond and then to Christopher; the latter shrugged and offered a weak nod.

"I agree," Hamond finally bellowed. "We can do it with twelve." He paused for a moment to run his eyes over the map before flashing a wicked grin. "Twelve fighting men against eighty unarmed villeins? We'll barely break a sweat." Thomas and James snickered loudly as they elbowed each other in the ribs.

"Boys," I chided them. "This is a time to be serious."

"My apologies, Sir Richard," Hamond said, raising his eyebrows in feigned regret.

"Men, it's approaching midday. You have one hour to be mustered in the courtyard and ready to fight. Master Edmund, see what we have in the form of spare armor down in the store rooms. We cannot afford for any man to even receive the slightest scratch from one of those vile creatures. See that Andrew receives the hauberks and any leg armor you can find to protect his archers. Distribute the rest between the three men from the levy."

"Men," I bellowed in a loud voice to the half-circle of soldiers arrayed before me. Although they stood silently stamping their feet upon the cold cobblestones, the cloud of ravens had not dissipated. If anything, it had grown in size. A number of the servants and refugees had braved the icy breeze to see us all off.

"I know you all would prefer to be sitting around a fire with a warm cup of wine in your hands, but that will have to wait a while. Right now, our friends are trapped inside Saint Wystan's. They have no food or water or supplies of any kind. They are holding out hope that we will not forsake them. I, for one, do not intend to let them down."

"We're with you, Sir Richard," Therry said without hesitation. He was clad in his dark maille and had a thick cleaver-like sword in his hands. "Just tell us where you want us to go." George Blythe stood next to him brandishing a sword and buckler. He had been loaned a sallet and plate leg armor to go along with his hauberk. His young companion, Robert Asheley, had likewise been given a sallet and steel legs as well as a pair of gauntlets. Miles Dirikson, the third man from the levy, stood in back with the rest of the archers. Andrew had given him a hauberk to go over his crudely made jack. He also had an open-faced sallet to protect his head.

"The church is too far for us to make it there and back on foot," I continued. "First, we need to get to the horses locked inside the barn. Even though it's not that far, it's sure to be a nasty fight." The small band of warriors gave a hearty shout.

With a nod to Lewys, he and one of his new grooms began pulling open the inner gate. The three men-at-arms, covered from head to foot in hardened steel, hefted their pollaxes and took their place on either side of me and Thomas.

"Are you sure you're ready for this?" I asked Thomas in a low voice, giving a brief nod to his leg. My son nodded a reply as he moved to stand shoulder to shoulder with me. He carried his pollaxe stiffly before him.

"Take a breath, Son. It's perfectly normal to feel a bit jittery just before a fight. Trust your armor and your training. If you keep your wits about you, those two things will keep you alive."

I looked around. Each man was giving one final test of his weapons and armor, making certain his steel-encased limbs had full range of motion. Satisfied, one by one they lowered their visors into place.

As if the creatures could somehow sense the living, the outer gates began to bump and creak as Lewys and his helper stepped inside to remove the cart. Once it had been dragged out into the courtyard, the press of men squeezed into the confines of the gatehouse.

"Remember what I told you, Thomas," I said quietly, leaning over to make sure my words could be heard. "Stick close to me. No matter what happens, never leave my side."

"Yessir," he said with a grin before raising his bevor plate to cover the lower portion of his face. With a soft click, it locked into place. I reached up and slapped his visor closed.

"Make way, lads," the master of the stables barked from behind. "Make a hole." He elbowed his way through the crowd to gain access to the outer doors. Reaching up and placing both hands on the crossbar, he looked back over his shoulder for my signal. Hamond and Christopher each placed a steel-shod foot against the base of the doors. Within a heartbeat, the clawing and pounding outside grew to a fevered pitch.

"Get that bar off, Master Lewys, and then get yourself out of the way." I slammed my visor shut, instantly turning day into night inside the shadowy confines of the stone structure. My hands tightened around the stout oaken shaft of my pollaxe as I prepared for the onslaught.

The next few minutes were a blur. As soon as the doors were pulled open, a bitter cold breeze chased the blinding sunlight through my visor slit to sting my eyes. Two dozen black shapes groaned as one as they surged forward into the gateway with surprising speed. I leveled my shaft and shoved back against the dark mass. Heavy axe heads streaked down from either side, cleaving skulls and pummeling the foremost creatures to the ground; the grisly business sounded like Butcher's Row in Gloucester.

With a small step, I quickly moved into the newly created space and drove a steel spike straight into a snarling bearded face. Thomas followed suit and stepped forward to hack at the ghoul to his front. Edward slashed a third monster, once again clearing ground to move ahead.

Bellowing a war cry, Hamond jumped forward and cut a wide sideways arc with his pollaxe, striking the chest of a snaggletoothed crone. He continued his defiant shout as the impact of his weapon toppled three of the creatures over the bridge railing.

Again we shuffled forward, taking slow, measured steps over the top of the corpses. An arrow struck through the eye of a rancid monk as it reached for Thomas. It could only have come from several feet above the press. Down the line to the right, an archer was precariously balanced atop the narrow railing of the bridge pulling another nocked arrow back to his ear.

Tottering fool! I thought to myself. *If you fall, no one's going to come pull you out of your watery grave.* As I looked back to the front, a tall, bony ghoul threw his arms around my helm. Taking a half-step back, I hooked it behind its neck and leveraged it down and to the ground between me and Edward. An instant later, Therry shouldered past an archer to cleave its skull with his sword.

Blow by blow, step by step, we managed to fight our way down the length of the bridge and onto the grassy slope of the manor green.

No words were spoken. No commands had to be given. Once free of the confines of the bridge, the squires and men-at-arms spread out to either side of me like a flock of geese taking flight. The archers remained only a step or two behind us, the three footmen protecting our rear with their broad-bladed swords. Whenever we cut down one of the devils, an archer would jump into the gap and let fly a deadly missile into the face of the next-closest monster.

It took no more than a half hour to cut a swath along the edge of the moat and across the open space to the large stone barn. The last fifty paces were at a near jog as most of the danger was in the direction of the village.

"Wheel to the right!" I shouted as we reached the corner of the structure. The deadly chevron of men pivoted around me to face the direction we had just come from. Before us, the dark path back to the manor was paved with mutilated bodies. Hundreds of ravens were already swooping down to noisily pick at the gray flesh of the corpses.

"Get those doors open," I barked as I lifted my visor and took a gulp of fresh air. The cold wind burned my lungs, but I did not care.

"Oh, that air feels good," Thomas heaved, raising his own visor. A broad smile was visible over the top of his bevor. "My arms are on fire." From behind came the sound of metal banging against wood.

"What's taking so long?"

"The doors're locked, Sir Richard," Therry spat.

"Don't keep us waiting out here all day." I scanned the field in front of our small formation. There were a dozen or more of the creatures moving in our direction from the edge of the village. "I said get them open!"

With a loud grunt, the footman began hacking at the doors with his sword. The noise echoed between the buildings and across the grassy expanse. Several more of the creatures appeared through hedgerows in the distance, scrambling through ditches and over berms.

"How many arrows do you men have left?" I called, glancing back over my shoulder at the archers. The steady pounding of steel on wood continued.

"Only nine," Leonard sneered, looking down under his right arm at the white fletchings sticking out of his belt.

"I've got twelve," Bertram responded.

"Six," Andrew said with a sigh.

"Seven—I mean, eighteen," the archer from the levy answered in a low voice as he touched each arrow nock with a finger.

"Miles, is it?" I addressed the man, turning my gaze back towards the village. "Give half of what you have left to the others, and all of you should be ready with your swords. The fight is far from over." A pale-faced monster in dark robes limped ever closer to our line. With the loud twang of a bowstring, a white-tipped missile streaked over my shoulder and struck the monster in the forehead.

"Almost got it," Therry exclaimed. With an audible heave, he splintered a thick board followed by another. "We're in!"

"Move!" I ordered. "Get inside." Scrambling through the opening, we dragged the heavy door closed behind us, choking off the main source of light and leaving us in a cavernous expanse. "Footmen, secure the door. Archers, find the horses."

Small rays of light filtered in around the edges of shuttered windows. The overhead beams were no more than thick dark lines against the thatched roof. Slowly the archers made their way forward.

"They're just outside the doors now," Therry reported. A faint clawing sound grew steadily louder. "Someone give me an axe." Christopher handed his pollaxe to the burly stone mason, who hooked it through the opening and held the door firmly closed from a distance. Hamond stepped forward and did the same.

"Don't let them through," I growled. An arm reached its way through the hole in the door and blindly groped at the air. Shifting his weapon to his left hand, Edward drew his sword and hacked through the forearm, spraying black blood across the inside of the door.

"Heaven help us!" gasped James as he pointed to the ground. Like a snake after its head has been cut off, the fingers of the hand continued to grasp in the air at some phantom prey. "It can't be! It can't be!" the young squire breathed as he repeatedly stomped the limb into a bloody mess. Edward finally threw an arm around him and led him away from the doorway.

"Heads up," Andrew called from the darkness. "We're driving the horses to you." Several large shapes of gray and brown and black trotted forward. The four archers were walking behind them with their arms stretched out to their sides. With nostrils flared and eyes wide with fright, the horses darted around in a circle between the two groups of men.

"Where are their saddles?" I protested. "We need them ready to ride."

"Sorry, Sir Richard, but we couldn't find any tack. I don't think they had time to bring it over from the stables. We found a bit of rope, but not nearly enough to fashion makeshift bridles."

"They're useless without their tack. The same goes for the ones brought to the manor last night." Turning back to the exit, I figured there had to be a dozen ghastly figures pressed against the doors. "We can't even leave them here now; the doors are busted. Ballocks!"

"We've come this far," Thomas shrugged. "Why not just cut our way through to the stables."

"He's got a point," Edward replied dryly. "It's further back to the manor than over to the stables." There was no real alternative. If we returned to the manor now, the horses would be killed and the barn overrun. It would not be easy, but we had to get to the stables, find the tack, and then carry it back here to the barn under threat of attack.

"Therry," I said, placing a hand on his maille-covered shoulder, "if we clear the front of the barn, can you hold the door closed with just one axe?"

"Yeah. I think so." He did not bother to look back.

"All right," I thought aloud as I scanned the faces. "We'll be one axe short on the line." Young James Berkeley was staring wide-eyed at a second arm groping through the opening.

"I'm leaving James in charge of the footmen," I concluded. Therry nodded in acknowledgment. He understood the squire's promotion was in word only.

"I'll be needing to borrow your axe," Christopher said as he walked over and stood next to James. The squire just blinked back at him.

"Yeah, sure," James finally mumbled as the man-at-arms gently tugged the pollaxe from the young man's hands.

"Form up, men," I ordered. Once again, Thomas and Edward stepped to my right. Christopher moved to my left, leaving just enough space for Hamond to squeeze in between us when it came time for him to step back from the door. Andrew shepherded his archers in tight behind us.

"George and Robert," I called, pointing my axe head towards the hole in the door that was now filled with several pale-skinned limbs, "see what you can do to create some space." The two footmen rushed to either side of Hamond and used their swords to hack off the exposed arms before thrusting their blades through the opening. "Get ready to open the doors."

Hamond unhooked his axe head from the door and hustled over to fill the gap between me and Christopher, creating a five-man wall of polished steel. My hand went instinctively up to lower my visor, but the darkness was already so thick inside the barn that I chose to leave it open.

"Shove, you poppets," Therry grunted as he shouldered the righthand door and muscled it forward against the press of the ghoulish attackers outside. Robert and George both had their backs against the other door, digging their heels into the soft ground for leverage.

Slowly the two doors parted and I was struck in the face with a massive bolt of light. A cold blast of wind carried the sweet smell of rain mixed with the revolting odor of rotting flesh. Squinting against the brightness, I rushed forward into the opening and delivered an overhead chop to the first monster. It slumped into the legs of the devil to its back, taking the clawing fiend with it to the earth.

Thomas thrust a spike into the face of a boy wearing filthy white robes. Hamond cleaved the skull of a stringy-haired woman to the left. Stepping forward, I dispatched the devil pinned below the first corpse, and so our wall of steel steadily advanced out of the shadows and into the light.

The repetitive sound of frozen raindrops pelting against my sallet began to drown out the heaves and grunts of the men around me. It only took a short time to hack and slash through the score of invigorated corpses. We veered to the right and slowly made our way towards the two-story house once occupied by the Sorel family.

About fifty paces ahead, several of the creatures had been scavenging around the outer corral. Upon our approach, one by one they turned their heads and bared their blackened teeth before charging forward like a pack of wild boar.

"At our backs," Andrew shouted suddenly from behind. "They're coming up on our rear." Stealing a backwards glance, I saw there were a half dozen more of the enemy scrambling across the grassy expanse from the direction of the village.

"Deal with it," I growled. "Hold the line, men." I twisted the balls of my feet into the slick grass in an effort to find some traction as I lowered the head of my pollaxe against the coming attack. From behind, the snap of bowstrings began to reverberate as Andrew and his men called out their targets.

A faceless woodsman dressed in green rags was the first to reach our line. The corpse found its chest impaled upon

Hamond's spike while its legs continued to surge forward; it was almost suspended in the air before the man-at-arms forced it to the ground. A heartbeat later, a feral groom leapt over the writhing corpse to land atop Hamond's shoulders, clawing against the hardened steel of his harness.

"Crazy bugger," Hamond bellowed as he reached up with one hand and slung the boy to the ground, never slackening his grip on the pollaxe that pinned the other creature to the ground. As I glanced down, Hamond stomped an armored foot onto its small throat.

Several more of the ghouls were cut down as they careened into the steel wall of armored men. The physical strain was beginning to take its toll on everyone. My arms burned from exertion, begging to put down the heavy pollaxe. As the last few of them were hacked apart, the men along the front row let out a collective sigh, their shoulders finally sagging under the weight of their armor.

"I'm out," Andrew shouted from behind.

"Last one for me," Leonard replied. A moment later, the familiar twang of his longbow meant that he, too, had just become a footman. Glancing back, I glimpsed there were several arrow-ridden corpses lying not far beyond them; only two or three attackers remained to our front.

"Advance," I ordered. We crossed the short distance between the Sorel home and the horse stables at a quick pace. With a sudden, furious cry, dozens of dark, winged shapes streaked into the air as we made our way around the paddock. Overhead, a swirling cloud of ravens followed us towards the stables.

The corpses of cattle and oxen were strewn about the outer enclosure. A thin white layer of frost had begun to grow across their bloody carcasses, and the cold needles of ice carried by the northern wind continued to drone atop our steel helmets.

"Heads up," Christopher hollered from the right. The mass of ravens that had been circling low above the dead cattle suddenly broke apart and took to the sky. An ashen-skinned old man with a long, bloodstained beard crossed the broken ground of the paddock and deftly clambered over the fence rails. With a high-arcing blow, Christopher cratered its skull.

"They're bloody everywhere," I grumbled.

"It's spreading like wildfire," Edward remarked. "There's no way all these fiends were from Stony Heath."

"I thought I recognized the old miller when we made our way out of the barn," Miles offered.

"Then the disease is not just within the village proper," Christopher added. "That means it's spread to the outlying cottages as well."

"Cut the chatter, men," I ended the conversation. "Let's finish this nasty business and get back to the manor."

The doors to the stable had been left wide open. Our wall of steel rushed through the opening and down the narrow corridor, quickly scanning the individual stalls along each side.

"All clear," Edward reported as we reached the back wall.

"Thomas, take the men-at-arms and hold the doorway," I said, pointing back the way we had just come. Turning to point to a door to the left, I gave the archers their instructions.

"Andrew, I want you and your men to start emptying the tack room. Make sure you get enough for at least eight horses. And make it quick!"

The archers rushed through the small door and began pulling saddles off the walls and throwing them into a pile on the floor, counting aloud as they worked. I lowered my bevor to finally catch a breath as I made my way slowly back towards the entrance. The air was heavy with the smell of manure and rancid meat. Five of the stalls contained the corpses of dead hackneys left to rot.

Thomas and the men were standing to either side of the entrance, taking occasional glances through the doorway but doing their best to remain unseen from the outside. Small clouds of steam rose from his damp hair when he pulled off his helmet and wiped his brow with a gloved palm. He flashed a quick smile as I approached.

"Don't get caught without your sallet on," I chided him, turning his grin into a narrow frown. "How does it look out there?"

"The devils are bunched up around the front of the barn, but they seem to have forgotten about us for the moment."

"That's great," Hamond said with feigned enthusiasm. "We'll have to clear them out again. And I was starting to think the fighting was over. Andrew dropped a pair of saddles on the ground next to Thomas. He had his bow slung across his back, and several bridles hung around his neck.

"That's two," he panted before turning to hustle back to the tack room. A moment later, Leonard, similarly encumbered with a bow and leather headstalls, tossed two more saddles to the ground next to the others. Before he could turn to leave, several desperate cries echoed through the doorway.

"Help! Help!"

"That sounds like James," Thomas blurted as he threw on his sallet and darted around the corner.

"Thomas, get back here!" I bellowed in vain. Rounding the corner behind him, at least a dozen ghouls were battering on the front of the barn. The hole in the door had been enlarged, and a slender corpse was wriggling through the opening. With a loud crack, several of the boards splintered and the dead forced their way inside.

"On me," I ordered. Thomas, Edward, Christopher, Hamond, and I quickly reformed our steel wall and, an instant later, began the charge straight across the open field to rescue the rest of our forces.

"Ballocks!" shouted Leonard from inside the stables. "Come on boys, we're getting left behind!"

The ragged mob continued to funnel through the opening. The hungry dead were driven into a rage by the terrified screams of those inside. The broken door swung open on its hinges to reveal Therry desperately swinging his heavy blade, its whirling arcs sending severed limbs flying into the air.

The ground was becoming slick with ice. We did our best to cover the distance between the stables and the barn, but the sudden sound of rolling thunder slowed our collective pace.

"The horses are stampeding!" exclaimed Christopher. Two and three at a time, the horses galloped out of the shadows, kicking and snorting their way through the press of bodies. A roan palfrey shied away from a snarling monk only to startle sideways into Therry, knocking him to the ground along with two of the ghoulish figures.

"Don't let them get away," Thomas yelled as a trio of horses bolted past our broken line. The rest fled in every possible direction.

"It's too late," I panted. "They're all gone. Just get to the barn." A few steps later, with a loud crash of metal and wood and a litany of indiscernible curses, Hamond lost his footing and tumbled across the frozen ground, nearly taking Edward down with him. Thomas started to slow his pace.

"Leave him," I gasped.

Not far ahead, Therry slowly pushed himself off the ground, first onto his hands and knees and finally onto his wobbly legs. Shaking his head, he reached down for his sword. A pale woman with long, greasy locks scrambled to her feet and pounced upon the dazed footman. With a painful howl, he stabbed his sword blade under his arm and slung the witch to the ground.

Before Therry could turn back, another ravenous corpse tackled him to the ground.

"No!" a voice bellowed from somewhere inside the barn. An instant later, George dashed from the shadows and began hacking down onto the monster's back. The old footman's livery was covered in dark blood and bits of flesh. There were huge gashes down his face and neck.

"They're done for," Christopher groaned.

"We're not leaving them," I breathlessly ordered him as we stormed across the final dozen paces to reach the barn.

"Get off him, you bloody fiend," I bellowed as I shattered the ribs of the corpse atop Therry with a steel-covered foot. The creature never uttered a sound as it flew past George and rolled across the hard ground.

Edward quickly cut down two monsters from behind as they advanced on Robert, who had been cutting the air with his sword as he backed away. The young footman's eyes were wide with fear as he looked down at the headless corpses.

"Thanks," he finally muttered.

"Do something! Help!" a voice squealed from the left. Turning, I could see several of the savage creatures pressed tightly into the dark corner next to the doorway. A blood-covered dagger in a steel hand plunged over and over into a mutilated shoulder, its owner hidden behind the wall of hungry dead.

Without a word, Thomas darted over, hooked the closest creature with the head of his pollaxe, and dragged it to the ground. With a quick thrust, he pierced the ghoul's forehead with the top spike.

"Hold on," Hamond growled as he sidestepped my son and buried what was left of his own pollaxe into the skull of another; the lower half of its shaft had been broken off. With a kick to the back of a knee, he toppled a third ghoul, allowing him to easily dispatch it with a follow-up strike. James, taking advantage of the open space, thrust his dagger into the temple of the final attacker.

"Are you hurt?" Thomas demanded as he moved to his friend's side. James's once-polished armor was streaked with blackened blood.

"No," he replied with something between a whine and a laugh. He fumbled with shaking hands to raise his visor. His entire body had been protected from harm by plate and maille.

"Look him over," I gestured to Hamond as I turned back to Therry, who was slumped motionless on the ground. There were no fewer than five pale-skinned corpses strewn around him. His blackened maille glistened with wetness in the pale light. Bright blood oozed between his fingers, which were pressed against the side of his neck.

"Therry?" I called quietly. He slowly opened his eyes.

"I'm sorry," he sputtered, letting his hand slide away from his neck. Immediately the blood began to spurt across the ground.

"Sorry for what?" I tossed my pollaxe to the side and dropped to a knee. "Don't take your hand away," I rebuked him, grabbing his wrist and pressing his hand back over his wound. The color was quickly draining from his face.

"I failed you." His eyes darted around the room at his companions standing around.

"Don't be foolish. You fought like a lion. Now let us get you back to the manor so brother Phillip can see to your wounds." The burly footman closed his eyes and shook his head.

"Too late for that," Therry groaned, once again letting his hand fall away from his neck. "Just don't let me become like them." He glanced over at the corpse of the greasy-haired woman lying a few feet away before painfully turning his head to stare out the door. "Make it quick," Therry finally whispered as he closed his eyes.

I gently placed a hand on the side of his face as I drew my dagger and positioned its tip behind his ear.

"Forgive me," I whispered through clenched teeth. An instant later, I mercifully ended his life. I slowly removed my hand and stared for a moment at the dead man, perhaps making sure that he would not rise again before sheathing the dagger. Looking up, I saw Edward and Christopher standing over another corpse several feet away.

"George?" I asked them. Their grim faces already relayed their answer.

"Dead," Edward replied sternly before plunging the top spike of his pollaxe into the back of the old footman's skull. Retrieving my pollaxe, I leaned on it wearily as I climbed to my feet.

"Where did Robert go?" I inquired. The men shrugged in response.

"Don't see him lying around here," Christopher offered as he walked around poking at the corpses.

"Robert!" I shouted down the dark corridor. Apart from the labored breathing of the men, there was only an eerie silence inside the barn.

"There are more coming down the road," Andrew warned as he and his men entered the barn. They had saddles tucked under each arm and headstalls hung around their necks. With their swords sheathed in their belts and their yew bows slung over their shoulders, they were not going to be able to defend themselves without abandoning the precious saddles.

"Form up and let's head for the back of the manor," I directed them. "Miles, grab what weapons you can off the dead."

"What about the corn?" Thomas asked.

"Forget it. We'll have to come back another time."

We started across the manor green. Tiny shards of ice continued to find their way into our helms to sting our exposed faces. We skirted the moat around to the right and followed its murky green waters around behind the hall. Christopher, Thomas, and I led at a brisk pace followed by the archers encumbered by the heavy tack. In place of the footmen, Edward and Hamond protected the rear.

"There," I wheezed, pointing towards a narrow wooden bridge spanning the far end of the moat. "Make for the garden bridge."

"They're gaining on us," Edward warned. Three or four figures were rushing to overtake our small force. Despite being slowed from exhaustion and extra weight, I was certain we could reach the manor in time.

"Keep moving." We half-sprinted the last few dozen paces to reach the bridge. "Open up!" I shouted at the stone wall ahead. "Open up!" We scrambled across the slick wooden slats only to stop abruptly before a locked portal. Thomas slipped and fell underneath my legs as I pounded a steel fist on the small door.

"Open the bloody gate!" I bellowed, my voice hoarse but filled with anger.

"At our backs," Edward warned. Glancing back, I saw that two ghastly shapes hurried down the edge of the moat only yards away from the bridge. An arrow struck the first one in the shoulder causing it to spin and crash into the brackish water, spraying the archers with an icy cold bath. Miles plucked his last bodkin from his belt and quickly let it fly into the cheek of the second monster. It collapsed heavily onto the frosty ground and slid into the railing.

"I said open the blasted gate!" I continued to pound on the door. Thomas regained his feet and added his own fist to the urgent hammering.

"Move aside. Move aside," a muffled voice growled from the other side of the door. A moment later, there was a loud bump as the wooden bar was removed. With a click, the latch was pulled back and the door swung open to reveal Edmund standing in front of several wide-eyed servants.

"Sir Richard?" he said, his brow furrowed in confusion. "Wha—"

"Get inside," I barked over my shoulder, ignoring the steward. Placing a hand on Thomas' back, I shoved him through the door and past Edmund. Christopher and James followed close behind. One by one, the archers turned sideways to squeeze past me into the manor with the saddles under their arms. As soon as Edward and Hamond had rushed through the narrow gateway, I shoved my way inside and slammed the door, pulling the latch closed.

"Home sweet home," Thomas panted with a broad grin as he dropped to his knees and tossed his sallet to the floor. He looked across the faces of the men-at-arms doubled over in front of him trying to catch their breath. Each man gave Thomas a slow, deliberate bow of the head, the kind of salute I had not witnessed since my days in France.

My son has earned their respect. My heart was filled with such pride in that moment to see Thomas not as the unruly boy who had chased his sisters around the hall with a wooden sword but as a man of honor. Leaning back against the door, I let myself slide down onto the hard stone floor. A strange feeling of comfort and safety began to slowly wash over me.

"So who's ready to go back out there?" Thomas suddenly blurted out, dispelling the seriousness of the situation. The corridor was instantly filled with the sounds of laughter.

"Sir Richard?" Edmund said forcefully, his face unusually somber.

"What is it, Master Edmund? What has happened?" The steward's mouth instantly turned downwards as he prepared to respond.

"Prior Gregory is dead." Edmund's report immediately quenched our brief moment of happiness.

"How long ago?" I demanded as I tried to push myself back up the door. My legs refused to obey.

"An hour. Maybe two," the steward replied. Perhaps sensing my alarm, Edmund gave the most important detail: "Master Lewys has seen to his passing. We were awaiting your instructions as to what you want to do with his body."

"Very well," I said, beckoning for my son to approach. "Thomas, come help your father to his feet." The young man quickly climbed to his feet and offered me his hand.

We made our way down the corridor, passing the kitchens and storerooms adjacent to the great hall. The cooks and bakers and carvers and servants all paused to silently watch the line of weary and bloodied soldiers shuffle past them.

As we entered the great hall, a large crowd of villagers were huddled together around the central hearth, staring lifelessly into the orange flames that leapt high into the air.

"No matter what differences we may have once had," I said in a low voice to my son as we crossed the room, "Prior Gregory was a good man. Let's see what we can do to honor his memory."

Large globs of snow began to fall heavily onto the smooth gray stones of the courtyard. The bitter cold stung my face and drove tiny daggers into my old joints. I stood on the steps of the hall, watching the solemn proceedings but keeping a respectful distance. Anne and the children were at my side dressed in their fur-lined cloaks.

You had no choice, I reassured myself. *Either you cremate him here in the courtyard, or you drop his body over the walls. There's nowhere to bury him inside the manor, and you can't just leave him to rot in his room.*

Prior Gregory's body was laid upon a small pyre covered in a white sheet. His exposed skin was marred by dark blemishes. Atop his head, Doctor Symond had reverently placed a white priestly hood to cover the hole left by Lewys's dagger.

"Requiem aeternam dona eis, Domine. Et lux perpetua luceat eis."

Brother Phillip stood shivering in silent prayer at his superior's feet but was otherwise immoveable. His tonsured head and sandaled feet were so ghostly pale that he could have been mistaken for one of the angels painted on the walls of Saint Wystan's. Even from across the courtyard, the dark circles under his eyes were plainly visible.

"Exaudi orationem meam. Ad te omnis caro veniet."

Standing to the left of the surgeon, brother Philemon stamped his feet and rubbed his arms. Although he kept his head bowed low, his hawklike eyes were scanning the faces in the crowd. Hovering a few feet behind the two monks, Alexander Ducworthe sniffled loudly and dabbed at tearless eyes with a strip of white linen.

"Like a couple of mummers putting on a show," I mumbled under my breath. "Your little act may fool this crowd, but it doesn't fool me."

"What did you say, husband?" Anne whispered.

"Nothing," I lied. "I was just complaining about the cold."

"Requiem aeternam dona defunctis, Domine. Et lux perpetua luceat eis. Requiem aeternam dona eis, Domine Et lux perpetua eis. Amen."

Upon hearing the final word of Doctor Symond's prayer, the villagers of Stony Heath promptly turned and shuffled back to the warmth of the great hall, passing wordlessly by me and my family. As the last man stepped through the door, Lewys walked over and touched a torch to the corner of the pyre. The oil-soaked wood quickly caught fire and engulfed the white sheet and dark figure atop it.

As the bright flames climbed ever higher into the air, Alexander stepped forward and whispered something into the subprior's ear. Brother Philemon nodded twice but did not turn around. With a chuckle, Alexander slapped the monk on the back and then waddled around the pyre to follow after his companions.

For the briefest moment, a thin smile began to creep across the subprior's face. Meeting my gaze, brother Philemon suddenly dropped his head and curled his mouth down into a mournful scowl. He stamped his feet a few more times, crossed himself, and then hurried to catch up with his rotund friend.

"Are you coming, Father?" Thomas asked. Anne and the girls were gone, leaving only me and Thomas standing alone. Brother Phillip had completely disappeared behind the billowing smoke.

"Yes. Yes. Let's go see what has been prepared for supper."

"I'll be black," Thomas said enthusiastically as he arranged the fifteen dark stone discs onto the starting position on his side of the board. The family had retired to the solar after supper, and my son had challenged me to a game of Tables.

"I know. I know. You're always black." I similarly placed a series of white discs on my side of the board. "It was good to see everyone turn out to pay their final respects to Prior Gregory."

"As cold as it was and as bad as he looked, I was surprised that anyone came out." He cast a sidelong glance as he picked up the ivory dice and rolled them across the table. "Five and three." He picked up one of his stone men and moved it across the triangles of alternating color.

"Prior Gregory was the rector of Stony Heath. It was their duty to be there." I scooped up the dice and tossed them onto the game board before moving two of my men from the starting position. "And those that did not want to go were abruptly shown to the door by Master Hal." Thomas smirked as he retrieved the dice for another roll.

"Father, have you ever heard of the three estates?"

"Of course I have. Those who fight, those who pray, and those who work. It's good to see that Sir John has provided you with a capable tutor. So which estate do you belong to?"

"Naturally, those who fight." He flashed a smile that lasted for only a brief moment. He stared wordlessly down at the board for several moments.

"What's troubling you, Thomas?" I pushed the dice over to him for his next turn.

"What would happen if there were no more laborers?"

"Well, I guess there'd be a lot of fields that would go fallow. Why do you ask?" He picked up the dice but only rolled them around in his fingers, studying the small dots carved into the sides.

"I'm afraid that if we don't find a way to stop this Plague, the world as we know it will cease to exist." His brow furrowed as he raised his eyes to meet my gaze.

He has a point. Almost every monk and most of the villagers in Stony Heath are gone. The same is happening here in Colleville. If it spreads beyond our valley, what will be left?

"That's why we have to keep it from entering the walls of the manor." I lowered my voice as I glanced around the room to see if Anne or the girls were paying attention to our conversation. They were busy doing needlepoint or reading a book or chatting with my squire. "We have to do whatever it takes to keep our family safe. It sometimes means you have to make difficult choices, but the family must always come first."

"But it's not enough just to keep it outside the walls. Without all the people in the village, there is no manor. Who in this room—" A stern look from me gave him cause to lower his voice. "Who in this room knows how to harness an ox to the plow or tend bees to pollinate the field or patch a loose stone in the wall or forge a weapon to protect ourselves with?" He paused for a moment to emphasize his next statement. "Without the third estate we will starve."

"We can always go hunting. The forest is rife with game."

"And how long do you think that will sustain us? With no wardens to protect the herds, poachers will clean out our chase in no time—if any people are even left to do the poaching."

"You've got too much of your mother in you, son," I said as I rolled the dice. "Just know that it won't come to that. And, to make certain of it, we need to be prepared for tomorrow when we ride out to relieve our tenants trapped inside the parish church." Thomas smiled weakly at the mention of a cavalry charge.

"We should've gone there as soon as we made it back with the saddles."

"No. We lost all of the horses we set out to retrieve, and some of our men were killed in the process. It's important that we keep up their spirits, even if we're unsure of the outcome."

"If you say so." He half-heartedly rolled the dice before sliding one of his men onto my side of the board. He passed the dice over to me.

"We'll have to continue this game tomorrow," I said, placing the ivory cubes down in the center of the board. "I still have much to do before then." Thomas gently nodded his head. With a frown, he pushed his chair back to stand and then walked over to where James and Bernice were sitting and talking.

"Cheer up, Son," I said as I pulled open the door to the stairwell. "You've been chomping at the bit for a cavalry charge. In the morning you'll get your wish. Now get some sleep. I don't want you and James to stay up late."

2 January

Feast of Saint Gregory

THOMAS, I WANT YOU TO HAVE Ebon." I held out the reins of my black charger to my son. He had been checking the girth of his replacement horse, ensuring the groom had properly saddled it.

"I can't take your horse, Father. He's been your favorite for the last—what, seven years?" The excitement on his face was undermining his protest.

"You're a man now and will one day soon have your own household. I wish I possessed the means to give you something more substantial, but fortune has not been on my side as of late. Ebon will have to do for now. Here." I pressed the reins into his hand. "Besides, Master William and I have been working with Goliath for some time now. Ebon is getting older and is a step or two slower. The time has come for me to pass him along to someone to learn on." We shared a short laugh together.

While I see you as a man and worthy of a knighthood, I wanted to tell him but could not, *I do not trust you to ride an untried horse into battle.*

"I am very pleased, Master Piers," I said, turning to the smith who was standing a few feet away. "The cloth barding looks like it just might work." I ran a hand over the red and yellow caparison the grooms had placed on Goliath. Its outer surface was embroidered with my golden bear crest, but its satin underside had been freshly quilted with several layers of linen. All six of the men-at-arms' horses were similarly protected from the base of the neck to the tail.

"Mount up," I ordered the nine warriors assembled in the courtyard. A wave of murmurs passed through the crowd of villagers that had gathered to watch the spectacle with morbid curiosity. Overhead, there were at least a dozen heads poking through the dormitory windows on either side of the gatehouse. The pungent odor of burnt hair and roasted flesh clung to the stone walls.

Jacob stepped forward and held out my sallet, his eyes cast down on the ground in front of him. "It's all right, lad. You're not coming along on this one. Have Master Edmund find you a proper coat." Although the snow had stopped falling, a cold northern wind still whirled around in the courtyard, creating small white drifts in the corners.

"Yessir," he said quietly, slowly lifting his gaze. There was a dark purple mark above his left cheek.

James, you bully. I'll deal with you when we return. For the moment, it was more important to get the young squire in his saddle. James was scared, and he had a litany of excuses why he should not ride out this morning with the rest of the men. It had taken Thomas's goading to finally shame him into donning his armor.

Taking the helmet from Jacob, I hurriedly buckled it on and climbed into the saddle. Wheeling Goliath around, I addressed my small retinue:

"My good fellows, I know you have already risked so much, but once more I must ask you to place yourselves in harm's way. If there were any others I could call on to take your place, I would." Leonard slapped Bertram on the arm and both men chuckled. They, like Miles, were mounted upon young geldings, each man also leading a second riderless horse. With their arrows all expended, the three archers had become swordsmen.

"Last night, I sent word to our friends in the church belfry to let them know we were coming. They reported that things are pretty grim over there. A fight broke out over the bread and wine; Sir Denis was hurt and one of his altar servers was killed."

"Be on your guard, men. There may be some inside the church who are infected, so do your best to stick together and take no chances."

"Prepare to open the gates," I called to Lewys. The courtyard quickly fell silent except for the sounds of horses snorting and shifting their feet. Even the ravens had forsaken the manor in search of a place to shelter from the frigid wind. The marshal hurried through the gatehouse and placed a hand on the tall outer doors before turning to look back. A low bumping and scraping sound began to grow outside the gates. Somewhere in the crowd, a young girl began to sob.

"To arms, men." The squires and men-at-arms drew their swords. Looking up, I saw Andrew Fowler standing atop the gatehouse, his eyes focused intently upon me. I gave him an exaggerated nod. The yeoman immediately turned away and began waving his arms high over his head. A few moments later, the bells at Saint Wystan's began tolling loudly, followed by loud hollering and shrieking. I kicked my horse and led the men to the edge of the gatehouse.

"It's working," Lewys said in a low voice. "They're moving away." Thomas reined Ebon alongside me. His grin was visible even behind his raised bevor.

"Let's give them a bit more time." Turning, I watched Edward and Hamond arrange the men into two columns behind me and my son. A number of the villagers were filing back into the hall. "All right, Master Lewys, open the gates and get yourself clear." The marshal removed the heavy bar and pulled the gates open.

"Hah!" I spurred Goliath down the empty bridge and onto the manor green. A short distance ahead, a pale-skinned ghoul was hobbling across a small patch of snow. Its lower left leg was badly maimed and missing a foot. With a downward slash, I lopped off its head and turned my charger to the left, leading the men away from the village and in the direction of the stables.

We skirted the edge of the moat. Several bloated corpses could be seen writhing around in its murky waters as we once again turned left and cantered towards the rear of the manor. Passing the garden bridge and rounding the northeast corner of the wall, I signaled for the formation to halt.

"We wait here," I instructed the men. The long line of cottages and hedgerows along Churchwell Lane made it impossible to see how many of the creatures had been drawn to the parish church, yet none were visible stalking around the manor either.

I looked back west; the yeoman stood atop the gatehouse in anticipation of his next command. I waved my sword back and forth high over my head. Andrew once again signaled to the men in the belfry. Almost immediately, the bells ceased their ringing.

The archer briefly disappeared before returning to the battlements with his yew bow in hand. He pulled it back to his ear and let fly an arrow. A tiny flame flickered from its tip as it cut a high, slow arc into the air before coming down onto a cottage just south of Market Cross.

"Are you planning to burn down the village?" Thomas exclaimed.

"Let's hope not," I replied without turning back. The arrow smoldered atop its thatched roof for several moments before dying out. "That's the most isolated cottage within range. If the roof is not too wet to burn and our little distraction works, it should lure some of the devils away from Saint Wystan's. I only pray that the fire doesn't spread and burn the whole village to the ground."

"How many arrows does he have?" Leonard wondered aloud as Andrew once again drew his bow and sent a flaming arrow high into the air.

"He *had* three," I grumbled as the second shaft stuck into the center of a narrow strip of white. A thin wisp of gray smoke quickly disappeared in the cold breeze.

"He couldn't make that shot again in a thousand years." I turned and glared at Leonard; his large smirk was quickly erased.

Last one. After a quick backwards glance, Andrew took aim and loosed his final arrow. It spiraled across the manor green in a low arc before striking just under the eave of the cottage.

"Ballocks!" I shouted. Andrew lifted his bow over his head and struck it against the battlements several times, the final one breaking the yew shaft in two. "For all the bloody good it's done you," I grumbled. Turning in the saddle, I addressed the men. "I guess we do this the hard way. Prepare to move. Archers, keep behind us and don't get caught up in the fight. Your job is to get those horses inside the churchyard for those who can't run."

"Sir Richard," Edward interjected, pointing back west. "Look."

A thin column of gray smoke began to roll out from under the eave before being caught in the wind and carried south. We sat and watched for a long while as the gray column turned into a black pillar and then into a giant orange blaze. Several small birds darted out of the burning thatch and began to flutter around the cottage. In time, the structure became an enormous, roaring flame.

"Your plan's working," Thomas cheered, pointing the tip of his sword towards the church tower. Several corpses were clawing their way through the garden hedges between several cottages. Their milky eyes were wide in astonishment as they lumbered across the open ground towards the crackling fire.

"Follow me!" I shouted as I spurred Goliath around the eastern edge of the village. The thunder of hoofbeats caused some of the monsters to turn and seek out its source, but the column was moving much too fast for them to overtake it.

The blustery wind whistled under my raised visor and stung my eyes as my stallion streaked around to the northern edge of the village. Veering sharply to the left, I led the column straight down Churchwell Lane to Saint Wystan's. There were still at least a dozen of the ghastly figures lingering around the base of the belfry. As we drew near, they turned and began rushing forward to meet our rumbling charge.

Edward and Hamond spurred their horses alongside me and Thomas to fill the road. With a downward slash, I cleaved through the hood and skull of a ghoulish villager before veering right to pick a path between the rest of the oncoming mob. I lopped the head off a grizzled farmer with a rising cut before reining towards a third corpse and trampling it with iron-shod hooves.

Within moments, we had fought through their ranks to reach the low wall ringing the parish church. Ahead, a large crowd of the hungry dead were surging down the road towards Market Cross.

"Keep your horses moving," I ordered as we cut a tight circle between Saint Wystan's and the smithy. "Circle around back." We galloped along the northern side of the churchyard wall before turning left.

"Open the gate!" I bellowed. "Open the gate!" An instant later, a large wooden door swung open in the center of the western wall. It was held open by a young man in a white smock who stared wide-eyed at the approaching horses.

"Archers, get your butts inside. The rest of you, form a bend and follow me." The men responded by reining their mounts into a single line angling back from Goliath. Glancing back, Leonard and the archers spurred their horses through the open gate before it was pulled shut.

"Saints preserve us," someone blurted from behind as we wheeled one final time to the left onto the road from Stony Heath. Stretched out before us, a dark wave of wretched corpses was swarming through Market Cross and headed directly for the churchyard.

"Charge!" I shouted, spurring Goliath down the southern edge of the wall.

"Hah-huh-huh-hah!" Thomas exclaimed as he trampled over the top of the first monster. A second creature raked its clawlike hand down the side of my charger an instant before I bashed in its head. Glancing down, I saw the horse was unharmed; the cloth armor had done its job.

The other men followed suit, and we cut a narrow swath through their foul ranks.

"Keep moving!" I shouted when we reached the corner of the wall. I reined Goliath to the left before slowing his gait to a gentle canter. "Is everyone all right?" All five men raised their swords in silent affirmation. "Catch your breath, men. The next time around we keep them engaged no matter what happens."

Rounding the next corner, I urged my stallion to pick up his pace. The base of his neck was covered in a white froth even in the bitter cold.

"Now! Make your escape!" I shouted as we rode past the gate. Looking back, the door swung open and Leonard rushed out, leading a horse with two small children atop it. Dozens of voices began yelling and screaming at one another inside the churchyard to hurry and run and flee.

"Have at them!" I bellowed, spurring Goliath into a charge. Ahead, one of the devils had climbed atop a headless corpse and was desperately trying to pull itself over the wall. A second ghoul dressed in a tattered black robe was attempting to scale the back of its vile companion.

"Keep them off the walls," Thomas shouted. Thundering forward, I reached over the top of my reining hand and delivered a rising cut, severing the forearm of the ghastly monk and removing the back of the other's skull. The black-robed figure just mounted the back of his crumpled partner and resumed his climb.

"Back around," I ordered, wheeling Goliath in a tight circle before spurring him towards the creature. With a sideways cut, its head instantly toppled to the ground.

"Rally on me," I called, reining my stallion around to the left to look for my men-at-arms. They were working in tight circles, hacking down to the left and right.

"Hah!" Thomas shouted as he spurred Ebon into a big-bellied merchant. The black charger groaned heavily as its forelegs suddenly doubled under from the impact, sending it crashing to the ground and vaulting Thomas over the top of its neck. He landed head first a few feet in front of the stallion.

"Thomas!" I screamed. He did not move. I stabbed my spurs into the side of Goliath, launching him forward into a full gallop. Two of the wretched devils immediately leapt on top of Thomas and began thrashing at his motionless body. "Thomas is down! Help him!"

Edward wheeled right and thrust a sword point through the neck of the closest monster atop Thomas; its dark blood sprayed across the ground, but it continued to claw at Thomas's throat. The esquire took the head off an approaching corpse and then spurred his horse around for another pass.

Reaching Thomas's side, I wrenched back on the reins, causing my warhorse to rear up and stagger sideways. Not waiting for him to fully stop, I threw myself off his back and landed hard on the frozen ground, sending a sharp pain up my leg. My son coughed loudly before he began to flail his arms and legs around underneath the weight of the two monsters.

Thank God, he's alive! I lumbered over and kicked one fiend in the side of the head, sending it rolling across the ground. I grabbed the second one by its long golden hair and peeled it off my son before slicing clean through its neck.

"Thomas!" I screamed, his name catching in my throat. He was frantically trying to pry apart his bevor and visor as he gasped and coughed. I dropped my sword and knelt over him.

"Rally to your lord!" Edward shouted. "Keep them back!"

All around the sounds of bones breaking, men grunting, and horses snorting quickly faded into the background as I drew my dagger and sliced through the leather strap behind Thomas's neck, which held the bevor in place. His face was covered in stinking blood and bile, and his eyes were wide with fear.

"Ugh," Thomas coughed loudly before turning and vomiting.

"Hold still, Son. You're going to be all right." Cutting off the hem of my coat, I did my best to wipe the filth from his face. Around us, the four defenders had turned their mounts to create a protective box. Scooping up both our swords, I stretched out my free hand to my son. "You have to get up, Thomas. We can't stay here any longer."

I pulled him to his feet, but his legs were still unsteady. I led him over to James's stallion, where I stuck my blade into the ground before sliding his sword into the sheath belted to his side.

"Climb up," I told him, clutching my hands together to form a step. Thomas slowly scrambled up behind his friend and threw his arms around James's waist.

He's safe now, I reassured myself as I snatched up my sword and scanned from side to side. The surreal calmness quickly melted away and the battlefield once again became a maelstrom of furious shouts and violent actions.

"The villagers are all well clear of here," Edward hollered over his shoulder as if he could read my thoughts.

"All right," I growled. "Let's get back to the manor." I slid between two horses and grabbed the reins of Goliath, who was angrily pawing and stomping the ground. Once in the saddle, I gave the command to disengage and quit the field.

It could've been worse, I reminded myself. When I glanced back, several of the wretched fiends were feeding on my expensive warhorse. There had to be at least three score of the rotting corpses strewn across the side of the church, but another two dozen were rushing down the road in pursuit. *It could have been much, much worse. Your son is alive, and your villagers are safe inside the manor.*

The courtyard was filled with people. I urged Goliath through the dense crowd, ignoring the groans and whispered curses of the men and women nudged aside by the large stallion. Reaching the steps of the hall, I hurriedly dismounted and helped Thomas down from the back of James's horse.

"Chris!" shouted a young woman as she squeezed past.

Placing my arm under his, I half-carried Thomas to the door of the great hall, where Edmund stood waiting. The steward's lower jaw was open in a look of shock.

"Edmund, fetch brother Phillip at once. Then see to all these people. No matter what, don't let the infection inside our walls." If he responded, his words were lost in the din of raised voices as a flood of villagers began to pour out of the hall to see the spectacle.

"Make a hole," I barked angrily at a trio of men laughing as they exited the door. "I said stand aside, you bunch of swag-bellied louts." They scowled with disdain but quickly parted without a word. I ushered Thomas through the great hall and up the stairs to his room.

"You're going to be all right, Son," I said to Thomas soothingly as I began to strip off his armor. His skin was pale by the time I placed him into his bed. Despite the chill in the air, beads of sweat ran down his forehead to moisten his hair.

"Where the devil is brother Phillip?" I yelled over a shoulder at the open door. "Someone fetch me that blasted monk or by heaven there'll be hell to pay."

Part Three:
Famine

3 January

Feast of the Holy Name of Jesus

S OMEWHERE IN THE DISTANCE, a door slammed shut, sending a sudden surge of panic through my veins. The echo quickly faded into the darkness leaving only the sound of my heart pounding in my chest.

How long was I asleep? I wondered. My mind reeled as if it were recovering from a long night of feasting. The dusky chamber was lit only by a thin ray of light that filtered through a narrow divide in the curtains in the far corner.

Where am I? How did I get here? When I turned my head, there was a sharp pain in the crook of my neck as if bone rubbed against bone. My limbs were strangely heavy. Looking down, I was clad in bloodstained armor and seated on a hard, cushionless chair.

Thomas slept in the bed to my right, his breaths short and labored. There were dark, purplish marks under his eyes and a small, sutured gash across the bridge of his nose. A mass of long, golden hair, loose and uncovered, lay atop the pillow next to him.

"Anne?" I whispered. Her eyes were bright red and brimming with tears. She blinked but did not look up; her gaze was firmly fixed upon our son. Anne softly stroked his cheek with a single finger.

"Do you know the hour?" I asked quietly. "I didn't hear the morning bells." A slow shake of the head was her only response. She gently combed back Thomas's dark hair. Small beads of sweat glistened on his pale forehead. "Is he doing any better?"

"No," Anne replied, her voice wavering. She placed her delicate hand on his chest. "He's shivering, Richard. Please build him a fire."

Rising from the chair, I crossed the room and began stacking small slivers of wood into the fireplace. Its embers glowed through a thin layer of ash. Once the kindling began to smolder and then finally to burn, I added several logs to help warm the room.

"There," I said, rising. "It'll be warm in no time." Anne continued her silent watch over our son. Outside the chamber, a pair of footsteps climbed the stairs before pausing before the door. After a faint knock, James craned his head into the room and looked around.

"What hour is it?" I demanded in a low voice. I walked over and joined him in the doorway.

"Huh? Oh, it's just after prime, Sir Richard. I came to see if there is anything you need. Anything I can do." The squire frowned as he eyed the motionless figure underneath a heavy wool blanket.

"Where the devil is brother Phillip? Why isn't he here?"

"He left just after you fell asleep," James stammered, taking a step back as if he wanted to run. "He said you needed your rest. If you want me to go and get him, he's in the solar with Bernice and the girls."

"Of course I want you to fetch him. He should be here." A low moan came from the bed. Slowly, Thomas opened his eyes and stared up at the ceiling. His eyelids were heavy. Brother Phillip had given him an elixir to help him sleep.

"Anne, you should go and see to the girls. I'll stay here and wait for brother Phillip." Her green eyes pierced me with an emotionless gaze, but she uttered no reply. Her hand continued to delicately stroke Thomas's face.

"Why are you still here, James?" I barked at the squire lingering in the doorway; he quickly spun on his heels and dashed down the hall. A few moments later, brother Phillip stepped into the room carrying a small lamp. His large satchel was tucked under one arm and the *Liber Medicinarum* under the other.

"How is he doing this morning?" brother Phillip inquired. The monk had a weak smile on his face and averted his eyes as passed by.

"He awoke a short time ago, but he still seems groggy from whatever you gave him."

"It's important that Thomas recover his strength." He sidled across the room to stand at the foot of the bed. "Has he spoken yet?"

"No," I said flatly.

Edmund appeared in the open doorway. His face was drawn and his clothes were disheveled, something very out of character for the jolly old steward. Behind him stood three teary-eyed girls.

"Please come in and shut the door, Master Edmund." Lizzie's chin began to quiver as she turned and buried her face into Bernice's side. I yearned to reach out to them, but I was not ready to answer the questions they would no doubt have. The steward turned and slowly pushed the door closed.

"With your permission, Lady Anne," brother Phillip said as he placed his lamp on the table next to the bed, "I'm going to examine your son." He moved around to the other side of the bed, obligating my wife to rise. She slowly sat up and slid down to the end of the bed. The monk gently lifted Thomas's head and placed the second pillow behind it.

"What happened?" Thomas groaned, doing his best to force a smile. "I feel like I was run over by an ale cart." He tried to push himself up on an elbow.

"Rest easy, Thomas. You've had a nasty fall and must remain in bed for the time being." Brother Phillip placed a hand on my son's forehead and held it there for a time. "Tell me, does your head still hurt?"

"Something fierce." His weak smile quickly faded. The monk pulled back the covers and lifted Thomas's shirt.

"Just continue to breathe normally." Brother Phillip placed his ear atop my son's chest. Closing his eyes, the monk listened intently for several moments. "Good," he finally said, replacing Thomas's shirt and covers. Ruffling through his satchel, the monk produced a small metal plate.

"Can you spit on this for me?" brother Phillip asked as he cradled Thomas's head with a hand and placed the plate under my son's chin. "From as deep down in your throat as you can."

With some effort, Thomas complied with the monk's request. Brother Phillip gently laid him back down on the pillow before turning and walking across the room to the window. Pulling back the curtain a few feet, he squinted from the bright glare as he studied the ball of phlegm.

"Very good, Thomas," the monk said as he wiped the plate clean with a sleeve and returned to the side of the bed. He took out a small glass jar from his bag and placed it on the nearby table. "If you are able, I need you to fill this."

"May I have a word with you, brother Phillip?" I asked the monk in a low voice as he began to rifle through his satchel. "In private?"

"Of course," he replied, closing the flap. We walked over to stand next to the window.

"How is he?" I kept my voice low. "The truth."

"It's still too soon to tell. Your son was thrown from his horse. If all he has to show for it are a couple of black eyes and a cut on the nose, he is incredibly lucky. After all, he could have broken his neck."

"It sounds as if there is more."

"I am pleased that he is coherent and able to speak, but head injuries can be very tricky to diagnose, and the migraines have me worried. They could be a sign of swelling of the brain. If that is the case, I would have to bore a hole in his skull to relieve the pressure." The monk pursed his lips as he looked to the floor.

"That's not everything, is it?" I asked, placing a firm hand on his shoulder. I pushed him through the door and into the hallway. "Out with it, man. What are you not telling me?"

"I am concerned about his breathing. His lungs sound as if they are filling with fluid. That is a sure sign of infection."

"Is there nothing else to be done?"

"You can pray," brother Phillip replied with a tender smile. "Apart from that, all we can do is wait and see."

"We have been waiting all night," I pleaded. "How long before you can know for certain?"

"I have yet to examine his urine. In the meantime, there are a few medicines I am going to prepare. If you'll excuse me, I'll get started on them immediately." With a nod, I sent him back to work. Across the room, Edmund was still waiting patiently next to the door. He gnawed anxiously at his lower lip.

More bad news. I motioned him out into the hallway before hearing his report.

"What is it, Master Edmund?" I finally asked with a sigh.

"Sir Richard, it has been very difficult to find enough room for all of the people that came from Saint Wystan's. There are many who are rather unhappy with their accommodations."

"I am not very concerned with their happiness. They have a roof over their heads and food on the table—my table. Let them know they are more than welcome to leave in search of better conditions if they feel so inclined."

"But there have been several physical altercations between your tenants and those from Stony Heath.

"Deal with it, man," I replied coldly. "You're the steward, so do your bloody job." Taking a deep breath, I bit back any further rebuke. "I know you are doing your best to treat everyone fairly, but do not let a bunch of knaves push you around. Call on Edward and the men if you need to. Now, if you will excuse me, I have more important things to deal with."

I stepped past Edmund to re-enter the room and pushed the door half-closed. Anne was reclining on her side next to Thomas, combing her fingers through his hair. Brother Phillip was standing next to the open window holding a glass jar up to his face, examining the light filtering through the dark yellow liquid inside.

"Slightly ruddy as if of golden alloy, not too cloudy, with very little foam," he said as he swirled the container around several times before placing it under his nose. "A bit pungent, but nothing to be overly concerned about."

A chamber pot sat on the floor next to the bed. The acrid smell of vomit emanated from it. Anne blotted a wet cloth to Thomas's face. His skin was even more pallid than before.

"He became nauseous when he rose to void his bladder," Anne said with a tone of remorse. "He must have sat up too fast." I walked over to Thomas's bedside and looked down at him. My son flashed a feeble smile.

"Still not feeling any better, Son?"

"No," he moaned with a deep, wet cough.

"Hang in there, Thomas. Brother Phillip is going to have you on your feet in no time." I did my best to look confident.

The monk paced back and forth in front of the fire holding a small stone mortar in one hand while forcefully working a pestle with the other.

"I'm grinding roasted eggshell and marigold into a powder," he explained. He used a finger to scrape out the ingredients into an iron pot. A rank, yeasty smell spread throughout the room as he opened a small vial containing a dark, syrup-like liquid.

"It smells wretched." The monk added a few drops of the pungent syrup into the pot before hanging it over the fire.

"I'm infusing it into a good ale to make it a bit more palatable. Thomas will need to drink it each morning and night."

"How long will it take to prepare?" I inquired.

"Not long, though it will be a while before we see any result."

"I'm going down to the chapel, Anne. I shouldn't be long." She did not bother to look up. She ran her hands along Thomas's sides, tucking the blanket underneath him.

"My sweet, sweet boy," she whispered as she began to softly sing a lullaby to him. Stepping out into the hallway, I slowly pulled the door closed.

First, I need to get out of this armor.

Jacob Stoney lurched from his bed as I threw open the door to my chamber. He rubbed the sleep from his wide eyes.

"It's all right, Jacob. You're not in trouble. Help me out of my armor." The young varlet quickly rushed over and began untying the leather laces that held the armor in place at my shoulders and elbows.

"How is Thomas?"

"Better, I hope. Thank you for asking." With a grunt, the boy helped me slide out of my heavy cuirass. Jacob sat it down on the floor and then began unbuckling the straps along the backs of my legs.

"Sir Richard?" the varlet said meekly.

"Yes, Jacob?"

"I'm sorry for what I said the other day, about you being a harsh lord. I didn't mean it."

"I know, lad. It's already forgotten, so let's speak no more of it." After removing the last of the armor, I was finally able to change out of the previous day's clothing. Pouring rose water into a basin, I did my best to wash off some of the sweat and grime. I then donned my brigandine and once again concealed it beneath a pleated coat.

"Have James scour my armor clean right away. Tell him not to wait until it starts to rust. If he gives you any trouble, you come straight to me."

"Yes, lord."

Turning, I made my way across the room and into the stairwell leading down to the chapel. Men's voices echoed up the narrow passage. The sounds grew louder as I neared the foot of the stairs. Opening the door, I was rendered speechless by what awaited me.

The chapel was located in a lower corner of the hall with a small, arched door leading out into the courtyard. Sunlight filtered through a series of stained glass windows above the doorway to illuminate the narrow, rectangular chamber. The floor was a checkerboard of pale yellow and white stone and was devoid of any furnishings apart from the altar at the far end of the room; a bleached linen cloth decorated with golden embroidery covered the altar.

Doctor Symond looked up and smiled softly as I stepped through the doorway. He was standing in front of the altar wearing his priestly cap and robes. Kneeling before him were Edward, Christopher and Hamond. Glancing back, they crossed themselves before standing and walking over to where I stood.

"I hope you don't mind," Edward said reverently, "but we came to pray for Thomas." His words squeezed the very air from my lungs.

"Thank you," I half-sputtered. "Please continue." I stood in the doorway for several moments taking deep breaths in an attempt to regain my composure. The three men-at-arms returned to the altar, where they knelt as one and resumed their heavenly petitions.

I, too, dropped to my knees before the altar and began to pray more fervently than I ever had before. I pleaded with every saint whose name I could recall to intercede on behalf of my son.

Eventually, Edward and the men stood and quietly made their way to the back of the chapel. A cold blast of air whipped through the room as they opened the door to the courtyard, causing the light from dozens of candles to flicker against the walls. Outside, several shouts reverberated through the doorway. It was impossible to discern the words, but I was sure that I would learn the nature of it soon. A short time later, the door was flung open and a pair of boots hurriedly shuffled across the stone floor.

"Sir Richard," Raulfe panted over my shoulder, his face red from exertion. "There's been a murder down in the servants' quarters."

"What are you talking about?" I demanded, making the sign of the cross as I stood and turned to face the archer. The image of a pale-skinned villager running amok in the dormitory immediately sprang to mind. "Who has been murdered?"

"The blacksmith from Stony Heath."

"Not Piers Smythe?" *There must be some mistake. Why would anyone want to kill him?*

"I'm afraid so." Raulfe wiped a sleeve across his sweaty brow. "His wife and son only just discovered the body. Edward's with him now."

"Was it the disease?" There seemed to be no end to its reach despite every precaution.

"No, I think he was killed with a knife."

"You think or you know?" My jaw clenched with anger.

"I only know what Edward told me. He said the blacksmith was stabbed in his room and to come and tell you straightaway. The crowd outside is getting bigger even as we speak."

"Will this nightmare ever end?" I groaned. I motioned the archer to the door. "Very well, lad, we had better go see what can be done to sort out this mess."

Outside, a mob of villagers filled the courtyard. They were pressed so tightly together that it was almost impossible to pass through their midst. Overhead, at least a dozen crows circled in the bitterly cold sky; their incessant droning was muted by the loud murmuring of the people.

"Get back!" Hamond barked. "I said get back before I start busting heads!"

"Make a hole," I growled as I pushed my way through the crowd to reach the dormitory entrance. Hamond, Andrew, Leonard, and Aleyn were standing shoulder to shoulder in front of the door. A look of relief instantly appeared upon the yeoman's face as I emerged from the press.

"Keep everyone outside," I instructed as I slid past them. Bertram was standing guard at the top of stairs.

"They killed him," Rebecca Smythe wailed as I rounded the corner. "They killed my Piers. What'd he ever do to hurt anybody?" She reached out and grasped the folds of my coat before burying her face into my chest.

"Who killed him?" I inquired, trying to lift her head, but she only pressed it harder into my chest as she sobbed heavily. "Let me go, madame. I need to see to your husband."

"Sir Richard doesn't need you pawing at him," Bertram said as he hurried over and placed his hands on her shoulders. Rebecca did not resist as the archer gently pulled her back. Instead, she turned and threw her arms around his waist and began to weep bitterly.

"What happened?" I asked, turning to Edward. The esquire was halfway down the hall standing in front of an open door with his arms crossed. He slowly rubbed a hand over his chin in silent reflection. I walked over to his side. A knotted kerchief had been discarded near his feet. Some coarse bread and salted meats could be seen in its folds.

"Stabbed clean through the heart," Edward stated without bothering to look up. "Doesn't even look like he put up a fight." The blacksmith's body lay only a few feet inside the doorway. The handle of a crude dagger was sticking out of his chest; a large, red circle stained his white shirt around it. Piers's face was contorted into a look of both fear and pain.

"Perhaps we should take a closer look inside," I said, motioning for the esquire to enter the room. We carefully stepped around the body and closed the door; the sobbing of his widow faded into the background. "I must confess that I'm more than a bit relieved it was not Plague. How bad have things become that murder is more palatable than disease?" I did not wait for him to answer. "I take it there were no witnesses?"

"Not a one. Nobody even reported hearing a single scream. At least, that is, not until his wife and son returned to open the door."

"And where were they at the time?" I knelt next to the body and checked the folds of his garments for any other cuts or visible wounds. *Nothing. Not even a scratch.*

"In the great hall," Edward replied, jutting his head towards the window, "apparently having dinner."

"Why wasn't he with them?" I stood and glanced around the room. Like the other refugees from Stony Heath, the blacksmith had not had any time to grab his personal belongings before fleeing his home. It was impossible to know if anything had been taken by the killer. "It's odd that a family would choose not to eat together, don't you think?"

"She said her husband was worried someone was going to break in and occupy the room while they were away, so he sent them to eat without him. They brought him something back."

"Why did he think someone would try to take their room?" My fists were clenched in anger. "He is a guest under my roof. Who would have the audacity to forcibly remove him?"

"She didn't say." The esquire looked down at Piers's corpse. His arms were stretched awkwardly over his head and there was a small pool of blood under his feet. "Do you really think he was killed over the room?"

"If that was the case," I countered, "why didn't anyone hear a shout or a scream or even a raised voice?"

"The attacker must have been quick with a knife. He burst into the room and caught the blacksmith by surprise. Stabbed him through the heart before he could react."

"Perhaps," I said, walking across the room and taking a seat in one of the chairs next to the bed. "If I were waiting for supper to be brought to me, I would likely be doing so at my leisure." I rose and walked past the corpse to stand at the door. "There is no sign of forced entry, so Master Piers must have opened the door for his killer." I pulled the door ajar and peeked around it into the hallway. Only my head and upper chest were visible from the outside. "He was stabbed through the heart and almost immediately collapsed just inside the room. The killer then dragged him out of the doorway before anyone might happen along and see what was going on."

"It makes sense," Edward said with a thoughtful nod of the head. I pushed the door shut and slid the latch closed.

"That leaves only one question in my mind: why would he open the door? I mean, if he truly believed that someone wanted to evict him and his family from the room, what would compel him to open the door?"

"The voice of a friend?" Edward responded with a shrug. "It could be that he was well acquainted with the killer."

"That would mean he was killed by someone from Stony Heath." I could not help but let out a small sigh of relief. "The men are stretched thin enough as it is just trying to keep this wretched disease from finding its way inside the manor walls. The last thing we need is for this to turn into open conflict between the two villages."

A soft knock on the door interrupted our deliberations.

"Enter," I said bluntly. A moment later, the door was slowly pushed ajar, and Christopher poked his head through the narrow opening. His furrowed brow gave him a pained look. "What is it, man?"

"Begging your pardon, Sir Richard," the man-at-arms finally said, "but Alexander Ducworthe insists upon seeing you." The name instantly caused my spine to stiffen.

"I'm in no mood to deal with him right now."

"He is most persistent," Christopher continued, gesturing out into the hall with his head. "He claims to have important information to share."

"Very well," I sighed. "Show him in." Pushing the door open, the man-at-arms stepped back and, with a wave of his arm, motioned for Alexander to enter. The reeve sauntered into the room, slipping around the body of Piers as if it were only a puddle of water on the floor. He wore ill-fitting clothes that only served to accentuate his spindly legs below his rotund gut.

You look like a four-legged spider. I could not help but smile at the thought. The man's face brightened, no doubt mistaking the sudden display of amusement as a sign I was glad to see him.

"My lord," Alexander said in a flourish with a slight bow. Only then did he half-turn and finally look down at the corpse. With a shake of the head, he continued his address. "What a pity. I wish I could say that I was shocked to hear the news, but I knew it was only a matter of time before violence broke out."

"Master Alexander," I interrupted, "what are you talking about? What information do you have to share?"

"Information? Oh, yes." He cleared his throat. "There has been so much quarreling in the great hall of late. At least, that is, ever since your tenants arrived. Many of them have been most unfriendly to me and my fellows. More than one has told me flatly that he thought those of us from Stony Heath should be thrown out to make more room."

"Please tell me that is not all you have to share. A man has been murdered in cold blood while under my protection. I am hard-pressed to find the killer."

"Might I suggest that your men search for the owner of the blade?" He fingered his own dagger, which dangled from his long, thin belt in a tooled leather sheath. "It shouldn't be too difficult to spot a man who's missing his knife. I would suggest that you look very closely at your household servants."

Why didn't I think of that? Edward and I shared a quick glance. *Could it really be so easy?*

"That is a good idea, Master Alexander, but I think you are focused on the wrong party. Why would one of my men want to kill him? We have reason to believe that Piers was killed by someone from Stony Heath." The reeve's eyes widened with momentary surprise.

"Really?" he swallowed hard. "Forgive me for saying so, lord, but that doesn't make any sense. What sort of evidence is there to suggest that it wasn't one of your tenants?"

"He told his wife that he feared someone wanted to forcibly remove them from their room, and yet he still opened the door. A terrified man would keep his door locked and only open it for someone he knew. Someone he trusted." The reeve's eyes narrowed as he considered the statement.

"If I heard a knock at my gate," Alexander replied with a shrug, "I would open the porter's squint to see who is standing outside the wall. But if I heard a knock on my inner door, I dare say I would just open it without a second thought. The blacksmith was expecting his wife to return. He heard someone at the door, and he opened it, never suspecting that a murderer was lurking in the hallway. Thanks be to God that your lordship was sleeping soundly in your chamber, where you are safe, for none of the rest of us will feel safe while a killer is on the loose."

"Remember that you are a guest in my house, Master Alexander. If you believe you would feel safer somewhere else, by all means, take your leave of Colleville. My men will see you to the gates."

"I beg your pardon, my lord," the fat reeve gasped. "It was not my place to comment on the mood of your tenants. I merely came here to offer my help in finding the assassin hiding in our midst."

"And so you have. You are dismissed." The spider spun around and ambled out of the room.

"I don't trust him," Edward said in a low voice once Alexander had gone. He pushed the door closed.

"Nor I. It would be foolish not to keep a close watch on him. Still, the man was right about one thing."

"And what is that, lord?"

"I have a house full of malcontents. They're only going to become more emboldened with each passing day. I dread to think what will happen when the food supplies begin to run low." I picked up a linen towel lying next to the wash basin.

"From what I just saw in the courtyard, they already seem rather united in their displeasure."

"We need to channel their anger in another direction. They need to see a demonstration of justice. It is vital that we find the killer. Soon." I knelt next to the body of Piers. Using the towel, I slowly eased the blade out of the blacksmith's chest before wiping it clean. "I want you to do everything you can to find the owner of this knife."

"I'll have the men start searching right away," Edward said, reaching out to take the weapon. "I'm afraid it won't be easy," he added as he twirled the blade in his hand. "It looks like a run-of-the-mill eating knife. There have to be a hundred others just like it hanging from the belt of every man in Colleville."

"Nevertheless, it's the only thing we have to go on at this time. I also want you to post a guard in each of the hallways as well as the great hall." The esquire sighed wearily.

"That will stretch the men very thin. As it is there are barely enough to man the walls and watch the gates."

"I really have no other option, Edward. I can't afford to let this kind of lawlessness go on in my own home. Piers Smythe had my guarantee of safety, and yet someone killed him in cold blood right under my nose." *I never even got a chance to thank him for the cloth barding.*

"I'll inform the men. They will do whatever is asked of them. You can be sure of it." With a nod of gratitude, I stepped over the corpse and opened the door. Christopher and Bertram were still waiting outside with Rebecca.

"What did you mean when you said 'they' killed your husband?" She wiped the tears from her cheek and straightened her back.

"That fat weasel, Alexander Ducworthe," Rebecca said with a sneer, "and his hangers-on. Ever since my husband came to you and informed on them, they have been looking at him with contempt in their eyes."

"Did you ever actually hear them threaten your husband with violence?" Her eyes narrowed in anger.

"Threaten him with words, lord? No. They didn't use words or warn him they were coming. They just waited until he was alone and then they killed him. How long before they come after me and my son?" She began to tremble with a mix of fear and rage.

"Mistress Rebecca, I mourn for your husband. I will not rest until his killer or killers are punished. Know that you and your son will be safe. I have already instructed my men to keep a guard posted here in the hallway night and day." Her eyes began to well up with tears as her chest shuddered with a ragged breath.

"It's my fault that he's dead," she wailed as she once again buried her head in my coat. "I pressed him to come tell you. He wouldn't have said anything if I hadn't pushed."

"It is not your fault, madame. You are not to blame." I gently pushed her back. "Now, please, you must excuse me. I have to go deal with an angry mob." On cue, Bertram stepped forward and took her softly by the shoulders.

I turned and started down the hall.

"Sir Richard?" the esquire called as I reached the stairwell.

"Yes, Edward."

"How is Thomas? Has he gotten any better?" A lump suddenly lodged itself in my throat. I had to swallow hard before replying.

"No. I'm afraid he's feeling worse." Edward nodded grimly but said no more. I spun around and strode down the stairs.

"You left my husband to die in Saint Wystan's," a woman shouted as I shouldered through my men and into the courtyard. She wore a mud-stained dress and had eyes as black as her unkempt hair. "You said you were going to save them all, but you just left him there to die at the hands of those monsters." Turning, I gave an accusatory look to Leonard, who was still guarding the doorway along with Aleyn, Andrew, and Hamond.

"We had no choice, lord. There were six or seven of them who had been injured in Monday's battle and were certain to be infected."

"So you just left them there to turn?" I seethed in a low voice. "Why the devil would you do such a thing?" For every ghoul we killed, another soon rose to take its place.

"Sir Denis wouldn't let us take care of them. He threatened us with eternal damnation if even one drop of blood was spilt on holy ground." As much as I wanted to, I could not fault them for their hasty decision.

"Good people," I said, turning to address the mass of villagers. "It is terribly cold out this afternoon. Why not take yourselves back inside where it is warm?"

"What happened to Piers?" a bearded man in a green hood demanded. "Who killed him?"

"Leave that to me. I will do everything in my power to find his murderer."

"It was one of yours who did it," a voice railed.

"Yeah, the fault lies in Colleville," another shouted.

"That is enough," I bellowed. *My son is sick. I don't have time for this nonsense.* Turning, I gave a final order to my men before forcing my way back to Thomas's chamber. "Clear the courtyard. Use force if necessary."

"Your son's humors are out of balance," brother Phillip explained as I entered Thomas's chamber. "I need to bleed him in order to let out the sickness."

Crossing the room, I took a seat next to the bed. Anne dipped a clean cloth into a small basin filled with a clear liquid, and the white towel turned a light shade of pink. Although there were a number of dark petals floating on its surface, the rose water emitted a strong vinegar-like smell. Anne started washing Thomas's head before working her way down his body.

"How are you feeling, Thomas?" He turned his face towards me. His mother continued to wash his brow, softly humming an indiscernible tune to herself.

"My whole body hurts," he groaned before coughing painfully. "Were you able to catch Ebon?" I did not have the heart to tell him that his beautiful black stallion had been killed.

"I'm afraid not. We'll have to look for him later."

"I"m sorry." He coughed again. "I should've been more careful."

"It's not your fault, Son. Now stop talking and rest."

Brother Phillip took a seat on the edge of the bed before rolling up the sleeve of Thomas's nightshirt. He took up a long, thin blade with his right hand. With his left, he pushed down firmly on the inside of Thomas's elbow for a few moments. Keeping the skin taught, the monk positioned the narrow blade onto my son's arm and made a small incision. Thomas looked away as bright red blood began to pulse through the opening. My stomach twisted into a knot.

"Good," brother Phillip said quietly to himself. Lifting Thomas's arm, he placed a metal bowl under the elbow and watched as his lifeblood throbbed into the container. "By opening the veins leading to the heart, the disease can be allowed to leave the body."

"How do you know how much to let out?" I had watched many men bleed out on the battlefield but had no idea where the invisible line might lie between life and death.

"It's not an easy thing to know. You have to eliminate as much of the disease as you can. A good surgeon can tell when a patient has reached his limit."

After several minutes, he picked up a small vessel containing a purple-hued paste, which he applied liberally over the top of the incision, staunching the blood flow.

"What now?" I asked, pulling up the covers to keep Thomas warm. His face and lips had even less color than before.

"Let's see how our medicine is coming along." Using an iron hook, brother Phillip removed the small pot from the fire and gave it a long sniff. "Just right," he declared as he gave it a quick stir and then poured a measure of it into a cup.

"Here you go, Thomas," the monk said as he walked over and sat on the bed next to my son. He gently helped Thomas lift his head before placing the cup to his lips. "Be careful. It's hot." Thomas took a small sip and made a hideous scowl. "I know it tastes bad, but it's important that you drink a cup each night and each morning." Brother Phillip stood and began to pack up his things.

"Where are you going?" I said flatly.

"Thomas needs his rest. I will be back at first light. You and Lady Anne should try and get some sleep as well."

"Thank you, brother Phillip, but I'm fine right here," Anne said as she placed the vinegar-water on the floor next to the bed. She placed a wet cloth over Thomas's forehead. "He still has a fever. I'm going to stay right here until it breaks." I knew it was pointless to argue with her. We sat there at his side for some time, watching his labored breathing slow as he thankfully drifted off to sleep.

"We should leave this place," she finally said quietly.

"Leave the manor?"

"Yes. As soon as Thomas is better, we should leave."

"And go where?"

"Far from here. It's not safe anymore."

"Anne, we've been over this before. The walls around Colleville Hall are high and strong. They could keep out a small army."

"And yet people keep dying every day. No matter what we do, whether by disease or murder, Death keeps finding a way inside."

"We can't just leave, Anne. We have a responsibility to the manor. What would happen to all of these people?"

"I don't know, but if we don't, this Plague is going to be the death of us all. We should go and find a place where the disease hasn't reached."

"Have you seen any merchants on the roads? Any peddlers since this wretched disease arrived? Any pilgrims even? How do we know that anywhere is safer than inside these walls?"

"It's too cold out for travelers," she replied in a voice barely more than a whisper. Without another word, she laid her head down on the pillow next to Thomas and closed her eyes.

I crossed the room and pushed open the window; the sun had already dipped well behind the western wall, painting the sky with hues of orange on a black canvas. Atop the gatehouse and along the perimeter, armed guards kept watch over the hundred or so villagers who had gathered in the courtyard. Some held small lanterns to illuminate the growing darkness.

A shrouded figure lay atop a small pile of timber in the midst of the assembly. Alexander Ducworthe worked his way through the crowd to stand beside the covered body. He wrapped his meaty fingers around the lapels of his ill-fitting waistcoat and scanned the faces of his audience. He held up a hand and noisily cleared his throat.

"Piers Smythe never met a stranger nor had a harsh word to say about anyone. He was a good man and a good friend to everyone. Everyone, that is, in Stony Heath." A wave of murmurs passed over the crowd.

The bloody coxcomb.

"His only crime was trusting too much." The portly reeve paused momentarily. "Believing he would be safe inside the walls of Colleville under the protection of its lord."

"Watch yourself," Edward growled from his place several steps behind Alexander. Hamond and Leonard stood to either side of him.

I should have him hanged. I partly feared that he was as popular as he claimed to be. *No, just let him wear himself out with his hollow words. If he did kill Piers, I'll put the noose around his neck myself.*

"No. No. Get away," Thomas murmured, waking me from a

restless slumber. I had once again fallen asleep in the chair by his bedside.

"It's okay, Son," I said, placing a hand on his shoulder. "It was just a dream." Thomas mumbled something as he rolled over.

The room was dark and cold. There was just a faint glow coming from the dying embers in the fireplace.

"Get up and make a fire," I grumbled under my breath. Padding across the room, I placed a bit of kindling atop the glowing ashes. The wood smelled of sweet wine. I had ordered some empty casks to be broken up as supplies of firewood ran low.

With a few puffs of breath, it quickly ignited. I stacked several slats atop one another to create a small pyramid. Soon the warmth of a roaring fire radiated throughout the room.

That's strange. Glancing to the right, I saw that the door to the chamber was wide open. The fire cast an orange hue across the bed where Thomas lay. Anne was nowhere to be seen.

"Anne?" I called in a raised whisper. I walked to the door and looked out into the hall. "Anne?" *Where would she have gone at this hour?*

I returned to the bedside and retrieved a candle. Lighting it in the fireplace, I stepped out the door and headed down the hall. Our chamber was empty; the girls were all sleeping soundly in their rooms.

Where the devil are you, Anne? I slipped down the stairs and found the door to the great hall slightly ajar. Passing through it, the massive room was dimly lit by the silver rays of the moon filtering through the vaulted windows. The sounds of raised voices echoed from across the room.

"Unhand me," a woman seethed from somewhere beyond the screens passage.

"But, m'lady," another voice sputtered. "You really should return to bed." I hurried through the maze of sleeping figures. Several times I stepped on an outstretched limb or bumped a head with my foot, but I ignored their angry curses.

Rushing through the screens and into the kitchens, I found Anne trying to get past Aleyn. The young archer had his arms spread out like he was trying to herd a wayward goose.

"I'll have you tossed out on your ear, young man, if you don't let me by." I almost burst out in laughter.

"Sir Richard," Aleyn exclaimed when he caught sight of me coming through the doorway. His face brightened as he let out an audible sigh.

"Anne, what in heaven's sake are you doing down here?" She turned and glowered in my direction. Her head was uncovered and her hair disheveled.

"I came down to check all the doors," she stated before pointing a finger at Aleyn. "But he manhandled me in the hall and wouldn't let me past."

"I was only—it's just that I thought," he stammered.

"It's all right, Aleyn. You can go back to your post." The young archer hurried past without another word. Once he had left the room, I turned back to my wife, who had her arms crossed in anger. "Why would you come down to check the doors, Anne?"

"I couldn't sleep. In the back of my mind, all I could think about was what if a servant left the doors unlocked. One of the monsters could get inside."

"They are all locked. I saw to it myself, and no one has been outside since Wednesday." I placed an arm around her and guided her back towards the hall.

"But I need to know," she demanded. There were dark circles around her eyes. "Please, Richard."

"Let me get you back upstairs, and I'll come back and check them all myself."

"Thank you," she said softly. Her muscles finally relaxed as she relented and let me lead her through the great hall. Dozens of voices whispered around us. Although the words were too faint to make out, in my head I could imagine their derision.

Climbing the steps of the dais and entering the private chambers, I turned and barred the door. Even with only a candle for light in the dark passage, I could see the lines of concern carved deep into her face begin to soften.

"You're safe now, Dear. Let's get you up to bed."

"I want to check on Thomas first." With a nod, I escorted her to our son's room.

"I'll be back in a moment," I said in a low voice as I pulled the door closed. I knew that I would find all of the gates barred and the doors locked, but I went and checked them anyway. *A promise is a promise*, I reminded myself.

4 January

Octave Day of the Holy Innocents

RICHARD, WAKE UP!" ANNE'S voice was low but its shrill tone sent a shock up my spine. I jumped out of my seat and blinked at the dusky room. Anne was on her knees bent over Thomas. There was blood down the front of her pale yellow dress. I rushed over and threw open the shutters to brighten the room.

"What's wrong?" I asked as I started back towards the bed.

"It's Thomas. He's bleeding." Reaching the bedside, I saw that the front of his nightshirt was stained crimson. Streaks of blood ran down from his mouth and nose onto the pillow. He had a pained look on his face, and his eyes glistened with tears.

"Father?" he moaned.

"Go get brother Phillip." Anne did not move. I quickly slid around the bed, took her by the shoulders, and led her to the door. "Go fetch the physician, woman, and make haste. Go!"

I returned to Thomas's bedside. He coughed fitfully.

"I don't want to die, Father." His eyes were wide with fear. I knew Thomas could see the desperation on my face, but, for the life of me, I could not conceal it.

"I know, Son. Brother Phillip will be here soon. Try and remain calm." I grabbed the rag and vinegar-water and began wiping the blood from his face. The rose-colored liquid in the small basin quickly turned bright red.

"I'm here," brother Phillip exclaimed as he rushed through the door. Anne was no more than a half-step behind him. The monk hurried over to stand beside the bed and looked down upon my son. His features instantly melted into a look of extreme sorrow.

"The skin is becoming necrotic at the fingertips," he stated, gently lifting one of Thomas's hands up to view the blackened fingers. The monk pulled open the front of his nightshirt. His chest was covered in red and black splotches. "This dark rash here is from bleeding underneath the skin. I'm sorry, but it is just as I feared. He has contracted the Plague."

"No!" Anne wailed. "He can't. You said so yourself. He just fell from his horse." Thomas's eyes widened with fear as his mother collapsed onto the side of the bed in a fit of loud sobs.

Please, God, no! Although my heart still prayed that my son might recover, my mind screamed out that there was nothing to be done. *No power on earth can stop what is coming.*

"What is it?" Lizzie pleaded from the open doorway. "What's wrong, Father?"

"Go to your room, Lizzie. Your mother will be in to see you in a moment." She started to enter the room but hesitated under my gaze. "*Now*, Elizabeth! And close the door behind you." She slowly turned and pulled the door shut.

Anne was right. I have to get our family out of here.

"Anne, I need you to go check on the girls." I walked around the bed and gently placed my hands on her shoulders. "Come on, Anne. Get up." I pulled her to her feet and wiped the tears from her cheeks. "Your girls need you right now. I will stay and look after Thomas. And, Anne, you should go and change your clothes before the girls see you."

Reluctantly, she turned and left the room. It was all I could do not to break down as I gazed down at my son lying helpless in bed.

Why, God? I prayed internally. *Why? What has my son done to deserve this?*

"Don't let me turn, Father." Thomas groaned with pain as he tried to sit up. I placed a hand on his shoulder to hold him down. "And please don't burn my body. I want to be buried in holy ground."

"You'll never be one of them, Son. You have my word." I gave the monk a shove towards the fireplace. "But you're as strong as an ox, Thomas, and as hard-headed as one, too. Keep taking your medicine. You're going to outlive this." With the last word I had to stand and wipe away a tear that started down one cheek. I joined the monk by the fire where he stirred the small iron pot that was beginning to simmer.

"Give him something to help him sleep," I said quietly. "I don't want him to suffer anymore."

"Why is God taking Thomas?" Lizzie demanded, wiping her nose on her sleeve. "What did he do wrong?" She was seated on my knee in the solar. I had asked Anne to gather everyone in the family room while I went down to give instructions to Edward.

"That's not the way it works," I replied. Around the room, Anne and Ellie were seated to her right; James and Bernice shared a window seat across the room. "Sometimes bad things happen to people even when they have been good."

"James said we're all going to die," Lizzie said with fear in her eyes. I cast a withering gaze at the feckless squire.

"James is as dumb as a barrel of rocks." The squire reddened with embarrassment. "You're not going to die, not for a long, long time. Do you hear me?"

"You promise?" she asked, throwing her arms around me.

"I give you my word." I swore to myself in that moment that I would move heaven and earth to keep the rest of my family safe. "In fact, that is why I wanted you all here right now." I stood and placed Lizzie down in the chair. "We are going on a little trip tomorrow. We will leave here at first light."

"Where are we going?" Bernice asked with a blend of excitement and fear.

"We are going to visit the place where your mother lived when she was a girl." Anne gave a subtle nod. She had inherited a meager estate at the death of her mother. The manor house was no bigger than a tithing barn, but it was far from any other towns or seaports.

"That sounds fun," Lizzie said cheerfully.

"When are we coming back?" Ellie asked with a tone of skepticism.

"When all of this madness has passed."

"But this is my home," she protested. "I don't want to leave. I like it here."

"Sweeting, you have to come. We're all going. You can't stay here by yourself." Giving Lizzie a playful poke in the arm, I turned and walked to the door. "Now go and collect your things. Pack only what you absolutely must. There is a trunk in your mother's chamber. Everything has to fit inside or it stays here." Leaving the solar, I climbed the stairs to the upper hall where, hopefully, Edward was waiting with good news.

"So what options do we have?" I asked the esquire seated to my left.

"There's a good-sized wagon outside of the barn. If we could get it back here, we could frame it up to create a carriage for the women. It would offer them a reasonable amount of protection."

"If we create a distraction by riding into the village, a few men should be able to run over and have time to hitch it up and bring it back to the manor."

"No good," I countered. "There's no way that everyone will be able to go, so I think it's best if you leave at daybreak before the rest know what's going on."

"You're not coming, Sir Richard?" Edward asked. He gave a worried look to the men on either side of him.

"No, I will not leave my son, and he cannot be allowed to leave the manor. I also have a responsibility to all of those who are lodged within my walls. I want you to see my family safely to Harrowford Manor."

"Don't worry, Sir Richard," Hamond declared. "We'll come straight back here afterwards."

"No, you will not. I want you to remain there and keep my family safe. For that reason, I want you to take your wives and children as well. Master Edmund and the other members of the household will be here to help me manage until such time as I can join you."

"That explains why they weren't invited to the meeting," Christopher said with a wry smirk.

"Never you mind that. Anyone who doesn't want to go can stay here. I will release you from your indentures right here and now."

"I don't have a wife or children," Miles said quietly, "but my parents are downstairs."

"And they will remain safely there; there will be precious little room inside the wagon. I know it's an impossible decision, but each of you has to make it alone."

"What if they walk?"

"Then they would stand very little chance against the white-eyed devils. No, it has to be this way."

"Then I will stay here."

"Same goes for me, my lord," Raulfe added. "There's no way I would leave my friends and family."

"Any others?" Each man looked around the room in silence, studying the faces of his longtime friends.

"I will see your family safely to where they need to go, Christopher said, "but afterwards I plan to return, alone if I have to. My parents are old and my sister lost her husband in the first battle." He nodded several times as he spoke as if to reassure himself of his decision.

"Very well. If there are no others, let's consider the logistics." I numbered what remained of my retinue: three men-at-arms, six archers, and a squire, though two of the men had chosen to remain behind. "I count eight of you. I am sending my wife and three daughters. How many more women and children must be accommodated for?"

"I have a wife and two young daughters," Hamond stated.

"I have a wife, a boy, and a girl," Andrew explained, "but my son can ride on my horse behind me."

"Nicholl, my varlet, isn't in here right now," Edward said, "but he has a horse of mine and he's coming with me."

"And I have a wife that'll be coming," Leonard declared.

"That's four women and six children," I tallied out loud. "Will they all be made to fit in the wagon?"

"Aye, lord," Leonard replied. "Leave it to me. I know my way around a hammer. There may not be a whole lot of room left for supplies, but I'll frame up that wagon so it'll keep them all safe from the monsters."

"It's just after the fourth hour now. Meet me downstairs in one hour in full kit." Everyone in the room stood and began walking to the door.

"One more thing, men. This should go without saying, but I will say it anyway just to be absolutely clear. There will be hell to pay if any one speaks a single word of this to anyone. In fact, I do not even want you to tell your families until late in the evening. It will go much better for us all if you are able to slip away unnoticed. Is that understood?" I looked at each man in turn and received a nod of acknowledgment before turning and leaving the room.

"Sir Richard," Edward called from behind as I started down the stairs. Turning, I was handed a thin leather sheath.

"What's this?" I responded, taking the object and turning it over to examine its features. The sheath was cut from cheap leather and bore no markings or decorations. Edward started to answer but paused and took a step back as the men began to file out of the room.

"The knife that killed Master Piers belonged to Luke Stoney," he finally replied after the last man had descended the stairs. I tried to visualize the small boy who regularly entertained my guests with his psaltery stabbing the hefty blacksmith.

"That's ridiculous. He's only a lad. How can you be certain?"

"He told me so. Luke said he heard we were searching for a missing dagger and asked if we would help him find his eating knife. He said he had it at supper last night in the great hall."

"It couldn't have been him," I said with a shake of the head. "The killer dragged the body out of the doorway. That boy is way too scrawny to have ever done it. So where is he now?"

"I instructed him to stay in his room for the time being. Lewys volunteered to keep an eye on him while we all attend the meeting."

"Well, I don't believe in coincidences. The killer took the boy's knife in hopes of throwing us off his trail. That means it was no crime of passion. No, this murder was well planned. I should have known it wouldn't be that simple." I slapped the sheath in my palm several times, trying to formulate a plan to find the culprit. It pained me to imagine a murder going unavenged.

"You've done well, Edward," I finally said, handing the sheath back to the esquire. "The bitter reality is that the killer is essentially trapped inside these walls along with everyone else. Time is on our side. As long as we keep guards posted, there shouldn't be any more murders. Right now, your priority is to get that wagon ready to go. Have the men ready to ride out within the hour."

Apart from the rattle of armor and snorting of horses, the air inside the gatehouse was eerily still. As the outer doors were pulled open, I spurred Goliath onto the bridge, where only a single corpse was milling around. It turned at the sudden sound of iron-shod hooves on stone, but I took its head off with a flick of the sword before it knew what had happened. I was clad head to toe in steel plate underneath a bulky overcoat to guard against the bitter cold; James and my three men-at-arms were likewise armored and mounted to my rear.

We veered sharply to the right once we reached the manor green and thundered around the moat, shouting and cursing at the hungry dead. Behind us, Leonard, Andrew, and the rest of the men sprinted across the bridge and towards the barn.

"Come get a bite of this," Hamond jeered at a rotting corpse that lumbered around a nearby cottage. We kicked our mounts back and forth across the open field between the manor and the village, whooping and jeering at the plodding devils.

"Do they seem a bit slower to you?" Edward shouted over the din of hoofbeats. A gray-skinned carcass stumbled across the furrows to where we circled our horses. Its legs were stiff and its face gaunt.

"As a matter of fact, they do appear more sluggish. Could it be the frost?" We reined our stallions to the left and thundered back across the field. Christopher cleaved the skull of the shambling ghoul as we passed by.

"I don't know, but, whatever it is, I hope it keeps sapping their strength." I scanned the village for danger. "We slew a good portion of them on Wednesday. There are far fewer of them lurking around the manor now."

Ahead, Leonard and Andrew were pulling the wagon by its hitch around to the front of the barn; the other lads were pushing from the rear. Upon reaching the open doorway, the archers were suddenly consumed by a raucous cloud of angry crows that billowed out of the barn and into the gray sky.

"By the saints," I blurted. "It looks like every bloody crow in the shire has been sheltering in there." The black mass swirled noisily around the barn while the men pushed the wagon inside.

"Come on, let's get over there and watch their backs." It took only a moment to gallop by the manor and reach the stone barn. Once inside, we went about securing its doors and searching for any hidden dangers.

"Board up the hole in that door," I ordered as I slid from my charger. "And get us some light in here." Leonard pried off the lid of a crate and broke its slats apart. He then rushed over and began nailing them across the opening.

Andrew scraped together a tuft of straw and placed a piece of char cloth in its center. Pulling a small band of steel out of his pouch, he struck it with a piece of flint several times in rapid succession until the material began to smolder. The yeoman blew on the source of the smoke for a few moments until the straw burst into flame. Rushing over to the wall next to the doors, Andrew lit a lantern before stomping out the burning straw.

"Behind you!" Edward shouted. A milky-eyed demon suddenly materialized out of the darkness and charged towards our steel wall. With a quick swipe, I took off the top of its skull. The monster collapsed a few feet away. Its red livery jacket was stained with muck and dark blood.

"Was that Robert Asheley?" Christopher inquired.

"I'm afraid so. At least we know what happened to him." I shouted back to Andrew. "Get that light over here so we can clear the barn.

He hurried over and placed the iron-framed lamp in my hand. Its panes were made from thin horn, which cast a pale yellow light.

"On me," I said as I started down the length of the barn. Its walls were made of stone, but the roof was timber-framed and covered in thatch. Along either side were sacks of grain, bales of hay, as well as barrels and crates of unknown supplies.

"Bloody crows have eaten up all of our corn," Hamond growled. Although the wooden containers were still intact, the grain sacks had all been pecked open and were riddled with feces. The straw-covered floor was littered with a mixture of wheat and barley and oats and dried beans.

"Keep moving." Further back there were clumps of dried blood scattered across the ground. A large, dark stain covered a stack of canvas sacks in the far corner. "This must be where Robert met his fate." Glancing around, was saw no other devils lurking in the shadows. The sound of hammering echoed through the barn. "Let's get back and see how they are making out."

It took a couple of hours, but Leonard built a sturdy frame atop the wagon and enclosed it with wooden slats. He constructed a narrow door on the back that was held in place by wooden pegs.

"It's the best I can do with what he have in here. We could break up a door in the manor for bars and hinges, or we could pull out some metal bars from a window or two if you want them to be able to see out."

"As long as they can get air, they don't need windows. It's safer without them. Lash down a few crates to hold supplies and serve as their seats. Other than that, it's perfect." I patted Leonard on the back. "Good work."

"What now, Sir Richard?" All of the men had gathered in a tight circle near the exit. Outside, several of the monsters were raking their claws down the face of the doors.

"The noise has attracted some visitors. It looks like it will be another fight to get out of here. Archers, I want you to grab whatever sacks of corn that can be salvaged and carry them back to the manor. That should dispel any questions about what we were doing. The men-at-arms will clear you a path." Andrew nodded in acknowledgment. He and his men went to work trying to find any unpolluted grain sacks on the bottom of the piles.

"Leonard, when we get back, I want you to pick out the largest two hackneys to pull the wagon and have them ready to go. You can all see that there is very little room. Only bring what you can carry on your person or on your mount." Each man nodded in response. "And let's shut the blasted doors this time!"

I met brother Phillip coming down the stairs from Thomas's room. He was wringing his hands as if wiping invisible grime off of them; his eyes began to glisten at my approach.

"Sir Richard," he sputtered.

"Is it Thomas?" I demanded, suddenly remembering my oath. "Don't tell me he's dead."

"No, he still clings to life, but only by a string."

"How long does he have?"

"It's hard to say. It's come on him so fast. Hours maybe. A day or two at most."

No father should ever have to endure the death of his son.

I brushed past him and hurried to Thomas's room. Anne was still there, seated on the bed, with his head cradled in her lap. The front of her golden dress was spattered with dark red. She had a moist cloth that she was using to wipe his brow. Every few moments he would be seized with a hard, wet cough. Anne would then wipe the fresh blood from his mouth and cheeks.

"Where were you, Richard?" she asked in a toneless voice.

"Anne, darling, I've been making the preparations that we discussed only hours ago. You know that."

"Can't you see that your son needs you right now?" She finally looked up and met my gaze. Her alabaster skin was stained by countless crimson freckles. I squatted beside the bed and carefully plucked the towel from her hand.

"Hold still," I said as I gently wiped her face. A moment later, Thomas was wracked by another choking cough. Anne retrieved the stained linen cloth from my hand and dabbed it around our son's mouth. I was utterly powerless to provide any measure of comfort to either of them. My heart ached as it had never before."

I turned to see brother Phillip kneeling at the foot of the bed, his head bowed, whispering an indiscernible prayer. I stood and made my way over to the window to stand alone; its curtains had been drawn to let in the light. The small panes of thick, leaded glass distorted the world outside.

"Pardon the intrusion, my lord," Edmund suddenly spoke over my shoulder. So severe had been Thomas's painful hacking that his entry had gone unnoticed.

"What is it, Master Edmund?" I replied, turning to face him. The steward's face was even more drawn than the previous day.

"I feel it is my duty to inform you that many had feared you were abandoning the manor when you left this morning. As I had not been privy to the details of the expedition, I could offer little by way of encouragement. The sacks of corn, at least, brought them some measure of comfort."

"Master Edmund, you yourself stated that there are not enough supplies inside the manor to sustain the large host now gathered under my roof. I rode out with the men in hopes of bringing back more food, but the bloody crows have beaten us to it. We brought back what little could be salvaged."

"Edward told me as much," he stated with a brief nod. "Although he described in great detail the condition of the provisions, he became rather tight-lipped when I asked him about the wagon and the sounds of hammering I heard coming from the barn."

"The esquire is not known for his patience. The original plan called for the wagon to be used to bring back a load of corn. As to the second part of your question, the doors were broken and had to be repaired." The furrows in his brow deepened, but he did not immediately reply. Instead, he stared at me for several moments with a look of sadness.

"My lord, how long have I been in your service?" he finally asked.

"Some twenty-odd years now, as best as I can tell."

"In all of that time, lord, have I ever given you cause to question my loyalty to you?"

"Heavens, no, Edmund," I replied, placing a hand on his shoulder. "I consider you to be a dear and trusted friend. Why would you even ask such a thing?"

"I have been taken for a fool. What kind of steward would I be if I did not know that you had called your men together in the upper hall for a secret council?" My face burned with embarrassment. "If I do not enjoy your trust, then I should expect to be soon relieved of my office."

"I am sorry, Edmund. I should not have thought to deceive you. I am sending Anne and the girls away to Harrowford. Edward and most of the men will provide them with safe escort. I, however, will remain here in Colleville Hall to keep order and defend the helpless within its walls." Edmund's brow softened as he nodded his head, and a gentle smile slowly spread across his face. Like the sun breaking through the clouds, his jolly countenance began to reappear.

He already knew, a voice whispered in the back of my mind.

"It has been my great honor to serve you, my lord, and I could not be compelled to abandon you here, now, for any cause." The steward paused to glance over to where Thomas lay as my son was seized by another round of bloody coughs; his momentary cheer quickly vanished. When he spoke again, it was barely above a whisper. "Has the surgeon given you any hope of Thomas recovering?"

"In truth, no. None at all. All we can do is wait for the end." A heaviness pressed against my chest, making every breath a struggle.

"Lady Anne," brother Phillip called softly, "are you feeling unwell?" She sucked in a quick breath but pursed her lips tightly together to hold back any response. The monk had ceased in his celestial petitions and instead turned his attention towards my wife. "Lady Anne?"

"I'm just a bit hungry and so very tired," she finally said. Her eyes were bright red from crying and ringed with dark lines from sleeplessness.

"May I?" the monk asked. With a nod, she allowed him to touch her on the forehead with the back of his hand. "Lady, how long have you been feverous?"

5 January

Vigil of the Feast of the Epiphany

A COLD WIND MOANED OVER the northern wall and nipped at the handful of torches silently darting back and forth across the courtyard underneath a black, starless sky. Owain Dun stood patiently near the gatehouse holding the reins of Goliath and two palfreys; all three horses had been saddled and made ready to ride.

The young groom's eyes searched my face for any clue as to why he had been roused from his bed so early in the morning. It was, after all, still an hour before Matins.

I am sorry, lad, I wanted to tell him but could not. He would learn the truth soon enough, as would everyone else. *The next few days will be a test for us all.*

"Everything is as you instructed, lord," Edmund spoke hoarsely over my shoulder. The blustering wind had masked his approach. "The men left about half an hour ago. They should be returning any time now."

"Take care not to catch your death, Edmund. I'll need to rely on you now more than ever." The old steward smiled weakly. His round, pale face and shadowy eyes gave him a ghostly countenance.

A young girl began to cry. Three women were huddled together in the far corner with their children clutched shivering to their skirts, all trying to find shelter from the damp chill. At their feet lay a mound of sacks containing everything they held dear.

"Open the gates," a voice bellowed down from above.

Too much noise! You're going to wake the entire hall.

Edward, Christopher, and Hamond cantered through the blackness of the gatehouse and into the courtyard. The caparisons on their wide-eyed stallions were streaked with dark blood. A moment later, the fortified wagon rattled through the gates with Leonard in the driver's seat and Andrew and his archers following close behind.

"Go fetch the girls, Matthew," I said to my varlet after I had waved him over.

"It's Jacob, lord," the Stoney boy mumbled. I patted him on the shoulder and then nudged him to the right of the hall.

"Use the chapel stairwell, lad, and try not to wake up the whole house." Jacob darted off into the darkness, his torch bobbing to and fro with every step.

"I'll see that the women and children are loaded into the wagon," the steward said before shuffling across the cobblestones. Edward reined his stallion around the steward and halted a few steps away.

"Did you encounter much resistance?" I asked the esquire. There were a pair of large crimson stains on the right side of his horse's caparison.

"I think they're really afraid of me now," the esquire smirked as he slid from his saddle.

"How do you mean?"

"The monsters didn't seem as eager to engage us this morning. We made short work of them."

"Have they slowed or has their hunger finally been sated?"

"In truth, all of the glory must go to old Jack Frost and his bloody north wind. We were practically on them before they even heard us coming." Edward nodded in the direction of the chapel. Turning, I saw James shepherding my three daughters across the courtyard; Jacob hustled along barely a step behind them with his flickering torch held aloft.

"Hurry along, girls," I chided them. "Let's get you out of this wind before you catch cold." I took Lizzie by her delicate hand and walked with them over to the wagon. Inside, the wives and children of the men were seated on two rows of wooden chests secured to the floor. Anne's trunk served as the rearmost seat, and it remained vacant, with a trio of heavy woolen blankets neatly folded atop its lid. I had little doubt that it had been Edmund who placed them there.

"My, you've gotten big," I groaned in mock pain as I lifted Lizzie into the rear door. "Now you behave and listen to your sisters."

"Where's Mother?" she protested, looking over my shoulder.

"She is going to stay here with me and Thomas."

"I want to stay here, too." Tears began to roll down her face. "Please don't send me away, Father."

"I'm sorry, poppet. It has to be this way. Now I need you to be a big girl and do as you're told. I'll come get you when it's safe to return home." Taking a step back from the doorway, I gave Ellie a hand up into the wagon. She had a book tucked tightly under her armpit.

"Thank you, Father." Bernie was waiting her turn, a strange look of warm contentment upon her face. James stood close beside her with his hand affectionately wrapped around hers. The squire nudged her forward, and she reluctantly complied.

"Now you look after your sisters," I instructed her as I helped her step up into the wagon. "All of you, listen to Edward. I had better not hear that you gave him any grief."

"Yes, Father," they replied as one.

"Mind your fingers," I said as I very slowly closed the door, inwardly longing for a bit more time to spend with them. Their teary eyes and trembling lips were soon shrouded in darkness.

"Sir Richard?" James called. I turned and the squire motioned to the windows along the inner side of the wall. Rays of light were beginning to trickle through a few of the shutters.

"We'll be off soon enough, James." I threw my arms around the squire's shoulders and pulled him into a fatherly embrace. It was the embrace I so wanted to give to Thomas but could not. Our metal shells clattered noisily together as I patted him on the back. Somehow he had grown older in the past few days.

I gave him my final instructions in a low voice: "I am entrusting you with the lives of my daughters. Treat them with the dignity and honor that they are due. Those three girls are all I have left in this world. And, James, know that it has been my great joy to watch you grow into the fine man that you are today."

"You have my word, Sir Richard." Parting, I turned and addressed the rest of the men who were gathered around the wagon.

"What are you all standing around here for? You have your instructions. To horse!"

"Are you sure you aren't coming with us, Sir Richard?" Edward asked as he climbed into his saddle. The rest of the retinue hurried to mount their own horses.

"You know I cannot. I will ride with you only to the edge of town and see you safely off." Owain led Goliath over and held him still until I had pulled myself up into the saddle. His eyes narrowed into baleful slits as he passed me the reins.

"What's happening?" a voice shrieked from the darkness. A moment later, the rotund figure of Alexander Ducworthe appeared in the doorway across the courtyard. "Have we been overrun? Are we abandoning the manor?"

I spurred my stallion across the cobblestones to the head of the column between Edward, Hamond, and James; all three men carried freshly lit torches in their reining hands. A half-dozen heads peered out from open shutters overhead.

"I will return shortly," I barked, drawing my sword. "It is best if you all remain secure in your rooms." Alexander hurried towards the gatehouse but stopped abruptly when he realized that no horses remained. The spider bared his teeth with unbridled disgust.

"Open the gates!" a voice shouted. An instant later, the heavy doors were pulled wide open, revealing a dark, stinking shape in the flickering torchlight.

"Hah," I bellowed to Goliath as I urged him across the bridge, splitting the creature's skull with a downward stroke. The cold wind stung my face as it whistled loudly through my sallet. Leonard whipped the reins of his team of horses, and the wagon lurched forward and quickly picked up speed as it crossed the manor green. Andrew and his archers kept a tight circle around the fortified transport with our families inside. Christopher and Nicholl guarded the rear of the formation.

The road ahead was quickly cleared; only three or four figures emerged from the shadows and approached the caravan. Turning onto Churchwell Lane, we made our way slowly towards Market Cross in the center of the village. The air was still pungent from smoke as we passed the handful of burned-out cottages. A thin streak of pale orange began to glow on the eastern horizon.

"Have they all departed?" Hamond wondered aloud.

"Quiet," I hissed. Although a thin streak of pale orange had appeared on the eastern horizon, the world was still blanketed in shades of dark gray. The torchlight from my men-at-arms did little more than light the path ahead.

The sound of snapping branches echoed from the right. Something large struggled to make its way through a hedgerow between two houses.

"On the right," I called, quickly turning Goliath towards the sound. Edward, Hamond, and James wheeled around to my left as Leonard instinctively halted the wagon and Andrew's men began to spread out defensively. Several muffled cries of terror reverberated from inside the wagon.

"Quiet!" Leonard hissed as he slapped the roof of the transport.

"I can't see a blasted thing," I complained, squinting my eyes at the darkness.

"Me neither," Edward said as he turned his horse and raised his torch. A moment later, a black shape lumbered past a mounted archer, veered around my own stallion, and then charged headlong at the esquire. Edward brought his torch into the top of the ghoul's head, sending a cascade of orange sparks flying through the air.

The monster tumbled downward and rolled underneath the protective caparison. Instinctively, his warhorse began to stomp and kick with its legs; the stallion's grunts were mixed with the crunch of breaking bones. I leapt from my saddle and delivered a killing blow as Edward spurred his mount forward.

"Now it seems they're more afraid of you, lord," Edward said with a chuckle as he circled back. He stuck out his torch to get a better view of his trampled attacker. The orange light reflected off the corpse's dull, white orbs. "Ugh, what a mess."

"Whoa!" Hamond bellowed as his horse suddenly startled and reeled to one side. An instant later, a second dark shape materialized from the other direction. It slashed with its claws at the rump of James's steed, causing the animal to groan and leap forward. Before I could react, Edward charged ahead and split its skull with a downward slash.

"They're focusing on the bright lights," I countered. "Lose the torches. The sun will be up soon anyway." The men tossed their firebrands to the ground while I hurriedly climbed atop Goliath. "Let's get moving."

As dawn approached, the hues of dusky gray softened into tones of orange and brown. The caravan rushed through the remainder of the village, moving as quickly as the wagon would allow. No more than a half-dozen of the shadowy figures challenged our armed formation in the roadway; the rest were quickly left behind, stumbling their way across the fields.

"Keep going," I ordered. "To the top of the next hill." A short time later, I signaled the caravan to halt and turned Goliath to face the men. The rising sun had painted long pink and purple lines across the beautiful morning sky, and Colleville was no more than a small, broken line in the distance. The creatures had been left far behind.

"This is where I leave you," I said, offering Edward an outstretched arm. He took it, and we locked forearms in a sign of mutual respect. "Take care of my family."

"Aye, lord, but we could still wait for you just over the next ridge. You could join us when you have—whenever you are ready." I slowly shook my head.

"And leave my daughters out here exposed? You know that's not an option I would ever consider. Besides, I have a responsibility to remain here. One day, when you have an estate of your own, you will understand."

"Do you want us to open the wagon so you can bid farewell to your daughters?"

You don't have the resolve to do it again, I warned myself.

"No," I replied, turning to James. "It's best if you men don't tarry here too long. Tell my girls that we'll all be together again before they know it." I clasped James by his forearm. "James, remember what I told you."

"Yessir," he responded with a nod.

"Hah!" I shouted at Goliath as I spurred him alongside the column and back down the road towards Colleville.

A dozen putrid monsters were already waiting on the stone bridge by the time I thundered across the manor green. They were raking their clawlike fingers down the wooden gates. It wasn't until I wrestled my stallion to a halt that I discovered what had lured them up to the front of the manor: scores of raised voices reverberated from inside the walls.

"Fie, you stinking vermin." I spurred to the base of the bridge before cutting sharp to the left. Five of the rearmost ghouls turned and began to pursue. Circling back around, I cut my way through their midst, alternately slashing down to the right and to the left.

Halting Goliath once again at the end of the bridge, I taunted the enemy. Three more turned their attention away from the angry shouts emanating from the courtyard and staggered forward. I tightened the reins to hold the courser in place; he angrily pawed his front legs at the air.

Now! I spurred my warhorse in one flank and jerked the reins, wheeling him in a tight spin that knocked two of the monsters to the ground and sent them tumbling into the moat. Circling Goliath back around, I lopped the head off the third.

"Who's still hungry?" The last four ignored my jeers and instead groped at the tiny window next to the gates. A sentry must have opened the porter's squint to look out and was too afraid to reach out and close it.

Best not end up in the moat, Richard. Sliding from the saddle, I snatched the reins and led Goliath down the bridge. It was too narrow to engage multiple opponents alone. I thrust a sword point through the back of the first one's skull. Its companions turned just in time to see the second one lose his head. I kicked the third back against the door a moment before the last one raked its bony fingers down my chest, rending the fabric of my coat and scraping down across the surface of the breastplate beneath. I cracked the devil's nose with a pommel strike before hooking its neck with the cross-guard and hurling the creature over the bridge railing.

"Easy boy," I said to Goliath, who was trying to rear his head. "Just one more." I once again kicked the final monster as it struggled to rise and pinned it to the base of the door with a maille-covered foot. With a quick thrust of the sword, I pierced its skull and ended its existence.

"Ballocks," I grumbled, looking down at the ruined coat. My anger was quickly diverted to the angry voices on the other side of the walls.

"Open the gates," I demanded. I pounded a gauntlet on the heavy doors. "Open the blasted gates." A moment later, the doors were pulled open by a red-faced Lewys.

"I'm glad you're back, lord," he gasped. "We've a riot on our hands." I handed him the reins and strode through the gatehouse. Edmund, Hal, and Doctor Symond were in the center of the courtyard surrounded by dozens of shouting villagers. Alexander was the first to recognize that the lord of the manor had returned. He instantly fell silent and took several steps backward. Soon, more and more caught a glimpse of my approach, and a hush quickly fell over the crowd.

Edmund turned to see what was happening. He practically shuddered with a sigh when our eyes met.

"What the devil is going on here, Master Edmund?" I demanded.

"I tried to assure them that you would be returning soon," the steward replied. "There were calls by some from Stony Heath to plunder the house and make an escape."

"By whom exactly?" Upon hearing my question, the fat spider retreated several more steps into the crowd. He was followed by Edmund's accusatory finger.

"The loudest voice came from their reeve, Alexander Ducworthe." The front ranks instantly melted away from their instigator.

"But, my lord," he stammered, waving his hands in front of him as if to fan away the charges. His gaze quickly fell to the sword still in my hand. "I never—it's only that—I mean, we thought you—"

"Silence, you paunching knave. I have had more than enough from you. Another word and I'll drag you up and throw you from the battlements myself." His face turned white as he clutched a hand to his mouth. I turned my head side to side, scanning the faces in the crowd. "As for the rest of you, I will tolerate no further dispute. If you are not content with my hospitality, you are more than welcome to depart."

"Sir Richard!" a voice called from above. Glancing up, I saw brother Phillip's head and arm sticking out of the upper window; he was beckoning with an outstretched hand. "Come quickly before it's too late!"

"Thomas," I blurted just before charging through the crowd. I barreled through a pair of villagers who were slow to move out of the doorway to the hall. I sprinted through the great hall and bounded up the stairs, where brother Phillip was waiting at the top. He could not meet my gaze; I knew my son had already died.

"How long?" I shouted as I elbowed the monk aside.

"A few moments ago," he cried. An instant later I barged through the door to find Anne crumpled on the floor beside Thomas's bed weeping loudly. There were several large bloodstains on his coverlets. Raulfe was standing a few feet behind her with a hand on his dagger.

"Richard," she sobbed. "Where have you been? Our son is gone." I rushed over to Thomas's bedside, waving Raulfe out of the room. Brother Phillip followed close behind.

"What should I do?" the monk asked.

"Get Anne out of here." I dropped the sword and flung my gauntlets to the floor before gently lifting her to her feet. She did not protest as brother Phillip escorted her out the door. I took a seat next to Thomas, and my chest began to shudder as I stroked his dark hair.

Your oath, man! I slowly drew my dagger, said a quick prayer, and then sent my son to the next life.

Lewys, Charles, and Morys helped me to pry up the stones next to the altar in the chapel floor. I insisted on doing most of the digging. The ground was hard and rocky, so it was past midday by the time Lewys helped me out of the hole.

"That's more than deep enough, lord," he said quietly.

A short time later, my son's body was carried down the steps in a wooden coffin. I never asked where they found the wood or who was responsible for constructing it. The ladies' maids had done their best to clean Thomas up, and Jacob had dressed him in a rich velvet robe along with his favorite riding boots. His sword was strapped to his side, and a wool cap had been pulled down low to cover his ears. I sent the varlet up to my room to fetch my golden spurs; they were the ones I had received the day I was knighted. With trembling hands, I buckled them on my son's feet.

The small chapel was filled with all of the household officials and servants, but I felt alone in my grief. Anne had swooned after brother Phillip had led her out of the room and was either unable or unwilling to rise from bed. I could not fault her; a part of me longed to be anywhere else but in that chamber.

Doctor Symond wore a golden stole over his priestly robes as he anointed Thomas's body and offered prayers for his immortal soul. I do not recall anything he said that day. His words faded into the background as my mind became consumed with the bittersweet memories of my son.

At the conclusion of the service, after the servants had been dismissed, Lewys and his grooms helped me fill the hole. It only took an hour to shovel in the dirt and replace the stones.

"Come on, lads," Lewys said in a low voice. "It's time we go now." He quietly ushered his grooms out of the chapel, leaving me standing alone at the foot of the altar. The despair was more than I could bear. My knees buckled and I collapsed onto the hard floor, where I wept more bitterly than I ever had in my life.

I cannot recall how long I lay there, sprawled across the cold stone, hearing only my ragged breaths. Eventually a hand knocked softly on the outer door, the sound reverberating through the still chapel. I managed to slowly drag myself to my feet before the iron latch was pulled back and the door gently pushed open.

A cold blast of air extinguished the candles atop the altar. Glancing back, I saw Edmund quietly slip inside and carefully close the door. He stood against the back wall, head reverently bowed, and waited patiently for me to acknowledge him; his brow was heavily creased with lines of concern.

"What is it, Master Edmund?" I sighed, crossing the floor to where the old steward waited.

"Forgive me, lord, for troubling you at this time," he began with his head still bowed, "but I felt that I should come and warn you about Master Alexander."

"What has he done now?" I said, shaking my head. Edmund drew in a long breath.

"Whether by fortune or not, he received the Twelfth Night cake with the bean in it and has been proclaimed Lord of Misrule. He is in the hall right now holding court."

"Is it Twelfth Night already?" I smiled, but there was no joy behind it. "I seem to have lost all track of time. The past few days have been a blur. It's a pity that it should be someone like him to rule over the feast, but it is important that we maintain our traditions. I trust that Master Hal has seen to all of the preparations?"

Each year, on the night before Epiphany, I would hold a giant feast in the hall, marking the end of the winter festival. As part of the ancient customs, small fruitcakes were served to everyone in attendance, one of which contained a dried bean baked inside. The man or woman fortunate enough to find it would preside over the feast.

"Oh, yes," Edmund replied grimly. "The wassail bowls are filled, and there has even been a makeshift tree set up in the center of the hall for everyone to toast. Your guests are singing and making themselves merry." His final word turned my stomach. I wanted only to be left alone in my grief.

"That is good news. There has been so much heartache and despair this past week. They need a diversion, a reason to laugh and sing." The steward's face reddened with anger.

"He made me kneel and do him homage. He did the same to all the other men of your household."

"The man is a weasel and does not know his place, that is for certain, but it would create a major disturbance if I were to remove him so early in the day. His reign will end at midnight. Come tomorrow, he will have to stand in judgment for his transgressions."

"That brings me to another matter, lord. After the blacksmith was found dead in his room, a number of the servants have sought me out in private to report that they greatly fear for their personal safety. Word has it that he had quarreled with Master Alexander only the day before." In all of the chaos, the murder had somehow slipped my mind.

"I had hoped that the dagger would have led us to the killer—and I still hope that it does—but it has so far been a dead end. I suspect Alexander Ducworthe knows much more than he has been willing to share. I will send Miles and Raulfe to fetch him first thing in the morning. In the meantime, invite the servants and their families to move into the private rooms where my retainers had previously been lodged. Maybe it will help placate the villagers some to have a few extra rooms made available to them. Now, if you'll excuse me, I want to look in on my wife." I turned and started towards the private stairs.

The fat little spider will soon be caught in his web.

"Wait," I called to Edmund as he reached for the outer door. "How many cakes were made?"

"There were more than enough for everyone. Perhaps a hundred or more."

"Where did they come up with that much flour and spices?"

"Master Charles and the lads spent all night grinding the corn that your men brought back from the barn yesterday. The dried fruit and spices came from the storeroom."

"How many of the lads from Stony Heath were assigned to help out in the kitchens?" Edmund's countenance grew more sour.

"Three," he growled.

"I trust you will soon uncover the source of the reeve's good fortune?"

"Aye, lord," the steward fumed as he turned on his heels and strode through the door. I took a moment to relight the candles upon the altar before climbing the stairs to my bedchamber.

"It seems the whole world has come undone, Anne," I spoke softly to my wife, but she did not respond. Her glassy eyes continued to stare blankly up at the bed canopy overhead.

"I think it's just after Vespers, but who's to say for certain? With no one to ring the bells at Saint Wystan's, my daily routine has been completely upended." I slid my chair a bit closer to the bed. Her skin had grown even more pale.

"We can't have you catching cold," I said as I gently pulled the fur-trimmed coverlets up to her chin. "I sent Sarah and Jacob down to enjoy themselves, so it's just the two of us for the moment. I know what you're thinking, but brother Phillip will be back soon. He went downstairs to fetch you a pottage. You know, that monk hasn't stopped doting after you."

Anne did not return my grin.

The door creaked a short while later as brother Phillip pushed it open with his backside. In his hands he carried a bowl and a narrow pitcher. He walked over and carefully placed them onto the small table next to the bed.

"And her cup?" I asked.

"I wouldn't forget," he smirked as he produced a clay drinking cup from under his arm.

"Thank you, brother Phillip. I trust you did not encounter any problems?"

"None at all. Your kitchen steward was most helpful." He hesitated for a moment. "May I make a request?"

"Anything," I spoke over my shoulder as I stirred the pottage to help it cool.

As you know, tomorrow is the feast of the Baptism of the Lord. Brother Philemon and I would like to utilize your chapel to celebrate mass."

"Doctor Symond will see that you have everything you need."

"With your permission, I will see myself out."

"Thank you again, brother Phillip." The monk stepped out into the hall and pulled the door closed behind him. I gently slid an arm under my wife's shoulders and tucked an extra pillow behind her head, but she only continued to stare blankly ahead.

"Come on, Anne, you need to eat something so that you can recover your strength. Your daughters need you." I dipped a spoon in the bowl and blew on it. "I need you."

Slowly, my wife turned her head and managed a weak smile.

"I just feel so weak, Richard," she replied before taking a bite.

"You heard what brother Phillip said. That's why you need to eat your supper and get as much rest as you can."

"Why didn't you go downstairs? You always loved Twelfth Night." I shook my head and placed the spoon to her lips.

"No, I would like it better if it was just the household celebrating. Edmund is at his wits' end. That coxcomb Ducworthe is ruling over the feast. I think I'd prefer to remain up here with you." She smiled as I offered her the last spoonful.

"Is it really that bad?"

"It's certainly not like last year when Sarah was the Lady of Misrule. She was every bit the gracious hostess. Come to think of it, you turned out to be a good lady's maid, waiting on her every need. Now, let's get you tucked in so you can get some rest."

I lay in bed for a long time watching only the rise and fall of Anne's chest as she slumbered peacefully, but the raucous shouts of men and women echoing faintly up the stairs kept me from finding any rest.

"I think I'll take a walk," I whispered to my wife before gently rising from bed. Pulling on a long coat, I slipped down the stairs to the chapel and into the courtyard. A man stumbled out of the hall and down the steps before turning aside and nearly collapsing against the wall. He let out a long moan as a puddle grew beneath his feet.

Drunken knave!

I thought to shove him into his mess but did not. Instead, I entered the open door and climbed the stairs in back of the screens passage. As I had expected, the minstrel's gallery was empty.

A large tree stood between the hearth and the head table. It had been hastily constructed from all manner of wooden scraps that could be found around the manor. A circle of men and women stood round about it singing and drinking.

"Wassail! Wassail! All over our town," they cheered. "With the wassailing bowl, we'll drink to thee." The ring of people lifted their mugs to the makeshift tree before singing another chorus.

In years past, folk sought out the oldest tree in the village and honored it with a toast. It was believed that, by scaring off the evil spirits, the tree would provide a good harvest in the next season. If they cared that the object of their adoration would never yield a single piece of fruit, it was not evident.

"Paunching canker blossom," I mumbled as I looked across to the fat lord who was sitting in my chair at the high table. His words were lost in the revelry, but his arms never ceased waving over the lads bearing trays of food and pitchers of drink. "He won't be satisfied until he's eaten every crumb in our stores."

The hall began to dim as all of the lights were extinguished one by one, leaving only a faint glow coming from the embers of the hearth fire. A small, flickering candle suddenly emerged from the screens passage and was thrust high into the air before going out. A boisterous round of laughter drowned out the curses muttered by the candle bearer.

After a brief, awkward moment, the small light was rekindled and lifted up by a long pole. Three young boys with towels wrapped around their heads slowly entered the hall behind the candle. Each had black paint smeared across his face for a beard and a bore wooden sword at his side.

"Look, a star," one boy said.

"It's a sign," another one added.

"We should follow it," the third advised.

The procession slowly made its way around the dim hall, eliciting more giggles and cheers. Eventually, the starlike candle came to rest at the foot of the dais.

"I am Herod the Great, and I order you to kill all the male children in the land," a large man shouted as he lumbered down the steps from beside the high table. He was wrapped in a linen sheet.

"No!" the three lads bellowed as they charged their adversary. The hall roared with laughter as the evil king flitted around the room, dodging the boys' sword thrusts.

"I am undone," Herod finally gasped as he clutched a wooden stave under his arm and collapsed onto the floor. The dying king's legs twitched in the air several times before flopping to the ground. The three young magi then danced a joyous circle around his corpse.

The room once again cheered as the once-dead man stood up and, along with his three assailants, bowed to the audience.

"Again!" someone shouted.

"More! More!" another hollered.

"Fools," I seethed under my breath. I could bear their happiness no longer. Turning, I made my way back to the courtyard and up to my bed.

Part Four:
Death

6 January

Feast of the Epiphany

IR RICHARD! SIR RICHARD!" A muffled voice called from the chapel stairwell as a fist pounded on the door. "There isn't much time. You really must hurry."

I sat up in bed and rubbed the sleep from my eyes. A thin shaft of light filtered into the room from between the curtains.

"Is everything all right?" Anne mumbled.

"Will you see him in, Jacob, before he wakes the entire house?" The varlet quickly crawled out from under his blanket and padded across the floor. He had barely pulled back the latch before brother Philemon clamored through the door. Doctor Symond was only a step or two behind him.

"What is it, man?"

"It's Alexander," the subprior stammered breathlessly. "He's saddling your horse, and he's planning on leading a group to safety."

"Don't just stand there, lad. Fetch me my sword." I hastily pulled on a pair of hose under my nightshirt and slid on my boots as Jacob scrambled to retrieve my sword. I threw on my robe as the varlet ran over with my blade. "Wake Master Edmund and the others. Tell them to meet me downstairs." I slapped a hand on Jacob's shoulder as I slipped between the monk and chaplain and hurried through the door and down the stairs.

A tall man was wrestling with Goliath near the gatehouse. He was not one of the grooms, and yet he had managed to saddle the warhorse. His eyes were wide with anxiety as the stallion tossed his head and angrily stamped the ground. He held a longbow in his off-hand.

The dusky morning air was filled with the sound of raised voices.

"Get back!" Raulfe shouted. He was standing defiantly with arms raised in the center of the inner gates, his young face reddened with anger.

"Step aside, boy," Alexander Ducworthe demanded, jabbing a meaty finger into the sentry's chest. Two thin farmers stood to either side of their reeve.

"Or we'll have to go through you," the man on the left spat. Both of the farmers were armed with short wooden clubs that they held low, concealed behind their legs.

"But no one is to be hurt," Sir Denis protested. He had a large wool blanket slung over one shoulder, his spindly frame bent under the weight of the contents stuffed inside it. "You promised we'd only take what we must in order to reach Gloucester and bring back help."

"Shut your mouth, priest," the other man growled as he glanced back. "And that goes for the rest of you." Perhaps two dozen women similarly encumbered were clustered a few feet behind the reeve and his two cronies. A couple of old men and a handful of sleepy-eyed children were mixed among their ranks.

"No one is leaving here," I shouted as I started across the cobblestones. "Did you hear me? I said no one is to open those gates." Raulfe met my gaze and sighed with relief. A moment later he was struck across the temple with a heavy club. Several women began shrieking as his legs buckled and he crumpled to the floor.

"Stop him," Alexander hollered, frantically gesturing in my direction, "unless you want to rot here alongside him."

"I'll skewer the lot of you!" I bellowed as I started to sprint towards them. Many in the crowd turned their heads right and left trying to decide where to flee.

"No!" Sir Denis cried as he started in my direction. He only made it a few steps before falling to his knees. "I swear I didn't know." He folded his hands tightly together as though he were begging for his life.

"I'll deal with you later," I growled at the priest as I rushed past him.

"But someone has to go for help," he whined.

As I neared the gatehouse, the villein archer wrangled Goliath within a few feet of the reeve and shoved the reins into the chest of the closest farmer. With his free hand he deftly pulled a crude arrow from his belt and nocked it on his bowstring.

I shouldered through the scattered ring of women and children as he drew back the string in a single, fluid motion.

Saints preserve me, I prayed inwardly as the arrow's black fletchings reached his ear and the missile was leveled straight at my head. I was close enough to recognize that its point lacked a steel bodkin but too far away to have any hope of reaching the assassin in time.

Staring directly at the knife-sharpened tip, I hauled my sword back and roared a final challenge. The archer's fingers relaxed and let the string spring forward, sending the deadly shaft hurtling towards me.

I slashed forward with all of my might. An instant later, a searing pain tore into my left shoulder like the horn of a charging bull. My momentum carried me forward as my blade cut down into the face of my killer, cleaving down through his cheek and jaw and neck.

Fie! There was a loud crack as I crashed into the archer, and his bow snapped between our bodies. The once-shadowy courtyard was suddenly bathed in a bright white glow that quickly faded into pitch blackness as I tumbled headfirst across the cobblestones.

"He's dead," a voice echoed in the distance. Pain surged through every fiber of my body.

"No turning back now," another interjected. "There's only a few of them out on the green, and they're moving slow. We can make it if we go now."

I willed my eyes to open. The inky blackness softened into hues of purple and orange. The world had been turned on its side.

"Murder! Bloody murder!" an old man shouted from somewhere behind. Several more cries were added to the alarm.

"Stop," I coughed, straining to lift my head. "Don't you dare open those gates." My shoulder throbbed as I pushed myself up onto my hands and knees. A bright red stain was quickly spreading across my white shirt.

"Don't just stand there, you idiots," a fat man squawked as he stood next to a large horse. "Help me up." Two other men soon appeared on either side and helped him crawl into the saddle. One handed the rider a short sword.

"Now, men, open the gates." The two men, followed by a score of women and children, rushed past the rider towards the gatehouse. They stepped over the body of Raulfe, who was still slumped on the ground, a small pool of blood collecting underneath his head. With a loud click and heavy thump, the outer doors were pulled open and the throng rushed out of the manor.

"Sir Richard," a familiar voice called. I stood and turned to face its source. Jacob ran up and threw an arm around my waist. Edmund and Hugh emerged from the hall a moment later, followed by a score of men and boys.

"Hah!" Alexander shouted at the warhorse as he kicked his heels into its sides. Goliath turned sharply to one side, throwing the fat reeve off balance. Every time the rider shifted his weight, the stallion would whirl in the opposite direction.

Suddenly, a series of terrified screams echoed from outside the walls. The reeve snapped his head around to look through the gates.

"Go, you stupid ox," he stammered. Looking back, his face was stark white. "Go!" he shrieked as he slapped Goliath on the haunches with the flat of the blade. The warhorse lurched forward and spun, toppling its rider to the ground.

"Shut the gates, Jacob," I ordered as I stooped down to pick up my sword. I then staggered my way to the inner gates.

"Have mercy," Alexander whimpered as he squirmed around on the ground. He smiled momentarily as I began to slowly back away from him. His joy quickly faded when the young varlet rushed past him, sprinting back into the courtyard.

"No," he mewed an instant before sharp claws tore into his neck. Alexander continued to squeal in pain as we backed away from the gatehouse.

"Get back inside the hall!" I shouted as a blood-soaked woman streaked into the courtyard. Three pale-skinned ghouls lumbered through the gates after her; fresh blood glistened across their cheeks. "I'll hold them off."

"Lord," Hugh exclaimed as I stumbled and fell to one knee, sending my sword clattering across the cobblestones. Before I could protest, Lewys and Edmund pulled me up and dragged me through the chapel door, and Jacob slammed it shut.

"Jacob, bar the lower door," Edmund barked. "No one gets in or out. Lewys, go find the surgeon, if he's still alive." The steward's face was red and covered in sweat. The light in the room grew steadily fainter and the voices more hollow.

"Richard," Anne sobbed. "Richard, stay with me." She was looking down over me, tears streaming from her eyes.

"Lady Anne, I need you to help me keep the bandages pressed tight around the base of the shaft."

"I—I don't know—" she stammered.

"If you want your husband to live, you must bear yourself up." The steward was calm as he spoke.

"He's coming," Lewys shouted as he rushed back into the room.

"Good," Edmund said flatly. "Now get that fire going. We're going to have to cauterize the wound. There's not much time."

Muffled screams echoed up the stairs and through the chamber door as dark shadows finally enveloped the room.

"Lady Anne," Edmund said hoarsely. "He's starting to come to." My wife blotted a wet cloth on my brow as I opened my eyes. She once again glowed with life. The color had returned to her lips and cheeks; there were only faint traces of the former dark lines that had encircled her weary eyes.

"Richard?" she whispered. "I'm so thankful you're alive. You've been unconscious for several hours. I feared I would lose you." My shoulder throbbed with more pain that I had ever known.

"It takes more than a bloody arrow to kill me," I smiled as I tried to sit up. Fire radiated from my shoulder, surging through my veins and forcing me to collapse onto the pillow. The edges of the room darkened momentarily from the strain.

"Lie still, Sir Richard," brother Phillip admonished. "You'll tear open your wound. Do you remember when you asked me how much blood a man can lose and still live? Well, you proved me wrong." The monk smiled weakly.

"If you're all going to coddle me like a babe, at least you could give me an extra pillow so I can see everyone properly." Edmund and Lewys gently raised my head while brother Phillip propped me up. Apart from the rays of the sun filtering through the open window, there were no other sources of light in the room.

"Why is it so dark in here?"

"Sorry, lord," Jacob replied, "but Master Edmund thought it best we begin to conserve our resources. It could be a while before help arrives."

"No!" a muffled cry screeched from somewhere downstairs. Moments later, a woman began to sob loudly out in the hallway.

"I'm sure Charles is fine," a second woman reassured her. "You'll see. In fact, I'll wager he's locked himself in a storeroom and is eating all the little cakes leftover from last night."

"Mum, I want a cake," a young boy whined. "I'm hungry."

"Shush," came a quick response. "We're all hungry, Powlis. You'll just have to be patient."

"Are there still some of the devils inside the walls?" I demanded, turning my attention to the men gathered around my bedside. No one had the courage to answer. I searched their faces.

Anne continued to blot my forehead. Doctor Symond bit his lip while brothers Phillip and Philemon dropped their eyes to the floor. Edmund, Lewys, and Hal looked back and forth at one another, none wishing to utter the painful truth.

"Some of the creatures made it into the chapel right after we carried you in," Edmund finally divulged. "From the sound of it, they managed to get inside the great hall as well. We barred the door downstairs and barricaded the one to the chapel." The steward motioned towards the door in the corner that led down to the chapel. The shaft of a pollaxe had been wedged through its pull ring to prevent it from being opened from the other side.

"What about the others?" I asked.

"Apart from those of us in here, there's no way to know who is still alive. Masters Charles and Morys were down in the kitchens."

"Where I should have been," Hal grumbled.

"And you'd likely be dead," the steward frowned. "Miles is downstairs guarding the door to the great hall. Sarah and

Mistress Clere are out in the hallway trying to comfort Mary, who is still very upset." Jacob stiffened his spine at the mention of his mother. "And my wife, Martha, is in the upper hall with everyone else."

I have to get all these people out, I told myself. *Even if it kills me.*

"Brother Phillip," I said, looking to the monk and his subprior, "would you see my wife to the solar?" Anne's brow furrowed with a mix of fear and anger. She opened her mouth to protest, but I shook my head firmly. "Please, Anne. I don't have time to argue."

"Lady Anne?" brother Phillip pleaded as he touched a hand to her elbow. My wife stood and shrugged off the monk's touch before solemnly walking out of the room. The two monks followed closely behind her.

"Jacob, help me into my armor." I eased my legs off the side of the bed and slowly stood.

"But, lord, you need time to recover."

"The boy's right, Sir Richard," Doctor Symond interjected. "It's only by God's grace that you aren't dead already." I limped across the room to the chest where my armor was stored before turning and addressing the remaining men.

"Do you hear that?" I pointed at the door to the chapel. A faint scratching noise was coming from the other side of it. "You all know that help is not coming, don't you? At least not in time to do anything more than bury our rotting corpses. We have had nothing to eat or drink since yesterday. Every hour we sit here recovering our strength, we in truth only get weaker. We have no choice but to fight our way clear of this place. If we stay here, we will all surely die."

The men all nodded grimly. Jacob hurried over to my side and opened the decorative chest. Beginning with the feet, he worked his way up my legs, encasing them in hardened steel. My mind wandered to the desperate fight that lay ahead.

"I suppose my blasted sword is still down in the courtyard? What weapons do we have left?"

"All of the serviceable weapons were handed out to the men," Edmund replied. "The only thing they left behind were their pollaxes. Although yours is stuck in the door, there should be four others that we can use. Miles has his sword and longbow, though he has no arrows left. That's it unless you count knives and daggers."

"What about the hunting weapons?" Lewys inquired. "There should still be several spears and a couple of swords and crossbows."

"Go see what you can find, Master Lewys."

"Care to lend a hand?" the marshal asked Hal as he turned and started for the door. When the chamberlain failed to immediately respond, Lewys grabbed Hal by the sleeve and gently led him out of the room.

"My lord, are you ready for the cuirass?" Jacob asked quietly. With a nod I sucked in a deep breath and gritted my teeth as Jacob strapped the breastplate in place. Intense pain seared my shoulder like a dozen firebrands while beads of cold sweat began to run down my forehead.

Who do you think you're fooling? a voice whispered in my head. *You're already panting like a dog, and you haven't even gotten your armor on. You'll be lucky to even make it down the stairs.*

"You have to," I muttered aloud.

"Sorry, lord?" Jacob replied with an upward glance while continuing to buckle the straps along my right hip. "Did you say something?"

"I said you have to hurry." The lad nodded and quickly stood. He turned and picked up the armor for my left arm. Without thinking, I raised a bent arm to allow him to slide the articulated plates into place. My knees almost buckled from the agony.

"What are you all standing around here for?" I said breathlessly, looking towards the steward and two monks. "We are wasting daylight. Master Edmund, begin assembling everyone down in the solar."

The men quickly filed out of the room. Jacob did his best to support my arm while he encased it in protective steel. The additional weight pulling on my shoulder was almost unbearable.

"One more thing, lad," I grunted as soon as he had finished buckling the bevor around my neck. "I need you to find a belt to make me a sling."

A pale, spiderlike ghoul ambled around the gatehouse hungrily sniffing the air. Its white eyes almost glowed with malevolence in the light of the setting sun. The devil stepped past a discarded sword—*my* sword—without so much as a downward glance. A score of other devils were lurking around the courtyard.

Craning my head further out the solar window, I could see that the cobblestones in front of the hall were stained dark with dried blood and clumps of matted hair. The kennel doors were wide open.

The buggers killed all my hounds, I groaned inwardly. "The doors to the hall appear to be securely shut. There are no fewer than two dozen of the creatures down in the courtyard. Even if we fought our way through the chapel, we would be immediately surrounded and killed if we tried for the main gate. Our best chance is to make for the back door."

I stepped back from the window and crossed to the small pile of weapons left unclaimed in the center of the room. Lewys and Hal had returned a short while earlier, each carrying an armload of axes and spears and swords.

"That means going through the great hall, lord," Lewys frowned. "There's nowhere to hide and no way of knowing how many of the devils may have gotten inside." I ignored his complaint. There was no alternative.

"The axes will be most effective," I continued, hefting my own pollaxe into the air. It would have been impossible to wield with only one hand, but Lewys had shortened the shaft making it a bit less cumbersome. "They should go to the men best able to wield them." Lewys, Edmund, and Hal stepped forward, and each selected a pollaxe from the pile.

"Jacob, I need you to carry our light. Stay right behind me and Miles. Take my hunting sword for protection." The varlet left his mother's side to scoop up the long, thin hunting sword and buckle it around his waist. The tip of its scabbard scraped across the floor as he then hustled over to the writing table and grabbed the brass lantern.

"The rest of you choose a weapon that you are able to carry." James Sorel grabbed a throwing spear. Jacob's younger brother, Luke, stepped around his mother and also selected a short javelin. Clere watched her son make a few practice thrusts with his spear, but she did not move from her place. Many of the older ladies were similarly reluctant to move and instead only exchanged looks of uncertainty. My wife, too, sensed their hesitation.

"Come along, Sarah," Anne said as she delicately took her maid by the elbow and led her over to the pile. "We must do our part." Together they picked up a pair of short swords normally carried by huntsmen. One by one the other wives slowly walked up and selected their weapons. Mary Barry and Margaret Massy had tears in their eyes; Martha Bromeley's hands trembled as though she were palsied; and Clere did so with her youngest son clutching the folds of her dress. Only the two monks lingered in the corner.

"No doubt some of you must be thinking that you cannot or will not fight," I stated calmly. "A few days ago, my son, God rest his soul, reminded me of the three estates: those who fight, those who pray, and those who work." I paused long enough to look into each pair of eyes. It was disheartening to realize that so few remained alive from a once-thriving manor.

"Well, that world is dead now. Dead and buried. There is no one left to fight your battles for you. Scared or not, we all must fight together, for if we do not, then we will all surely die."

"Sir Richard," brother Philemon said humbly, taking a step forward, "with respect, we are not cowards. Please understand that our holy vows prevent us from shedding man's blood. No matter how dire the situation in which we find ourselves, we cannot use your implements of war to take a life."

I hate you. But I respect you.

"Those things down there are no longer men. Neither are they still alive. Are you really going to jeopardize the lives of everyone here for the sake of your own conscience?"

"Just as Daniel trusted in God to keep him safe in the lions' den, we, too, must place our faith in the Almighty to deliver us from certain death."

"I wish I had your faith, but I must deal with the lions in my own way," I growled as I feigned a chop with the pollaxe. Turning my back on the monks, I addressed the others:

"The time has come for us to make our escape. Lewys, you and Edmund will follow behind Jacob." The steward was outfitted with my brigandine, and the marshal wore my spare hauberk for protection. I had first offered them to my wife, but she had refused, saying that she could not take more than a dozen steps under such weight.

"Anne, darling, I want you to stay right behind Lewys and Edmund. Sarah, keep a close watch over my wife." The maid nodded, looking down at the huntsman's cleaver in her hand.

The other women positioned themselves behind Sarah. Martha, large and red-faced like her husband, carried a boar spear like it were a distaff. Mary hefted a horseman's mace into the air with both hands and rested it on her shoulder. Margaret cradled my hunting crossbow in her arms.

"Are you sure you can span it?" I inquired. Margaret wedged both feet into its stirrup and, with a cry that was a mixture of squeal and grunt, she slowly hauled back the string until it locked in place. Margaret reached into the quiver on her belt and plucked out a quarrel.

"Nicely done," I said with a laugh that was shared by the other men. Lewys waved her off.

"Best not load it just yet, dear," Lewys said as he hurried over and pointed at the underside of the crossbow. "If you bump that lever, it might stick a quarrel in something tender like my backside."

Clere Stoney had Thomas's crossbow. She passed the quiver to her youngest son, Powlis, before trying several times to pull back its string. Her thin frame did not possess the strength to do it.

"I can't," she cried, tears running down her cheeks. Lewys took the crossbow from her and easily spanned it.

"Here you are," he said softly as he handed it back. "Mind the lever. It's rather touchy. If you have a reason to let loose a quarrel, just hand it back to Hal. He'll help you respan it."

"It would be wise for you to take another weapon along," I advised her. "If we get in a press, there might not be anyone able to lend a hand." Clere looked down at the few remaining weapons. Apart from a couple of heavy boar spears she could not hope to effectively wield, there was a warhammer, a shortened lance, and a pair of wooden clubs from my tourneying days. After chewing her lip for several moments, Clere stooped down and fished out one of the clubs.

"Very good," I said to her with a smile. I let it wane before turning to the monks. "Brothers, you can arm yourselves with torches and fall in behind the women. They will do their part to keep you safe." I suddenly realized there were only two clergymen instead of three. "Wait, where is Doctor Symond?"

"He said he had to go back upstairs to get something," brother Philemon reported.

"What the devil is so important?"

"He didn't say." I was still angry with the subprior.

"Very well, brother Philemon, you can go find him. I would highly encourage you to make it swift unless you truly want to test how far you can make it through the hall alone and unarmed."

"What about us?" James inquired. He and Luke stood shoulder to shoulder near the doorway. Both were armed with throwing spears.

"You lads have a very important job. I need you to stick close to Hal and protect our backs. Everyone will be counting on you to keep them safe."

"Yessir," the boys said in unison.

"Jacob, bring me my sallet."

The clatter of armor echoed noisily ahead of the column as it cautiously descended one step at a time. Soft golden light flickered from the lantern, casting long shadows down either side of the stairwell.

"Keep that lantern raised as high as you can," I instructed the varlet in a low voice. From behind came the faint sobs and whimpers of women and boys. "Everyone needs to keep quiet."

A stout wooden door waited at the bottom. Despite Miles's assurances to the contrary, I had half-expected to find it ajar. Sheathing his sword, the archer took a final moment to readjust his maille shirt and check the tightness of his chinstrap. Satisfied, he quietly lifted the bar from its socket and set it to one side. Miles then placed his buckler hand against the door and reached for the latch with the other. Just as I prepared to give him the signal to open the door, the rapid peal of sandaled feet thundered down the stairwell.

Doctor Symond appeared in the torchlight, red-faced and out of breath. He had a large satchel slung around his neck. Brother Philemon was no more than a step behind him.

"Silence!" I chided them in a raised whisper. Turning back, I gave Miles an exaggerated nod. With a loud click, he pulled the latch and the door slowly creaked open. The cavernous room beyond the doorway devoured the flickering light of Jacob's lantern; only the edges of the high table could be discerned.

I can't see a bloody thing, I complained inwardly. *If only we had not wasted the last few hours of daylight.*

"Hold," I whispered to Miles. Apart from the short, labored breaths resonating inside my helmet and the scraping of shoes on the stone steps echoing from behind, the great hall was quiet. I cautiously stepped through the doorway and motioned to the right with my axe. Miles remained close to my side as we slowly shuffled along the back side of the high table.

Jacob passed through the door and slowly made an arc across the room with his lantern. Several sets of eyes twinkled in the light.

"Lord!" the varlet gasped. The glowing orbs suddenly streaked into the light, clambering up the dais to reach the high table, their guttural moans filling the hall like the drone of a beehive.

"Fall back," I ordered, taking a backwards step. An instant later, a stocky she-devil lunged from atop the table with clawlike fingers slashing through the air. I cut her down with a wide arc that sent her corpse crashing onto my feet. Three others leapt atop the table as Miles and I backed closer to the door. Jacob's lantern clanged against my backplate, momentarily eclipsing the room with darkness.

"Light!" I shouted. "We need that light!" The varlet lifted the lantern high over my shoulder just as two other grotesque women charged. Miles punched the first in the mouth with his buckler before hacking down into its neck with his sword. I stabbed the second in the face with the top fluke of my axe before we both took another step backwards.

"Ugh!" I groaned as something wrenched my leg. Looking down, a ghoulish boy had crawled under the table and was violently grating his teeth against my armored calf. I kicked him free and quickly chopped through the back of his skull.

"Get back, woman," Lewys barked from behind. "Back up the stairs." A heartbeat later, the lantern grew a bit more faint.

"Hurry up," I ordered Miles. "Get into the stairwell." A ghastly farmer and a blood-soaked shepherdess rushed towards us. A searing pain ripped through my shoulder as the archer and I collided into one another, desperately trying to wedge ourselves through the door at the same time.

"We'll use the doorway to our advantage," I grunted as I thrust a spike into the farmers forehead. The monster dropped to its knees and flopped against the wall. Miles cleaved the skull of the other creature while I jerked my axe free, readying myself for the next attacker.

The droning grew louder.

Three more devils rushed into the light. Their corpses were gnawed upon and covered in dark blood. They converged on the doorway and fought each other hungrily to be the first through the portal. We hacked them apart.

"You're hurt, Sir Richard," Jacob called from behind.

"I know." A ravenous orphan bounded over the pile of corpses only to have its head removed by a savage chop to the neck. My heart was beginning to race, and it became harder to catch a breath.

"You're bleeding," the varlet warned.

"I know." Two more monsters surged through the door and over the growing mound of bodies. Miles backhanded the first with his buckler and hacked through its knee, causing it to flop to the ground. I sunk an axe head into the second as the archer plunged his blade into the skull of his assailant. "It's too constricted in here. Help me out of my bevor."

The varlet unbuckled the strap at the back of my neck and the protective plate fell to the ground at my feet. Looking down, something was still moving underneath the pile.

"Heads up," Miles called as several more of the devils poured through the door. We had no choice but to slowly back our way up the stairs, hacking and slashing as we moved. Their mangled bodies littered the narrow passage.

Suddenly I was on my back.

"Richard!" my wife screamed. Looking down, I saw the face of a snarling ghoul; it had me by one leg, its claws scraping against the steel surface of my armor. Lewys quickly stepped over me and pierced its skull with the fluke of his pollaxe while Miles cracked the skull of another.

A pair of hands slipped under my arms and dragged me noisily up the stairs. Edmund and Jacob pulled me to my feet. The world began to swirl as darkness closed in around me. A moment later my legs gave out and I fell to my knees.

"Richard?" Anne cried out in alarm.

"I'm fine. I just got up too quickly."

"We should see to your wound," Edmund cautioned. There was a small stream of red running down my breastplate from my left shoulder. From the amount of pain I was suffering, I had imagined a river of blood to be pouring out.

"It'll waste too much time," I groaned. "I'll be all right. You can pamper me all you want when we are good and far away from the manor."

"Very well, my lord, but Lewys and I will take the lead for a while." His tone was fatherly. Even if I had possessed the strength, I doubt I would have argued with him.

Miles, Lewys, and Edmund carefully made their way over the pile of mutilated bodies. Jacob and I followed close behind. More than once I nearly lost my footing; only the narrowness of the passage saved me from further embarrassment.

We paused several steps beyond the doorway. Again an an eerie silence had fallen over the great hall. Our column slowly made its way around the high table and off the dais. Once the monks entered the chamber with their blazing torches, the walls around us were bathed in a soft orange glow.

"Keep moving," I said in a loud whisper. Miles raised his buckler and sword and slowly made his way along the wall. Lewys and Edmund followed a step or two behind. Jacob kept his lantern high above his head, scanning back and forth for any sign of danger. Behind us, Anne and Sarah were huddled close together. Their eyes were wide with terror.

A blood-curdling scream pierced the still air from somewhere beyond the screens passage. A series of panicked shrieks erupted an instant later from the rear of our column. I threw my head around to see what was going on. Two of the women had clasped their hands over their mouths in an effort to silence their uncontrollable cries.

"More're coming," a voice bellowed from the front. As I turned, several shadows streaked through the screens and into the hall. There was nowhere to flee to. A long row of trestle tables stood between our column and the exit; the outer wall was to our backs.

"Use the tables," I ordered. We all rushed forward and began flipping the tabletops over to form a low, angled wall.

Hal immediately began pushing the women down into the protective space it created. The rest of the men instinctively retracted to form a human shield.

A pack of the hungry monsters rounded the edge of the makeshift wall and careened into the shadowy figures of Miles and Lewys. Blades glinted in the faint light, but it was impossible to perceive who had the upper hand. Edmund hurried over to help hold the line.

Suddenly, a woman screamed from behind. Turning, I saw a pair of claws hauling the gaunt face of a monk over the tabletop. Margaret let loose a quarrel that lodged deep into the rim of the table, and, for a moment, the black-robed creature struggled to move. Mary swung her mace in a wide arc, taking the monster across the side of its face.

Undaunted, the devil continued to crawl over the low wall, dark blood streaming from its shattered cheek. Mary squealed and let her weapon fall to the floor. The rest of the women began to shriek and wail.

"Keep your heads down," I bellowed, sliding past Anne and Sarah to split the creature's forehead open with an axe. Two more ghastly faces suddenly appeared to either side of the dead monk. Wresting the pollaxe free, I heaved it back and prepared to deliver a lethal blow to the plump devil on the right.

"No!" Mary cried, throwing her hands into the air and moving. "It's my Charles."

"Get out of the way, woman," I shouted, taking a step forward. Mary's eyes flared wide as they focused on the pollaxe poised high overhead. Despite the pain, I quickly wriggled my left arm free and grabbed Mary by her sleeve to pull her aside.

"Argh!" she howled as a ghoulish hand suddenly seized her by the hair, savagely jerking her out of my grasp and back against the table. Darting forward, I plunged the axe into Charles's meaty arm, the crack of splintered bones reverberating through the hall, but the gray-skinned hand refused to release its victim.

"It's me, Charles," Mary whimpered, weakly tugging at her husband's hand. "You're hurting me." An instant later, a second set of talons stretched forward and shredded the side of her throat. Mary sputtered loudly as she writhed and kicked against the table.

The slender corpse of a kitchen boy scampered over the wall and flopped headfirst to the floor between Mary and Clere. The widow could only stare, mouth agape, as the gruesome imp quickly crawled to its feet.

"Saints preserve me," gasped Phillip as he thrust a torch into the lad's blood-spattered face. In a wordless rage, the devil-child slashed at the firebrand, knocking it out of the monk's hand and across the floor. The darkness crept ever closer.

I thrust a spike into the kitchen boy's smoldering face; his body immediately collapsed to the ground at Clere's feet. She recoiled, shrieking, and toppled over her youngest son, who had been cowering behind her. With a groan, the widow landed hard against the stone.

An instant later, Doctor Symond yelped with pain as he clutched his thigh and dropped to his seat. A crossbow bolt was embedded so deep into his leg that only the leather vanes were visible.

"I'm sorry. I'm sorry," Clere stammered.

Anne screamed from behind. I turned to see Jacob thrust a sword point through the face of a ghastly woman mere feet from where Anne stood. Two other monsters were clambering over the makeshift wall.

I lunged forward and cut down the nearest one, but the other leapt atop Sarah and began mauling her like a wildcat. With a spike through its head, I ended its miserable existence.

"Are you all right, Anne?" My wife was as pale as a ghost, her eyes twitching with fear. She dropped her sword and clamped her hands over her gaping mouth.

"I said are you all right?!" Anne blinked and then nodded.

A hand suddenly reached for my wife. Jacob sliced through it, the blade cleaving down into the creature's knee. The witch wobbled briefly and then fell to the ground. Martha stepped forward and impaled the creature with a heavy spear to its chest.

"It can't be," Martha stammered as the monster clutched the shaft and tried to pull itself up.

"The head," I warned her. "You have to stab it in the head to kill it." A moment later, Jacob thrust his sword through its eye.

"Fire!" a voice rasped from the left. Hal was defensively slashing side to side in front of two approaching devils, backing away step by step. Several other corpses were strewn about his feet. To his side, a young lad frantically jabbed his spearpoint several times at the air in front of him.

The room began to brighten as an orange glow slowly filled the room. To my left, fire quickly surged up the large tapestry hung along the side wall.

Soon it will reach the timber beams and bring the entire roof down upon our heads.

A loud crash caused me to whirl back around. One of the tables had collapsed under the weight of several monsters, creating a wide breach in the makeshift wall.

The two monks struggled to help Doctor Symond to his feet; a long wide stain covered the front of the chaplain's robe. As the devils struggled to stand, Clere crouched low to the ground and closed her eyes, clutching her son's head tightly to her chest. Margaret heaved back the string of her crossbow before fumbling to load a quarrel.

"Forget it," I said as I approached her. She quickly raised the bow and let loose the steel-tipped bolt; it cut a long gash down the cheek of the first corpse that had risen. "Go with Anne. Make for the kitchens."

I kicked the wounded devil backwards before hacking down at another still climbing to its feet. In the growing light, several more of the monsters stood and rushed towards the gap in the wall.

"Hurry up," I called to Hal and the others with a wave of the axe. "Else we all die here." With the aid of the two monks, Doctor Symond stumbled forward as fast as he was able.

"Right behind you, lord," the chamberlain said as he hacked down another devil and then turned to run. "Come on, boy," he growled at James Sorel as he shoved the lad forward using the shaft of his pollaxe. Clere and her son remained huddled together on the ground.

"By the virgin," I seethed. Grabbing the boy by the collar, I dragged him to his feet and drove him forward; his mother quickly rose and dashed after him.

Lewys, Miles, and Edmund were still fighting shoulder to shoulder, the pile of bodies growing in front of them. Jacob hurried to join them. Anne and Margaret hitched their skirts and chased after him.

"Protect the women but keep pushing forward," I called ahead. "We are running out of time." The hall was bathed in bright orange as the flames continued to climb higher along the wall. Much of the upper beams were concealed by a cloud of black smoke. Several more ghastly faces were visible over the top of the low wall.

"Push through them," I ordered as I rushed around the men and their pile of mangled corpses. Clearing the last upturned table, a half-dozen monsters materialized out of the darkness of the screens passage. They were only a short distance away.

Instinctively, I ducked an instant before colliding with the first. Intense pain radiated from my shoulder as the devil toppled over my back and fell to the floor. There was no time to turn and deliver a killing stroke; I had to trust that my men would do so. Rising, I thrust a spike into the nose of the next before quickly cleaving a third's skull.

"Left flank. Left flank," Miles warned as he punched his buckler into the face of a creature charging from the side. With a loud crack, teeth showered across the floor. He immediately chopped down with his sword to drop his attacker to the ground.

Glancing over my shoulder, I saw that the few remaining monsters that had been clambering over the tables had turned and were charging for our center.

Our only chance is to get to the door, I told myself. *Miles and Lewys will have to stop them.*

I cut through the last two and ran for the passage of the great hall. The light from Jacob's lantern bobbed across the floor as he hurried to keep up.

"Lord!" a boy's terrified voice called from somewhere above. "Up here, lord. Don't leave me." Jacob lifted his lantern towards the minstrel gallery overhead. Peering over the wooden rail was the face of Owain Dun.

"Get down from there, lad, and hurry!" I did not stop. I cracked the skull of another ghoul as I barreled into the narrow passageway underneath the gallery and quickly slammed shut the door leading to the kitchen. Turning, I fell against the door and braced it with my back. A series of shouts erupted out in the hall.

"Watch our backs," I panted at Jacob, struggling to catch my breath. Anne and Margaret suddenly raced through the opening in the screens; their faces were white from terror. A heartbeat later, Martha and Clere and Powlis darted inside. Doctor Symond with the aid of the two monks soon followed.

"Hold the gap," Lewys barked as he shoved young James behind him and took up a position between Miles and Edmund in the doorway. Together, they cut down four more of the creatures.

"That's the lot of them, lord," Miles reported over his shoulder.

"What about Hal?"

"Gone," Edmund muttered with a shake of his head. Anne shrieked as a door flew open behind her. A haggard-looking groom spilled out onto the floor at her feet. James pulled Owain to his feet before giving him a quick embrace.

"Anyone else up there?" I questioned the groom.

"No, lord. Just me."

So few remain.

Margaret stood close to my wife. She still carried the crossbow, but no bolts remained in her quiver. Martha paced back and forth in the narrow passage, the shaft of her spear dragging along behind her. Clere was once again huddled together with her son. They sobbed quietly behind the other women.

Doctor Symond's skin was deathly pale and his head wobbled back and forth; it was only with support from the monks that he managed to stay on his feet. The subprior was to his left and had a torch held aloft in his free hand. Brother Phillip was under the chaplain's right arm and was wielding a wooden tournament club.

"Where did that come from?" I asked him.

"I tucked it in my robes just in case someone might need it," he smiled sheepishly. "Besides, it's not a real weapon. How could the bishop object?"

"You're bleeding pretty bad, lord," Jacob said softly. He held his lantern close to my shoulder. A long, wide stain of blood ran down the side of the breastplate.

"It'll have to wait." The air was already becoming heated as wisps of gray smoke swirled around overhead. "Time to press on. We'll all roast like pigs if we tarry here much longer."

"Let us take the lead, Sir Richard," Lewys said as he and Miles gently pulled me aside. Jacob took a position to my left, while Edmund and the two grooms fell in behind the women and clergy.

Miles pulled the door open and immediately pummeled a charging servant with his buckler. Lewys hacked down with his pollaxe to cleave through the head of a small, gray-skinned scullion. I thrust my axe between the two men to impale a third ghoul.

It was a hard fight. A handful of the devils were crowded into the short but narrow passage. There was little room to swing axe or sword as even more rushed out of the kitchens and pantry in twos and threes. We hacked and chopped our way slowly down the hall, carefully stepping over the corpses until we were through the press.

The air became increasingly more acrid with smoke even after the orange glow from the hall had faded into the background. With no windows to provide ambient light, an ominous darkness loomed ahead.

"Get that lantern up here," Lewys whispered as we crept past the kitchens and paused at an intersection. "I can hear something down the hall to the left.

"Just storerooms down there," I cautioned him. "Avoid another fight if you can. We're almost to the exit." The two men moved aside to let Jacob shine his light down the dark corridor. Several devils were clawing furiously against a closed door. Muffled cries could be heard from inside.

"Ballocks," I growled. "We can't leave them to burn. Slow and deliberate, men."

A blood-soaked witch turned and cast a baleful look in our direction; her milky eyes glimmered in the light. The other four monsters were too captivated by the frightened screams of their prey to notice our party shuffling down the hallway. Miles cleaved her skull and we crept on.

Gray smoke roiled along the low ceiling, forcing everyone to stoop down. We passed the narrow steps descending to the buttery. Pausing only long enough to shine a light down the passage, we silently paced ever closer to the pack of ghoulish creatures.

We cut into the monsters with a flurry of blows without giving them a chance to turn and face us.

"No!" a voice howled from the rear of the column. "Morys, no!" Jacob whirled around to investigate, shining his lantern down the hazy corridor and leaving Miles and Lewys to fight in the darkness.

"Light, blast you!" Lewys bellowed. The varlet whipped back around just as Miles groaned in pain and collapsed to the floor. A lanky corpse glared hungrily down at the archer.

Several more screams rang out from behind as a voice howled with pain.

"On your right," I panted as I stepped over Miles to take his place next to the marshal. I spiked the devil through the forehead while Lewys nearly decapitated the final creature.

I turned to see a portly ghoul straddling a prostrate Edmund; bright red blood glistened from its maw. The steward's shrieking wife, mad with rage, was pummeling the devil with her bare fists.

I rushed through the midst of the column, out of breath and head spinning, but I was determined to reach the monster before it could claim another life. Shoving Clere aside, I reached for Martha to pull her back. I was too late. The ghastly butler snatched hold of her with both hands and sank his teeth into the side of her neck. A heartbeat later, brother Phillip cracked open his skull with three solid blows from the heavy club. The butler flopped to the floor still embracing his victim.

On the floor, Edmund lay in a dark puddle staring blankly at the ceiling, pink foam gurgling from his throat; his poor wife shuddered and died a few feet away. Brother Phillip stared down blankly at them. His lips moved as if he were speaking, but no words could be heard.

"You only did what you had to do," I offered, but the monk did not look up. Finally, after several moments, he opened his fingers and let the club drop to the ground.

"Brother," Doctor Symond coughed. He was seated awkwardly on the floor, the color completely gone from his face. The subprior pulled on one arm as if he alone could get the man to his feet.

"Take it, brother," the chaplain wheezed again as he clutched the hem of brother Phillip's robe. He pushed his satchel across the floor towards the monk. "I can't go on. Pray for me." With a long exhale, the chaplain's head slumped forward.

"I will," brother Phillip responded as he knelt beside Doctor Symond. He shifted his surgeon's bag aside before hefting the chaplain's satchel onto his shoulder.

"Ledgers," he said with a tone of surprise as he lifted the flap and peered. "That and a small box—"

"We haven't the time, brother," I chided him. The corridor was growing ever darker with smoke. It stung the eyes and burned the lungs. "You can tend to his effects later. It's long past time for us to leave this place."

"Lord," a voice interrupted from behind. As I looked back, Miles emerged from the haze and squeezed between Lewys and Jacob; a small trickle of blood ran down his brow from under his helmet.

"I thought you were dead," I coughed.

"So did I. Nasty bugger walloped me good." He jabbed a thumb back over his shoulder. "We found a woman and boy from Stony Heath hiding in the storeroom. The other one was empty."

Only two? I wanted to shout. *I sacrificed my oldest friend and his wife for a couple of strangers?*

Anne began to cough violently.

"Good," I replied tersely, grabbing Miles by the sleeve and pushing him back down the hall. "Now lead us out of here before it's too late." The archer quickly wormed his way through the crowded passage. Lewys and Jacob remained close behind him. The dark cloud quickly choked away the light from the varlet's lamp.

"Come on, Anne." Ignoring the pain in my shoulder, I took my wife by the hand and we groped our way slowly forward. We had to crouch low in order to escape the thickest smoke. Several steps later, the wall fell away to the right, and I knew we had reached the intersection. There was a faint orange glow struggling to cut through the black cloud. I quickly pulled Anne along.

"How can you see anything?" she asked hoarsely. There was barely any visible light coming from Jacob's lantern. I was simply following their hacking coughs and muttered curses.

"They're just ahead of us. Keep walking." A latch was pulled and a door squeaked open several feet ahead. Passing through the portal, the air ahead was much clearer, but the smoke at our backs was quickly swirling inside. Miles, Lewys, and Jacob stood waiting at the rear gate.

"I need to make sure everyone makes it through before we secure the door," I said to Anne as I released her hand and pushed my back against the wall to allow those behind to pass. She immediately clutched my forearm and tried to pull me forward.

"Stay with me," Anne whimpered. I no longer had the strength to argue. We shuffled forward as the rest of the group crowded inside. James slammed the door and jerked the latch closed behind us.

One final door, I sighed inwardly.

Miles lifted the heavy bar from its fittings, and Lewys slowly pulled open the door.

In the distance, the horizon was dark and almost starless, but the wooden bridge and grass were brightly lit. To our right, large flames billowed through the windows of the great hall. The rooftops above were completely hidden by smoke.

"Stay sharp, men," I wheezed. "We're not out of the woods yet." We slowly crept along the bridge, keeping our eyes focused ahead. The shifting flames made every shadow dance with life. The heat from the inferno was stifling.

"I need a moment to catch my breath," I called over the roar of the fire as I reached the end of the bridge. My heart was racing uncontrollably.

"Are you all right?" Anne asked as she turned back. Her mouth fell open in alarm as soon as her eyes fell upon my face. "Richard?" she gasped. A moment later, the world began to spin as darkness fell over me like a blanket. My legs buckled and I started to fall.

I dreamt I was once again aboard a ship bound for the coast of France. Strangely, I was lying on the deck as it pitched and rolled atop black seas on a starless night. Faint lights twinkled on the horizon in and out of view, except the world had been turned upside down.

"Hurry," a voice squeaked. "He hasn't much time."

I strained to lift my head. Lewys and Miles were to either side of me, their arms under mine, while Jacob and Phillip were carrying my legs.

"My house is not far," Lewys said, motioning somewhere ahead. Behind them, enormous flames had engulfed the manor. With a loud crash, a ball of smoke and fire was spat into the sky as the hall roof collapsed.

Once again, the dazzling lights faded into darkness.

"Please, lady. I know it's not much, but you must eat something."

My eyes blinked open to reveal Anne weeping over me. She had a wet cloth that she was using to clean the dried blood from my bare chest. My young varlet was crouched at her side holding a small basin of water. Lewys was standing across from her with a clay pitcher and basket of old bread in his hands. "I wish there were more, but Margaret's never been the best at keeping house." He smiled briefly.

"Is there no wine?" I groaned. My shoulder throbbed in pain. Strips of bloody blanket had been wound tightly around it, but the torment was almost unbearable.

"Richard!" Anne cried. "They said you'd never wake, but I knew you wouldn't leave me like this." She dipped the cloth in water and wrung it dry before gently dabbing my forehead. I did my best to smile.

"Where are we?" I inquired, looking around the room. A single candle flickered on a table next to my head. The small chamber was unfamiliar in the dim light.

"We're in Master Lewys's home," Anne said softly. "The men carried you here after we fled the manor. Miles sounded confident that we would be safe, at least for the night."

"We saw nary a soul outside," Lewys added. "I think they're all gone, burned up in the fire. As for the wine, I'm sorry, but the best I can offer is a cup of warm ale."

"I hope you're right, Master Lewys," I said with a nod. The marshal filled a small cup and pressed it to my lips. The ale was bitter and thick with sediment, but I sipped it heartily.

"I must ask one thing more of you," I coughed when the cup was finally taken away.

"Anything, lord. Just ask, and I'll see that it's done."

"Swear to me that you will see my wife safely to Harrowford Manor."

"You're coming, too," Anne cried. Her words lacked conviction. I sighed from fatigue more than from sorrow.

"No, Anne. My life is spent. But I want you to know that I do not grieve my passing. I will live on through you and the girls. My only regret is that I have nothing left to leave you."

"Don't say that, Richard. You're strong, and you still have life left in you." I shook my head wearily.

"My death is the only thing that everyone here is certain of. Right, brother Phillip?" The monk was hovering at the foot of the bed, the corners of his mouth turned down with pity. He had Symond's golden stole draped around his neck and a small cross-shaped box cradled in his arms. I had seen enough men die to know the box contained the consecrated hosts and oil to prepare my body for its final journey.

"I—uh," he stammered, looking down at the floor as he fingered the edges of his stole.

"Don't worry, brother. You'll get your chance soon enough."

"God may still answer the fervent prayers of the faithful," the monk retorted. His mouth was still drawn tight with sorrow.

"Save your prayers and your tears. If you must mourn something, mourn for our beloved Colleville. I fear it will soon become nothing more than a blight on the countryside, just like all those villages abandoned and left to ruin after the first great mortality."

"Very well," brother Phillip said, finally lifting his eyes from the floor. "If it be the will of God that your soul be taken during the night, where would you want your body to be buried on the morrow?"

"Don't waste your time. Just set me alight like all the others and make for Harrowford. Let my ashes be scattered by the winds across my land."

"I would hear your last confession so that you may be absolved of your sins," the monk stated solemnly.

I confess that I am guilty of avarice, I thought to say but did not. Instead, I closed my eyes and clenched my jaw tight to contain my grief. My heart ached with bitter resentment. *My entire life's work has been consumed by fire in a matter of hours. It should have all gone to Thomas, my son.*

"No," I finally said with a heavy sigh. In the span of a few heartbeats, I witnessed the entirety of my life pass before my mind's eye. "I have led as good of a life as I was able."

"You have, Richard," Anne whispered, placing her hand in mine and giving it an affectionate squeeze. "No one here will ever forget that. If not for you, we would all be dead now." Lewys and Jacob murmured in assent.

"If not for me?" I coughed. "What about Thomas? And Edmund? And Adam? And William? What about the scores of others whose names already escape me?" With every ounce of energy I could muster, I propped myself up on my elbow and set my gaze on brother Phillip.

"I changed my mind, brother. There *is* one more thing I would like to ask of you. I need you to tell the world of all that happened here. Of the men who died and the horrors that we endured."

"It's true that I carry quill and ink," the monk offered as he turned and rifled through his bag. "I'm afraid I only have a few scraps of paper left on which to write. Not nearly enough to record your account."

"Account, you say?" I suddenly recalled the heavy ledgers brother Phillip had discovered in Doctor Symond's satchel. "What if you used the parchment from the manor rolls?" The monk's eyes brightened at the idea.

"That should be more than enough. I'll get started right away scraping the parchment clean." He rushed over to a table on the far wall and dumped out the three large tomes. With the help of Lewys, the table was pushed noisily across the floor until it bumped into the side of the bed. Jacob appeared moments later with a short bench. Finally, brother Phillip reached into his own bag and produced a small wooden box that he offered to his subprior. "Brother Philemon is a much better scribe than I am."

The elder monk nodded as he accepted the box and quickly opened its lid to remove its contents. With skillful ease, he used a short blade to sharpen a quill, which he then dabbed into a clay jar that was almost black with dried ink.

"Rest easy, Sir Richard," brother Philemon said as he adjusted himself on his seat. "Just close your eyes and think back. Try to remember how it all started."

"That's easy," I smiled, slowly easing myself back onto the pillow. "It began with Thomas. We were hunting together in Colle's Chase."

Postscript

Philemon, by the grace of God sub-prior at the priory at Stony Heath, although unworthy, with piety in Christ.

REVERENT FATHER, IT IS WITH glad tidings that I am able to report to you that Sir Richard de Colleville has miraculously survived the night despite all of our doubts to the contrary. He is most determined to be reunited with his family before he dies.

As if we required a further sign of the providence of Almighty God, one of Sir Richard's men discovered his master's warhorse grazing out in the field just behind the house where we had sheltered. Even now, his servants are preparing to place him and his wife atop the horse and lead them to an obscure manor called Harrowford to the west.

I am sending Sir Richard's account with brother Phillip Sewelle. If it pleases you, Sir Richard has asked that it be delivered to his lordship, the Duke of Gloucester. He desires that the duke should hear straightaway of the terrible fate that has befallen the estate of Colleville. I myself plan to travel first to our beloved priory and see if any of its priceless tomes might be salvaged from the scriptorium.

I beseech Almighty Jesu to have you eternally in His merciful governance. Written in haste by my own hand on the manor of Colleville on Monday following the Feast of the Baptism of the Lord, in the year of Grace 1436.

Philemon Capell

Acknowledgments

There are so many who helped me along this long and difficult journey. First and foremost, I must again thank my wife for tirelessly reading page after page of something that was definitely not Jane Austen. Lacey, you inspired me to pick up a pen and start writing. Beth, you once said that I was smart enough to read a book; you were beneficial in translating my text from Texican into English. Leah, you worked your editing magic and made it possible for others to comprehend the story I had to tell. Jack and Owen, I appreciate your enthusiasm and the lessons in modern zombie lore. Finally, thanks to Randy, Dan, Mike, Ray, and so many others who provided critical feedback along the way.

Glossary

Arcade A covered walkway enclosed by a succession of arches.

Barding Protective covering or armor for a horse.

Bevor An articulated piece of armor that protects the neck and lower face; its hinged upper plate can be lowered to the chin.

Bill, or billhook Polearm weapon with a long, axe-like head that curves into a hooked bill, a small fluke on the back, and a long spike jutting from the top.

Book of hours A collection of texts, prayers, and psalms, usually in Latin, for personal devotion.

Brigandine Close-fitting, sleeveless body armor made of small overlapping steel plates riveted between two layers of fabric.

Buttery Room where large barrels, or butts, of ale and wine were stored; overseen by a butler.

Caparison Decorative cloth covering for a horse in parades and tournaments usually adorned with the heraldry of its rider.

Corn Grain, specifically wheat; not the North American plant.

Courser Swift and powerful horse used for hunting and in war.

Cuirass Generic term for the armor covering the torso.

Esquire Gentry rank below that of a knight.

Flux Dysentery.

Garth A central yard or garden courtyard in a monastery.

Halberd A polearm weapon with a broad axe-like head.

Hauberk A shirt of maille, with or without sleeves, often worn under plate or over fabric armor.

Hue and cry A loud outcry alerting others of a fleeing felon; all able-bodied men were obliged to assist in his apprehension.

Jack A heavily padded defensible jacket made of as many as 30 layers of quilted linen. They were known to stop arrows of war.

Maille, or mail Armor made from thousands of interconnected metal rings; often called *chain mail* in modern times.

Man-at-arms Professional soldier well-trained in the use of arms; may refer to either knights or fully armored soldiers.

Mantle A short, cloak-like covering for the shoulders attached to the bottom of a hood.

New Year's Day Although Julius Caesar established January 1 as the first day of the year, in Christian Europe, Annunciation Day (March 25) was regarded as New Year's Day until 1582.

Psaltery A musical instrument consisting of a sounding board, often trapezoidal in shape, with strings stretched across it.

Quarrel Ammunition used in a crossbow; also called a *bolt*.

Rache A scent hound used in packs to run down prey.

Reeve Chief official in charge of the day-to-day labor on a manor.

Rood screen A partition of wood or stone separating the chancel from the main part of a church.

Sallet A round helmet with a vision slit or moveable visor and with a projection over the neck; commonly worn with a bevor.

Saracen Pagan or devil-worshipper.

Scullion Menial kitchen servant.

Solar Room in a manor reserved for the family's comfort.

Steward Chief official overseeing the work done on a manor's land.

Tables, Game of The medieval name for backgammon.

Varlet Personal attendant to a man-at-arms who provided assistance in donning his armor.

Villein Commoner, specifically a tenant subject to a lord or manor to whom he paid dues and services in return for land.

Yeoman Freeman who owned or rented the land he worked.

About the Author

Lonnie Colson lives in Texas with his wife and children. He earned his Bachelor's degree from West Texas A&M. Lonnie has enjoyed a 20-year career in public service, but his true passion is historical re-enactment. He recently commissioned a suit of fifteenth-century tournament armor with every intention of one day using it in an international jousting competition.

Lonnie cannot say with any certainty when his fascination with knights and armor first began. He grew up watching Arthurian movies such as *Gawain and the Green Knight* and *Excalibur* as well as reading Malory and Tennyson. As a boy, Lonnie's only outlet was dueling friends with trash can lids and cane poles.

Lonnie has a tiltyard in his backyard where he practices the knightly skills-at-arms with lance, spear, and sword. When he is not riding, he enjoys conducting interactive educational demonstrations to groups ranging from kindergarten classes to high school cooperatives and children's homes.

Find him on Facebook: http://www.facebook.com/lonniecolson.

Follow him at: http://www.twitter.com/lonniecolson.

For more information, please visit: www.lonniecolson.com.

Thanks for reading!
This was my first full-length novel to be published.
Please add a short review on Amazon and let me know what you thought!